Praise for *The Never List*

"A perfect breezy thriller for a hot day at the beach."
—*Entertainment Weekly*

"This is one scary throat-grabber. . . . As twisted and terrifying as any novel in years."
—*Parade*

"This summer's most breath-stealing thriller."
—Elle.com

"Thrilling, super smart, witty, and just about the most distracting thing in my recent life. I've stayed up past my bedtime, missed whole subway stops, left children at the playground. *The Never List* is a perfect entertainment."
—Darin Strauss

"A nonstop psychological thriller with heart-wrenching twists."
—Jed Rubenfeld

"Cleverly plotted and highly entertaining, *The Never List* is a haunting psychological thriller that begs to be read in one sitting. Be prepared."
—Alafair Burke

"From the first page of *The Never List*, you have to know how this terrifying book will possibly end, and my advice to the reader is to only pick it up when you have the time to devote to it, because it's impossible to put down. Even a casual glance will tell you this is no ordinary thriller: you WILL lose sleep over it. A book to devour in one sitting!"
—Elizabeth Haynes

"A chilling premise that sucked me in from the first page and had me gripped all the way to the end as I tried to guess what was going to happen next. An impressive debut!"
—Chevy Stevens

"*The Never List* got its sticky, sharp talons into me in the first paragraph and wouldn't let go until I'd finished it in less than two days. . . . A stylish and impressive debut thriller."
—S. J. Bolton

"A dark psychological thriller, it will touch every nerve you have."
—Tami Hoag

"A novel with powerful and poignant psychological insights. Zan's razor-sharp debut combines the very best of page-turning suspense with classic head-game thrills and chills. Not to be missed."

—Lisa Gardner

"Throat clutching from the outset! *The Never List* stands as a sterling example of psychological thriller writing at its best. Cancel appointments and give up on sleep. It's that kind of book."

—Jeffery Deaver

"Sent icicles down my spine. One of the scariest thrillers I've ever read. This should be on every mystery reader's must-read list!"

—Tess Gerritsen

"As gripping as *Gone Girl*—but darker, and with an eerie timeliness—Koethi Zan's debut novel . . . is this year's edge-of-your-towel beach read."
                                                                    —*Elle*

"This fast-paced, disturbing thriller boasts a chilling premise as well as a layered first-person narrative full of shocking twists and turns."

—*Library Journal*

"Zan's first novel is a haunting depiction of the emotional scars left on women held in captivity."   —*Kirkus Reviews*

"Zan's debut novel is shocking and disturbing. The intense psychological thriller combines a horrifying plot, well-developed characters, thought-provoking psychoanalysis, and some great phrasing. Read it if you dare."   —*RT Book Reviews* (4½ stars)

"This story is a twisted tale of a courageous woman trying to make sense of a madman's mind. . . . For readers looking for a psychological thriller, *The Never List* will be hard to beat."   —*BookPage*

"A fast-paced, don't-dare-put-the-book-down read that will leave you cringing as your darkest fears emerge from the shadows as Zan takes you to the places you never wanted to go."

—*Suspense Magazine*

PENGUIN BOOKS

THE NEVER LIST

Koethi Zan was born and raised in rural Alabama, then moved to New York City after earning a JD from Yale Law School. She practiced entertainment law for more than fifteen years, working in film, television, and theater, most recently at MTV. She now lives in upstate New York with her husband and children.

Koethi Zan

THE NEVER LIST

PENGUIN BOOKS

PENGUIN BOOKS
Published by the Penguin Group
Penguin Group (USA) LLC
375 Hudson Street
New York, New York 10014

USA I Canada I UK I Ireland I Australia I New Zealand I India I South Africa I China
penguin.com
A Penguin Random House Company

A Pamela Dorman / Penguin Book

First published in the United States of America by Viking Penguin,
a member of Penguin Group (USA) Inc., 2013
Published in Penguin Books 2014

THE LIBRARY OF CONGRESS HAS CATALOGED THE
HARDCOVER EDITION AS FOLLOWS:
Zan, Koethi.
The never list / Koethi Zan.
pages cm
ISBN 978-0-670-02651-7 (hc.)
ISBN 978-0-14-312558-7 (pbk.)
1. Female friendship—Fiction.   2. Kidnapping—Fiction.
3. Bondage (Sexual behavior)—Fiction.   I. Title.
PS3626.A629N48 2013
813'.6—dc23   2013007348

Printed in the United States of America
1 3 5 7 9 10 8 6 4 2

Book design by Amy Hill
Set in Sabon LT Std and Cresci LP

For E.E.B., who always believed

"Human beings are so terrible. . . . They can bear anything."

—From the film *The Bitter Tears of Petra von Kant*,
Rainer Werner Fassbinder, director and screenwriter

THE
NEVER
LIST

CHAPTER 1

There were four of us down there for the first thirty-two months and eleven days of our captivity. And then, very suddenly and without warning, there were three. Even though the fourth person hadn't made any noise at all in several months, the room got very quiet when she was gone. For a long time after that, we sat in silence, in the dark, wondering which of us would be next in the box.

Jennifer and I, of all people, should not have ended up in that cellar. We were not your average eighteen-year-old girls, abandoning all caution once set loose for the first time on a college campus. We took our freedom seriously and monitored it so carefully, it almost didn't exist anymore. We knew what was out there in that big wide world better than anyone, and we weren't going to let it get us.

We had spent years methodically studying and documenting every danger that could possibly ever touch us: avalanches, disease, earthquakes, car crashes, sociopaths, and wild animals—all the evils that might lurk outside our window. We believed our paranoia would protect us; after all, what are the odds that two girls so well versed in disaster would be the ones to fall prey to it?

For us, there was no such thing as fate. *Fate* was a word you used when you had not prepared, when you were slack, when you stopped paying attention. Fate was a weak man's crutch.

Our caution, which verged on a mania by our late teens, had started six years earlier when we were twelve. On a cold but sunny January day in 1991, Jennifer's mother drove us home from school, the same as every other weekday. I don't even remember the accident. I only recall slowly emerging into the light to the beat of the heart monitor, as it chirped out the steady and comforting rhythm of my pulse. For many days after that, I felt warm and utterly safe when I first woke up, until that moment when my heart sank and my mind caught up with time.

Jennifer would tell me later that she remembered the crash vividly. Her memory was typically post-traumatic: a hazy, slow-motion dream, with colors and lights all swirling together in a kind of operatic brilliance. They told us we were lucky, having been only seriously injured and living through the ICU, with its blur of doctors, nurses, needles, and tubes, and then four months recovering in a bare hospital room with CNN blaring in the background. Jennifer's mother had not been lucky.

They put us in a room together, ostensibly so we could keep each other company for our convalescence, and as my mother told me in a whisper, so I could help Jennifer through her grief. But I suspected the other reason was that Jennifer's father, who was divorced from her mother and an erratic drunk we had always taken pains to avoid, was only too happy when my parents volunteered to take turns sitting with us. At any rate, as our bodies slowly healed, we were left alone more often, and it was then that we started the journals—to pass the time, we said to ourselves, both probably knowing deep down that it was in fact to help us feel some control over a wild and unjust universe.

The first journal was merely a notepad from our bedside table at the hospital, with Jones Memorial printed in Romanesque block letters across the top. Few would have recognized it as a journal, filled as it was only with lists of the horrors we saw on television. We had to ask the nurses for three more notepads. They must have thought we were filling our days with tic-tac-toe or hangman. In any event, no one thought to change the channel.

When we got out of the hospital, we worked on our project in earnest. At the school library, we found almanacs, medical journals, and even a book of actuarial tables from 1987. We gathered data, we computed, and we recorded, filling up line after line with the raw evidence of human vulnerability.

The journals were initially divided into eight basic categories, but as we got older, we learned with horror how many things there were that were worse than Plane Crashes, Household Accidents, and Cancer. In stone silence and after careful deliberation, as we sat in the sunny, cheerful window seat of my bright attic bedroom, Jennifer wrote out new headings in bold black letters with her Sharpie: Abduction, Rape, and Murder.

The statistics gave us such comfort. Knowledge is power, after all. We knew we had a one-in-two-million chance of being killed by a tornado; a one-in-310,000 chance of dying in a plane crash; and a one-in-500,000 chance of being killed by an asteroid hitting Earth. In our warped view of probability, the very fact that we had memorized this endless slate of figures somehow changed our odds for the better. Magical thinking, our therapists would later call it, in the year after I came home to find all seventeen of the journals in a pile on our kitchen table, and both my parents sitting there waiting with tears in their eyes.

By then I was sixteen, and Jennifer had come to live with us full time because her father was in jail after his third DUI. We visited him, taking the bus because we had decided it wasn't safe for us to drive at that age. (It would be another year and a half before either of us got a license.) I had never liked her father, and it turned out she hadn't either. Looking back, I don't know why we visited him at all, but we did, like clockwork, on the first Saturday of every month.

Mostly he just looked at her and cried. Sometimes he would try to start a sentence, but he never got very far. Jennifer didn't bat an eye, just stared at him with as blank an expression as I ever saw on her face, even when we were down in that cellar. The two of them never spoke, and I sat a little away from them, fidgeting and uncomfortable. Her father was the only thing she would not discuss with me—not one word—so I just held her hand on the bus back home each time, while she gazed out the window in silence.

The summer before we went to off to Ohio University, our anxieties reached a fever pitch. We would soon be leaving my attic room, which we shared, and go into the vast unknown: a college campus. In preparation, we made the Never List and hung it on the back of our bedroom door. Jennifer, who was plagued by insomnia, would often get up in the middle of the night to add to it: never go to the campus library alone at night, never park more than six spaces from your destination, never trust a stranger with a flat tire. Never, never, never.

Before we left, we meticulously packed a trunk, filling it with the treasures we had collected over the years at birthdays and Christmases: face masks, antibacterial soap, flashlights, pepper spray. We chose a dorm in a low building so that, in the event of fire, we could easily make the jump. We painstakingly studied the campus map and arrived three days early to examine the footpaths and walkways to evaluate for ourselves the lighting, visibility, and proximity to public spaces.

When we arrived at our dorm, Jennifer took out her tools before we had even unpacked our bags. She drilled a hole in our window sash, and I inserted small but strong metal bars through the wood, so it couldn't be opened from the outside even if the glass was broken. We kept a rope ladder by the window, along with a set of pliers to remove the metal bars in the event we needed a quick escape. We got special permission from campus security to add a deadbolt lock to our door. As a final touch, Jennifer gingerly hung the Never List on the wall between our beds, and we surveyed the room with satisfaction.

Maybe the universe played out a perverse justice on us in the end. Or maybe the risks of living in the outside world were simply greater than we had calculated. In any event, I suppose we stepped out of our own bounds by trying to live a semblance of regular college life. Really, I thought later, we knew better. But at the same time the lure of the ordinary proved to be too irresistible. We went to classes separately from each other even if we had to go to opposite ends of the campus. We stayed in the library talking to new friends well after dark sometimes. We even went to a couple of campus mixers sponsored by the university. Just like normal kids.

In fact, after only two months there, I secretly began thinking we could start living more like other people. I thought maybe the worries of our youth could be put away, packed safely in the cardboard boxes back home where we stored our other childhood memorabilia. I thought, in what I now see as a heretical break from everything we stood for, that maybe our juvenile obsessions were just that, and we were finally growing up.

Thankfully, I never articulated those thoughts to Jennifer, much less acted on them, so I was able to half forgive myself for them in those dark days and nights to follow. We were just college kids, doing what college kids do. But I could comfort myself knowing we had followed our protocols to the bitter end. We had, almost automatically, executed our protective strategies with a military precision and focus, every day a continuous safety drill. Every activity had a three-point check, a rule, and a backup plan. We were on our guard. We were careful.

That night was no different. Before we had even arrived on campus, we had researched which car service in town had the best record for accidents, and we'd set up an account. We had it billed directly to our credit cards just in case we ever ran out of cash or had our wallets stolen. "Never be stranded" was number thirty-seven on the list, after all. Two months into the semester, the dispatch guy recognized our voices. We only had to give him a pickup address, and moments later we would be safely shuttled back to our dormitory fortress.

That night we went to a private party off campus—a first for us. Things were just getting going at around midnight when we decided we'd pushed the limit far enough. We called the service, and in record time, a beat-up black sedan arrived. We noticed nothing out of the ordinary until we were in the car with our seat belts fastened. There was a funny smell, but I shrugged it off, deciding it was within the realm of the expected for a local livery company. A couple of minutes into the ride, Jennifer dozed off with her head on my shoulder.

That memory, the last of our other life, is preserved in my imagination in a perfect halo of peace. I felt satisfied. I was looking forward to life, a real life. We were moving on. We were going to be happy.

I must have drifted off too because when I opened my eyes, we were in total darkness in the backseat, the lights of the town replaced by the dim glow of stars. The black sedan was hurtling forward on the now-deserted highway, with only the faint trace of the horizon ahead. This was not the way home.

At first I panicked. Then I remembered number seven on the

Never List: Never panic. In a flash, my mind retraced our steps that day, pointlessly trying to figure out where we had made a mistake. Because there had to have been a mistake. This was not our "fate."

Bitterly, I realized we had made the most basic and fundamental error of all. Every mother taught her child the same simple safety rule, the most obvious one on our own list: Never get in the car.

In our hubris, we'd thought we could cheat it—just a little—with our logic, our research, our precautions. But nothing could change the fact that we'd failed to follow the rule absolutely. We'd been naïve. We hadn't believed other minds could be as calculating as ours. We hadn't counted on actual evil as our enemy rather than blind statistical possibility.

There in the car, I drew three deep breaths and looked at Jennifer's sweet sleeping face for a long, sad moment. I knew as soon as I acted that, for the second time in her young life, she would wake up into a life utterly transformed. Finally, with great dread, I took her shoulder in my hand and shook it gently. She was bleary-eyed at first. I held my finger to my lips as her eyes focused and she began to process our situation. When I saw the look of realization and fear dawning on her face, I whimpered almost audibly, but stifled the sound with my hand. Jennifer had been through too much and suffered so hard. She could not survive this without me. I had to be strong.

Neither of us made a sound. We had trained ourselves never to act impulsively in an emergency situation. And this was definitely an emergency.

Through the thick, clear plastic partition dividing us from the driver, we could see very little of our abductor: dark brown hair, black wool coat, large hands on the wheel. On the left side of his neck, partially hidden by his collar, was a small tattoo that I couldn't quite make out in the dark. I shivered. The rearview mirror was angled up so we could see almost nothing of his face.

As quietly as we could, we tested the door handles. Safety-locked. The window mechanisms were disabled as well. We were trapped.

Jennifer slowly leaned down and picked up her bag from the floor, keeping her eyes on me as she rummaged in it silently. She pulled out her pepper spray. I shook my head, knowing it was of no use to us in our sealed-off space. Still, we felt safer having it.

I dug into my own purse at my feet. I found an identical canister and a small hand-held alarm with a panic button. We would have to wait it out, in silence, in terror, with our shaking hands clutching our pepper sprays and sweat beading our foreheads despite the October chill outside.

I scanned the interior of the car, trying to come up with a plan. And then I noticed it. There were small open air vents in the partition on my side, but those in front of Jennifer were connected to some kind of homemade metal and rubber contraption. Valves were connected to a pipe that disappeared from our view into the front floorboard. I sat very still, gaping at this intricate mechanism, my mind racing but unable to grasp a coherent thought for a moment. Finally, it sank in.

"We'll be drugged," I said at last, whispering to Jennifer. I looked down at the pepper spray in my hand with regret, knowing I'd never be able to use it. I stroked it almost lovingly, then let it drop to the floor, as I stared back up at the source of our impending doom. Jennifer followed my glance and registered at once what it meant. There was no hope.

He must have heard me speak, for just seconds later, a slight hissing sound told us we were about to get very sleepy. The air vents on my side slid shut. Jennifer and I held hands tightly, our other hands gripping the outer sides of the faux leather seat as the world slipped away.

When I came to, I was in the dark cellar that was to be my home for more than three years. I roused myself from the drugs slowly, trying to focus my eyes in the sea of gray that swam before them. When they finally cleared, I had to shut them tightly again to stop the panic that threatened to take over. I waited ten seconds, twenty, thirty, and opened again. I looked down at my body. I was stripped naked and chained to the wall by my ankle. A chill prickled up my spine, and my stomach lurched.

I was not alone. There were two other girls down there, emaciated, naked, and chained to the walls beside me. In front of us was the box. It was a simple wooden shipping crate of some sort, maybe five feet long by four feet high. Its opening was angled away from me, so I couldn't tell how it was secured. There was a dim bulb hanging from the ceiling over us. It swayed just slightly.

Jennifer was nowhere to be seen.

CHAPTER 2

Thirteen years later, anyone who didn't know me—and let's face it, no one did—might think I was living the dream life of a single girl in New York City. They might think everything had turned out all right for me in the end. I had moved on. Gotten over it. Survived the trauma.

Even all that early work in probability had paid off, and I had a stable, if not very glamorous, job as an actuary with a life insurance company. I found it somehow fitting that I now worked for a company that made bets on death and disaster. Not only that, but they let me work from home. A virtual paradise.

My parents couldn't understand why I had moved to New York City so quickly in the first place, while I was still recovering and especially considering all my fears. They didn't understand how much safer it felt to have crowds of people right outside my door at all times. In New York City, I tried to explain, there is always someone to hear you scream. And better still were the glorious advantages of a doorman building in a city that never slept. There I was, on the Upper West Side of Manhattan, surrounded by millions, yet no one could reach me if I didn't want them to.

Bob at the front desk would buzz up, and he knew that if I didn't answer, it meant I didn't want to see anyone—no matter what. He would bring me my food deliveries personally, because he felt sorry for the crazy woman in 11G, and because I gave him triple what everyone else did at the holidays. In fact, I could stay home all day, every day, and have every meal delivered and every errand outsourced. I had raging Wi-Fi and a premium cable television package. There was nothing I couldn't do from the privacy of the well-appointed junior six my parents had helped me buy.

The first years out had been madness, literally and figuratively, but thanks to five sessions a week with Dr. Simmons, the therapist they'd provided for us, I had been able to go back to college, get a job, and function passably in the real world. But as time went on and the relationship with my shrink stagnated, I discovered I couldn't move beyond a certain point.

And then I went into reverse. Retrenching. Slowly, imperceptibly. Until I found it harder and harder to leave my apartment at all. I simply preferred to stay safely in my own cocoon in the midst of a world I perceived as spinning out of control. A world whose evils were driven home to me more each day as I documented them with increasingly sophisticated software.

Then one day the buzzer rang, and Bob said it wasn't a delivery but a flesh and blood man. Someone from my past. I shouldn't have let him up, but I felt I owed this particular visitor at least that much. That's where it all began again.

"Caroline." Agent McCordy was rapping at my door, while I stood frozen to the spot on the other side. I hadn't spoken to him in two years, since the last letter came. I wasn't ready for another communication from that other life.

It was when that last bit of correspondence from the prison had arrived that I had stopped going out entirely. Just touching something he had touched, reading something he had thought, was enough to send me spinning into that circle of despair and fear I thought I'd left behind. Dr. Simmons had started making house calls at that point. For the first month afterward, though she wouldn't say it, I knew I was on quasi-suicide watch. My mom flew in. My father called every night. I was invaded. And here it was, beginning again.

"Caroline, can you open up?"

"Sarah," I corrected, through the door, annoyed that he was following protocol, using that other name, the one I reserved for the outside world.

"I'm sorry—I mean, Sarah. Can you let me in?"

"Do you have another letter?"

"I need to talk to you about something more important, Car— Sarah. I know Dr. Simmons has talked to you about this a little already. She said I could come by."

"I don't want to talk about it. I'm not ready." I paused, but then, feeling it was inevitable, I methodically unlatched the three dead-bolts and the regular lock on the door. I opened it slowly. There he stood, badge in hand, held wide open to me. He knew I'd want to confirm that he was still official. I smiled at that. Then I folded my arms, defensively, my smile disappearing, and took a step back. "Why does it have to be me?"

I turned, and he followed me into the room. We sat down across from each other, but I didn't offer him anything to drink for fear he'd get too comfortable and stay awhile. He looked around.

"Immaculate," he said with a slow smile. "You never change, Sarah." He took out his notebook and pen, placing them carefully on the coffee table, at a perfect ninety-degree angle.

"Neither do you," I said, noticing his precision. I smiled again, despite myself.

"You know why it has to be you," he began slowly. "And you know why it has to be now. This is it."

"When is it?"

"In four months. I came early to prepare you. We can prepare together. We will work with you every step of the way. You won't be alone."

"But Christine? Tracy?"

"Christine won't speak to us. She won't speak to her social worker. She has completely cut us off. She married an investment banker who doesn't know about her past or even her real name. She has an apartment on Park Avenue and two daughters. One started preschool at Episcopal this year. She won't go near this."

I had some vague knowledge about Christine's life, but I could never believe how thoroughly she had managed to cut the whole experience out of her existence, to isolate and excise it like the cancer it was.

I should have expected it, given that Christine had been the one to suggest we change our identities when the press couldn't get enough of our story. She had walked out of the police intake with a purpose, as though she hadn't been starved for the past two years and hadn't been crumpled in a corner crying for the past three. She didn't look back. Didn't say good-bye to me or Tracy, didn't fall apart like Tracy did, didn't hang her head in defeat, battered from the years of humiliation and pain. She just walked.

After that, we knew only the outline of her story through the social worker who met with us all, and who each year tried to get us together on the questionable theory that we could help one another recover. The message back from Christine was that she had already recovered, thank you very much. And good riddance to us all.

"Tracy then."

"Tracy is coming, but you have to understand it can't be Tracy alone."

"Why not? She's stable, brilliant, articulate. You could even call her a small-business owner of sorts. Isn't that legit enough?"

He chuckled. "I suppose she is a productive member of society. But she isn't exactly the local greengrocer. More like your local radical feminist activist. And because that journal she publishes focuses on violence against women, she might just appear to have her own agenda.

"And yes," he went on, "she is articulate. After all those years in grad school, she'd better be. But in these circumstances she manages to go on the offense. She doesn't exactly inspire the pity we need the parole board to feel. Not to mention that she has a shaved head and forty-one tattoos."

"Wha—"

"I asked. I didn't count." He paused. "Carol—"

"SARAH."

"Sarah, when was the last time you left this apartment?"

"What do you mean?" I turned away from him. I looked around at this prewar gem bathed in white as though it shared my guilt in some way. A little heaven of my own making. "It's so beautiful. Why would I want to leave it?"

"You know what I mean. When did you last leave? To go anywhere. To walk down the block. To get fresh air. To exercise."

"I open my windows. Sometimes. And I exercise. You know. In here." I looked around. All the windows were shut and locked, despite the beautiful spring day outside.

"Does Dr. Simmons know this?"

"She knows. She isn't 'pushing me beyond my own boundaries,' she says. Or something like that. Don't worry. Dr. Simmons is all over it. She's got my number. Or numbers, as it were. OCD, agoraphobia, haphephobia, post-traumatic stress disorder. I still see her three times a week. Yes, I see her here in this apartment; don't look at me like that. But you know, I'm an upstanding citizen with a solid job and a lovely home. I'm just fine. Things could be much worse."

Jim stared at me for a minute with pity in his eyes. I looked away from him, feeling a little ashamed of myself for the first time in a while. His voice turned serious again when he finally spoke.

"Sarah," he said, "there *is* another letter."

"Send it to me," I replied, with a fierceness that surprised us both.

"Dr. Simmons is not sure it's a good idea. She didn't want me to tell you."

"It's mine. It's addressed to me, isn't it? And therefore you *have* to send it to me. Isn't that federal law or something?" I stood up and started pacing the room, biting my thumbnail.

"It doesn't even make any sense," he started. "It's more of his ramblings. It's mostly about his wife."

"I don't doubt that it makes no sense. None of them do. But one day he's going to slip up, and there'll be a clue. He'll tell me where the body is. Not in so many words, but he'll let something out, something that will tell me where to look."

"And how will you do that? How will you look? You won't even leave the apartment. You won't even testify at the guy's parole hearing."

"And what kind of a freak woman marries a guy like that anyway?" I interjected, ignoring him as I paced faster. "Who are these women who write letters to prisoners? Do they secretly *want* to be chained up, tortured, and killed? Do they *want* to get close enough to the fire to get burned?"

"Well, apparently she got his name through her church. They set this up as some kind of mission of mercy. According to him and his attorney, it worked. According to them, he's a true convert."

"Do you believe that for one second?" He shook his head, as I went on. "I'm sure she'll be the first one to regret it when he's out."

I walked back around to the sofa and sat down, putting my head in my hands. I sighed.

"I can't even have sympathy for this person. Such an idiot."

In ordinary circumstances, I'm sure Jim would have patted my shoulder or maybe even put his arm around me. Normal acts of comfort. But he knew better. He stayed right where he was.

"You see, Sarah, *you* don't believe he's had a religious conversion, and *I* don't believe it. But what if the parole board believes it? What if this guy serves just ten years for keeping you all locked up and—killing one of you? Ten years. Is that enough for you? Is that enough for what he did to you?"

I turned away from him so he wouldn't see the tears forming in my eyes.

"He still owns the house," Jim continued. "If he gets out, that's right where he will be going. That house. In four months. With his Southern Baptist jailhouse wife in tow."

Jim shifted in his seat and leaned forward, changing tack. "Your best friend, Sarah. Your best friend. Do it for Jennifer."

By then I couldn't hold back the floodgates. I didn't want him to see my tears, so I stood up and quickly walked to the kitchen to get a drink of water. I stood running the faucet for a full minute, pulling myself together. My hands gripped the edge of the sink until my knuckles were as white as the cold porcelain under my fingers. When I came back, Jim was standing up to leave. He slowly gathering his things and putting them back in his case one by one.

"I'm sorry to push you, Sarah. Dr. Simmons won't like it. But we need you to make this victim impact statement. Without you, I'm worried. I know we let you down. *I* let you down. I know the kidnapping charge wasn't sufficient for all he did. At the end of the day we just didn't have the proof to charge him with murder. With-out a body, and with DNA evidence that was . . . contaminated. But we have to make sure he serves at least the full sentence on what we've got him for. We can't take any chances on that."

"It wasn't your fault. It was the lab—" I started.

"My case, my fault. And believe me, I've been paying the price ever since. Let's get through this and put it behind us."

Easy for him to say. I was sure that's just what he wanted, to put this mess in his past. His big career mistake. For me, it was a little more difficult.

He held up his card, but I waved it away. I had the number.

"I will prep you here at your apartment. Anywhere you want. We need you."

"And Tracy will be there too?"

"Yes, Tracy will be there, but . . ." He looked over at the win-dow, embarrassed.

"But she made it a condition that she doesn't have to see me, talk to me, or be alone with me, right?"

Jim hesitated. He didn't want to say it, but I could see right through him.

"You can say it, Jim. I know she hates me. Just say it."

"Yes, she made that a condition."

"Okay. Okay, I'll think about it, not just 'okay.'"

"Thanks, Sarah." He took an opened envelope out of his note-book and placed it on the table. "The letter. You're right, it's yours. Here it is. But please talk to Dr. Simmons before you read it."

He walked to the door. He knew not to try to shake my hand. Instead, he gave me a quick wave from the other side of the room and closed the door quietly behind him, then stood right outside, waiting for me to fasten the bolts. When he heard the final click, he walked away. He knew me well.

CHAPTER 3

I spent three days alone in the apartment with the letter. I put it in the center of the dining room table and walked around and around it for hours, thinking. I knew I would read it, of course. I knew it was the only way I could get closer to the truth. I had to find Jennifer's body. It was the least I could do for her, and for me. As I stared at that letter alone with my fear, I could just imagine Jennifer looking up at me with her empty eyes, pleading without a word, *find me*.

Ten years ago the FBI had put their best men on the case. They questioned him for hours, but he didn't give them anything. I could have told them that. He was cold and methodical and, I knew, totally unafraid of any punishment they could mete out. No one could touch him.

This was a man who had fooled the administration at the University of Oregon for more than twenty years. The image that stuck in my head was of him at the lectern, with all those eager co-eds writing down every word he spoke. He must have loved that. I could just picture the teaching assistants sitting so close to him, one on one, in that stuffy little office I visited later with the prosecutor.

When Christine went missing, no one even remembered that she had been one of his favorite students. Good old Professor Jack Derber. What a great guy he was, a wonderful and brilliant professor. He had built a nice life for himself, and he even had a little mountain retreat nearby that his adoptive parents had left him. No one knew it had such an ample cellar. His parents had used it for pickling and canning. But not Jack.

I pulled myself out of my reverie. I was here. Safe in my own apartment, staring at this letter. I had practically memorized the crinkle of the paper, the soft line of the tear from when the lab tech had opened it with some sharp instrument. The seam was flawless. Derber would have liked to see that. He always admired a clean cut.

I knew they had studied the contents carefully, but I also knew there would be something in there only I would understand. Above all things, that's how he operated. He wanted that personal relationship. Very deep and very personal. He got inside your mind, crawled in like a venomous snake slithering into a hole in the desert, then twisted around in there until he was fully comfortable and at home. It had been hard to resist him when physical weakness made you turn to your attacker as a savior. Harder to push him away when, after taking everything away from you, maybe forever, he doled out the only things you needed to sustain you—food, water, cleanliness, the least sign of affection. A small comforting word. A kiss in the dark.

Captivity does things to you. It shows you how base an animal you can be. How you'd do anything to stay alive and suffer a little bit less than the day before.

So I was scared looking at that letter, remembering the control he'd had, and in some ways might always have, if it was put to the test. I was scared that that envelope might contain words powerful enough to take me back there.

But I knew I couldn't betray Jennifer again. I would not die letting her body sink deeper into the earth, alone wherever he had put her.

I could be strong now. I reminded myself that now I wasn't starving, tortured, naked, deprived of light and air and normal human contact. Well, maybe normal human contact, but that was of my own choosing.

And now, after all, I had Bob the doorman downstairs and a whole city of saviors out there, shadowy forms far below my window down on Broadway, shopping, laughing, talking, never knowing that eleven stories up a ten-year-old drama was unfolding at my dining room table. Me against me, *mano a mano*.

I picked up the envelope and eased out the single piece of thin paper. The pen had been pushed so hard against it, I could feel the letters like Braille from the back. Sharp letters. Nothing curved, nothing soft.

Jennifer had been gone from the cellar only a few days when he started taunting me. At first I dared to hold out hope. Maybe she had managed to escape and would send for help. I would spend hours imagining how she had broken free, that she was just beyond the cellar walls, with the police, their weapons drawn, surrounding the house. I knew how unlikely that was, given that she'd barely had the strength to walk up the stairs when he pulled her from the box that last time, with her head covered and arms chained. Still I hoped.

He left me to my own imagination for a while, then slowly it dawned on me what his strategy was. He started smiling at me knowingly when he came down to bring us food or water. As if we had a secret together. He gave me extra each day, as though he were nursing me back to health, as a reward for something. Christine and Tracy began to look at me suspiciously. Their voices sounded guarded when they spoke.

I was disgusted at first, but in the end, this new form of torture provided the germ of the idea that would save me.

After nearly two months, in a gesture of what might have even been compassion in his twisted worldview, he told me she was dead. I could not believe the emptiness that fell inside me in that instant, as if a black cloth had dropped over our cellar diorama. Despite the fact that Jennifer had not spoken a word in nearly three years, and I hadn't seen her face for the last one because of the ever-present black hood, still her presence had defined my day-to-day existence. She had been there, silent, like a deity.

When Tracy was upstairs and Christine asleep, I could whisper to Jennifer safely without being heard. Prayers, supplications, musings, memories of our life were all spinning out into the darkness to her, my quiet goddess in the box. Her suffering was so much greater than mine. Maybe that was what gave me the strength to keep fighting, and, indeed, to stay alive.

He took exquisite pleasure in watching the pain on my face when he told me she was dead. I tried to hide it. For three years he managed to use my love for her as a component of my regular punishment. In those rare instances when I tried to fight back and even pain wouldn't make me give in, he knew all he had to do was threaten to hurt her more than he already had. I suppose he did the same to her, but I wouldn't know because after that first night we were never to speak again. She was kept bound and gagged in that box. Our only communication in those early days was through a rudimentary code she tapped on its sides. It only took a few months for the tapping to stop altogether.

Of course, my suffering over Jennifer did not end with her death. He made sure of that. He liked to tell me how he would dig her up to look at her sometimes. She had been so beautiful in death that he wanted to see it, even though it took him hours to unearth her body. He loved to tell me how, in killing her, he'd been careful not to damage her pretty face, which had more eloquently than anyone else's expressed the terror and loneliness of captivity. Her fragility, the unique quality of her vulnerability, made her his true favorite. It was why, he said, he chose her for the box.

So now here I was, with this letter in my hand. Touching what he had touched, reading what he had written. I spread the sheet out flat on the table before me and prepared myself to withstand the force of his words.

Dearest Sarah:

I wish you could understand the secret as well as I do. If only you had read in the Book Room that beautiful passage, scrawled in the mind's eye in the darkness.

On the banks of the lake in the flat, low land by the ocean, danger lurked for so long, silent, waiting, and then it struck. If only you will be brave enough to shed your costume and walk with me into the holy sea where there is no weakness or sorrow or regret.

Sylvia can help you. She can show you the path. She has seen the innermost recesses of my heart. I have shown her the landscapes and vistas of my past, all of it. And she has forgiven me. She has opened my eyes and blinded me from evil. She is an angel of mercy with a candle in the darkness, filling my heart not with shame but with redemption.

Soon—I can feel this—we will be reunited. I will come for you and together we will walk through the valley of death, unharmed.

Like the Apostles, we must learn. We must sit at the feet of the Master and learn. Only listen to the teachings, Sarah. Read the teachings. Study the teachings.

Amor fati,
Jack

I read the letter slowly, five times, trying to find the meaning hidden in it. The only thing that was clear was that if they let him out, he was coming for me.

But there was also something new here—an urgency in this letter that I had not detected in the others. He was trying to tell me something else, the sick fuck. Probably sending me on some wild-goose chase, which would be just like him. But at the moment I had nothing else to chase. There was something here. I just needed to think. Only thinking could save me.

CHAPTER 4

The first day in the cellar was probably the hardest, even though he did not come down at all. It was my orientation into a life of total disorientation.

The cellar looked exactly the way I would have expected a dungeon full of abducted girls to look: stark, dismal, forbidding. I had been left on a small mattress covered with a white fitted sheet that seemed clean enough. Cleaner in fact than any we'd had in our dorm room. The room was large, and the steep wooden steps that ran along the right-hand wall led up to a solid metal door. I would learn to memorize the creak of those steps.

Our prison had dingy gray walls, dark stone floors, and a lone bulb hanging from a cord above us. The box stood in the smaller space to the left of the stairs.

Tracy, whose name I would learn later that day, slept next to me, chained to the same wall facing the cellar steps. She looked deceptively frail that first time I saw her, balled up tight in the crevice where the wall met the floor. She scowled in her sleep, the grimace on her pallid face visible beneath her overgrown bangs, blackened at the tips from some long-ago dye job.

Between Tracy and the wall to the right was a small corridor. I couldn't see where it led from my vantage point, but would discover soon that Jack had installed a serviceable but spare bathroom, containing only a toilet and a sink. I would quickly come to realize how immaculately clean we were expected to keep ourselves with only those bare-bones facilities.

Christine was shackled to the wall on the right, about five feet from the steps. She lay on her side, asleep or dazed—it was hard to tell—her limbs contorted awkwardly, splayed across the floor. Her matted blond hair had been twisted tightly and draped over her shoulder. The combination of her position and the tiny, even features of her face gave her the appearance of a china doll that had been played with too roughly and then discarded.

Each of us was tethered with one long, heavy length of chain—it would vary whether we were fastened by the wrist or ankle—and each link, one inch by two, was rusty enough for its coppery dust to rub onto our skin, leaving false scrapes all over our bodies as we hauled it around. The left wall was empty, but I saw a small metal circle jutting out, just so. Room for one more if he wanted.

I knew it was morning only because of a small crease of light that crept between the slats of the single boarded-up window. I would have screamed, but I was too afraid. I couldn't even get my first words out when Christine and Tracy finally woke up. I was obviously in shock, but even in my confused state, I was glad I was not alone.

Tracy rubbed her face and turned to me sadly. Without a word, she crawled over to Christine and shook her awake. Christine turned the front of her body toward the wall, then buried her face back in her hands, mumbling.

"Christine, come on, meet the new girl. She's up now." Tracy turned to me and gave me a half-smile. "I'm very sorry you've had to join us. You look like a nice kid. It's a shame. The other girl—you know her?—has saved one of us from something we were very afraid of, and so, I must admit, for that we are very glad."

"Where is she?" was all I could muster, my voice choked off by fear.

At that Christine sat up, her translucent blue eyes glittering as they slid nervously to the box. I followed her glance and started to cry.

"Tell me. Tell me. Where is Jennifer? Is she in *there*?" I was still whispering, afraid of what was lurking upstairs.

Christine turned over to face the wall again. This time her shoulders were heaving, so I could tell she was crying. It was enough to bring tears to my own eyes, and I wondered if I would be able to hold back the sobs building up inside me. When she turned back to me again, though, she was smiling, even as the tears poured down her cheeks. It was then that I decided she was not crying over the horror of my condition and hers. These seemed more like tears of relief.

Tracy adjusted her chain so she could get closer to Christine, carefully twisting and folding it over to make a solid loop on the floor. She knelt down beside her against the wall, maneuvered Christine into her arms, and shushed her quietly.

"Relax, Christine," Tracy said soothingly, as though she were her only child who'd just had a bad, but not dangerous, fall.

Tracy gave Christine a small kiss on the cheek, then started in my direction, pulling her chain and recoiling it carefully at her feet in a slow, methodical rhythm, as though she were engaged in some kind of avant-garde dance. The chains clinked almost musically. Drag, lift, settle. Drag, lift, settle.

She came close, very close, and I instinctively drew back as she continued. "I'm afraid your friend has not been lucky. But you are lucky. I mean, considering."

I started crying, wondering what kind of perverse world it was down here. I squeezed my eyes shut tight, willing it away.

"Where is Jennifer? Where is my friend?" I had found my voice at last and was practically screaming now. "Jennifer? Are you in there? Are you okay?"

Tracy ignored my question and went on, "You have one thing going for you. Christine and I are very experienced cellar residents. We'll show you the ropes, as it were." She laughed as though she'd made a joke. Christine also made a noise apparently intended to indicate amusement. I didn't find it funny at all, and in that moment I wasn't sure whether to be more afraid of my captor or of these thin, dejected girls stuck here at the end of the world with me.

Not taking her eyes off me, Tracy walked over to the stairs, pulling her chains along behind her. Drag, lift, settle. There was a cardboard box at the bottom of the last step. She lifted out two worn-out but clean-looking green hospital gowns. She tossed one to Christine and pulled the other around her shoulders. She reached back into the box and pulled out a third.

"Ah, see, he is providing for you already." She threw it over to me. It was soft from many washings and smelled freshly laundered.

"Your royal robe," she said dramatically. "And our weekly provisions. Good thing you arrived on a Sunday night. Mondays are good days for us."

I grabbed the gown and put it on following Tracy's example, with the opening in the front, but wrapped tightly around me. Tracy lifted more items out of the box—canned goods, a loaf of bread, a gallon jug of water—and placed them along the wall in neat order.

I was now crouching on the floor, clutching the thin mattress like a child clutches its doll, staring at the box and wondering why Jennifer wouldn't answer. Tracy continued, ignoring my state.

"For the most part, we're left to our own devices down here during the work week. It's different in the summer and during holiday breaks. Those are tough times in Cellar Land. The weeks are short in any event. Four days of freedom—a term I am using very loosely, obviously—then three days back in the trenches. You see—get ready for this one—our man is a psychology professor at the University of Oregon, with an emphasis on the 'psycho' part. He has *classes*. He attends *conferences*. Meets with *advisees*. Presumably they have graduation ceremonies and parent visiting day and other special occasions. And during all those events we are spared his presence, and we live here in peace and harmony. As long as he has left us enough food and water, that is."

"How do you know all that?"

"From Christine, of course." She looked over at Christine, who seemed to have fallen back asleep, though it was hard to tell. At any rate, she was very still, her knees tucked under her body, her chains neatly coiled beside her. "Christine was his star student. Well, that was over two years ago. He may have a new star now, for all we know, right, Christine?" Christine opened one eye. It darted from me to Tracy as she whimpered quietly.

All I could hear ringing in my ears were the words *two years*.

"His name is Jack Derber." Tracy said the name deliberately and clearly, but at the same time she scanned the room warily, as though afraid the very walls might reach out to grab her as punishment for saying it aloud.

"And since we know that juicy little tidbit of information," she continued, "we can rest assured that he will never, ever, ever set us free. We are supposed to die here when he's finished with us. Christine and I speculate that that will be when we get too old for what he wants, or sooner if we are too much trouble. That is why we behave very, very well. We are such good little girls, aren't we, Christine? He can, after all, replace us quite easily, can't he?" She looked at me pointedly. "And he only has so much room down here, as you can see. It can't be cheap to keep us all alive and kicking."

I could barely follow her drift, but it suddenly didn't seem so friendly. Then something stirred in the box, and all three of us jerked our heads toward it. Silence again. Tracy went on.

"I have developed a strategy down here, which I urge you to adopt. Christine, I'm afraid, has not been very adept at it, and as I think you will see, her failure to follow my advice has worked to her detriment. You must stay strong, physically and mentally, and learn whatever you can. We, my dear, are waiting for our miracle."

Miracle. I winced at the word, so contrary was it to everything I believed in. Tracy noticed.

"Yes, I know, a miracle is not such a great thing to have as your only option, but I have given the matter a great deal of thought, and that's all we have. All we can do is ready ourselves for it. I have a simple motto: 'Eat whatever you're fed, sleep whenever in bed, don't let him fuck with your head.'" She laughed jaggedly at her own sad joke again before continuing.

"The most important part of your body right now is your *brain*. As you will soon see, our enemy's favorite—not only, but favorite—form of torture is psychological, so you need your mind to *work*. You have to keep him out of your head. Never tell him anything about your life before. Never."

"A Never List," I whispered, more to myself than to her. "And Jennifer? What will happen to her?" I was finally able to ask the question without becoming hysterical.

Both of them looked away. Christine, her eyes cast to the floor, whispered something under her breath that I thought I could just make out.

"Forget her as soon as you can."

CHAPTER 5

After I read the letter, I spent another three days alone in my apartment. I canceled my shrink visits and didn't answer the phone. Dr. Simmons left three messages, and Agent McCordy four. I knew they were worried, but I could not explain to them that I was gearing myself up for a major break with my post-traumatic lifestyle, a break I was only halfway ready for myself.

I didn't have the courage to tell Dr. Simmons that after ten years of our psychological struggle together—the tears, my long stares off into the distance while she waited patiently, the circles and circles we spun in as we churned through the facts of my life, picking over every memory except the ones I still couldn't touch, the ones she most wanted to delve into—she couldn't do anything more for me. We were at a dead end. I needed to do something real.

After the first year of therapy, I was able to recite the facts of my captivity by rote. It was as though they had happened in some alternate universe, to some other person. A litany of terrible things I could mumble out across the room to keep Dr. Simmons at bay. New details whenever the conversation seemed stale, whenever she started demanding more of me.

It was a history I revealed in isolated images. Me, blindfolded, my feet in chains hanging from the I-clamp bolted to the ceiling. Me, on the table, spread out like an insect for dissection, a catheter running to my bladder, filling me up milliliter by milliliter. Me, in the corner, strapped to a chair with my wrists cuffed behind me, a surgical needle piercing my tongue.

Facts. Details. Specifics.

Things that happened to someone else. Someone not here anymore.

Ostensibly, I was opening up to Dr. Simmons, telling her my darkest secrets. But she always seemed to know that in reality I was pulling away. I could tell the stories, but I couldn't feel them anymore. They were like poems repeated over and over until all the meaning had drained out of them.

So for years now we had stood at a stalemate. Hours of sessions wasted, while she waited for me to make a move forward. But now, maybe, that's what I intended to do.

On the fourth day I called McCordy. He answered on the first ring.

"McCordy here."

"Are you sitting down?"

"Car—Sarah, is that you?"

"It is. Listen, I wanted you to know that I am fine. I read the letter. You were right. Mumbo jumbo. I promise not to freak out like I did before, okay?"

"So why wouldn't you answer your phone?" A hint of suspicion sounded in his voice. "A second longer, and we would have sent in the paramedics. You would not have liked it if we'd had to break down your front door."

"Why didn't you then?" Silence on the end of the line. "You talked to Bob, right? You knew I was still ordering in and therefore not dead. Clever. Anyway," I began, trying to sound carefree, "I've been thinking about what you said and . . . I'm going on a little trip."

"I'm glad I am sitting down. That's . . . wonderful news. But are you sure you're ready to do that? Shouldn't you start with something simple, like the grocery store?"

When I didn't answer, he went on. "May I at least ask where you are going?"

I sidestepped his question.

"I need to think, and to do that I need to get away. I'm taking some time off from work. I happen to have a lot of vacation days left."

"Not surprising. About the vacation time, I mean. Have you, um, talked to Dr. Simmons about this?"

"N-n-no. Not yet. But she's my next call."

I took a deep breath as I hung up. After all, I was not a prisoner. They were not my jailers. I *could* go on a trip, and I *did* have a lot of accrued time. These things were all true.

What was not true was the actual vacation part. I had an idea. The letter had not given me any distinct clues, even though something about it tugged at the back of my mind. I decided, however, that three days was enough to wait for the memory to jog, and since nothing was forthcoming, I had to move on to Plan B. I would listen to Dr. Jack Derber. His wife, Sylvia, was supposed to "show me the path." Well, maybe he was on to something. Though not necessarily what he intended. *Sylvia, show me*, I whispered resolutely as I put the phone in its cradle. *Show me*.

It took all of three-tenths of a second for Google to tell me Sylvia's full name and the town where she lived. The benefit of having a famous archenemy was that he couldn't get married without the world knowing the details. *Sylvia Dunham, Keeler, Oregon.* She lived not too far from the prison, convenient for her but unfortunate for me, because I believed I would be able to feel his presence through reinforced concrete and steel bars as easily as I had through the cellar door.

I ran a Google Earth search on the penitentiary and stared for a moment at the tiny yard, a smudge of tan on the screen, where surely he must walk every day. I could just make out the indistinct image of the guard tower, and even the minuscule line marking the boundaries of the prison with what must be razor wire. I shut down the Web page with a shudder. I didn't want to push my psychological limits too soon.

I hadn't even been back to the state since my escape, and I had solemnly vowed never to return. But Jack's letter made me realize what the price of my inaction might be. Even the remotest possibility of his release stirred up emotions I'd been fighting back for years and forced me to confront what I knew I finally needed to do, no matter how terrifying.

At Jack's trial, the prosecutors had "been pragmatic," they'd "done what they could." And their strategies had worked to an extent; he was in jail, after all. But that didn't change the fact that Jennifer's story had been left open-ended, a case that might never be closed. Over the years I'd come to accept it somewhat, thinking there was nothing I could do. But Jack's letter made me believe that Sylvia might be the key to it all, that she might know something concrete. Now duty was calling me, and for the first time in ten years, I felt I could answer it. Maybe it was all that therapy finally working after all. Or maybe somehow I knew this mission *was* the therapy.

Before my courage could fail me, I pulled up another Web site and booked my flight, a room in the nicest hotel in the area, and, pausing, a rental car, knowing that as much as I hated to drive, there was zero chance I could get into a cab. I booked under Caroline Morrow, my "real" name now. My practical side was taking over. I started making lists.

This would be the first trip I'd taken in five years, since visiting my parents back in Ohio, and, frankly that hadn't gone very well. Despite the ensuing three-hour layover in Atlanta, I had booked a flight that put me on a Boeing 767 because it had the lowest mechanical failure rate in the fleet. Even with that security, I'd had a full-blown panic attack as I'd boarded. The airline crew had forced me to deplane, thereby delaying the flight and raising the ire of a number of vocal passengers, who would have, I'm sure, been much more understanding if they'd known my real name and remembered me from the newsstands. I'd had to wait six more hours at the airport before the paramedics were convinced I could keep it together enough to get on a later flight.

This time my rigid aircraft requirements put my detour through Phoenix, and the circuitous route would take me a full twelve hours, six hours longer than was strictly necessary for efficiency's sake, but nevertheless utterly required for my mental condition.

I packed light but well. The next day, as I clicked my suitcase shut, I felt, once again, fully prepared. Ready. Sure of my mission. And then, as had happened last time, right before walking out the door, I felt that old familiar feeling—thoughts spinning, chest tightening. I fought it back, but as I struggled for breath, I made my way back to my bedroom, over to the white-painted bureau.

I pulled out the bottom drawer, the one I never looked in anymore, and dragged out a battered blue photo album. It fell open naturally to a page in the center, and in the upper-right-hand corner, under the peeling laminate, there she was, Jennifer, at thirteen.

Above her unconvincing smile, her eyes looked sad, as they always had in the years after the accident. She looked serious, as if she were thinking hard. I was standing next to her, leaning over, caught there with my mouth open, talking to her animatedly. She was lost in her own world, and I hadn't even noticed.

I studied the picture of myself at that age. Despite our fears, I looked so confident, happy even. Now, sitting safely in my room, if I leaned back on the rug, I could see myself at thirty-one in the mirror over the bureau. My sharp, angular features had been softened somewhat by age, but my dark brown hair was the same shoulder-length no-muss-no-fuss bob I'd had since high school. My brown eyes looked nearly black against my pale skin that had only the pink flush of panic to infuse it with life. I looked distraught, even when I forced a smile back at myself. No wonder they deliver up the shrink to my door, I thought, looking at the frightened creature staring back at me.

Slowly I stood up, and as I started to replace the album, I paused and pulled out that one photo of the two of us. I tucked it into my wallet and picked up my bag. Then I pushed the album far to the back, carefully closed the drawer, and smoothed my clothes. Jim was right. I did need some fresh air. I collected my things, double-checked my flight time and number, and put into my bag the sandwich I had wrapped earlier. I could do this.

It was only as I triple-locked my apartment door from the outside, with my bright red suitcase at my feet, that I remembered I hadn't called Dr. Simmons. Well, I shrugged, McCordy will tell her, and then we can talk about my avoidance strategies for three or four sessions. Nothing like a new narrative to keep the relationship alive.

CHAPTER 6

I had never lost the trick of closing my eyes to shut out reality, and I spent most of my flight to Oregon with my cheek pressed against my inflatable pillow. The stewardess supposed I was sleeping, so other than the routine seat belt checks, she had left me alone. I had felt the anxiety rising up in my throat as the plane took off, but knowing I didn't have time to waste with airport medics, I swallowed it back.

In truth, though, I didn't sleep at all. My heart was beating faster than ever. The sights and sounds of travel were overloading my brain, which hadn't taken in this much visual and aural information at once in five years. But it was more than that. My mind was racing as I was hatching my plan.

It would be a lot for me to meet with Sylvia, and I wondered if I was crazy to do this without Jim. But the FBI had spoken to Sylvia before and had not been able to break through to her. Now Jack had made it very clear in his letter that she was his confidante. That she knew all the details of his past. I hoped coming face to face with his victim would make her realize whom she had really married, and that I could persuade her to reveal something she might not tell anyone else.

I was staying in Portland, even though Keeler, where she lived, was about forty miles outside the city. It was a little inconvenient, but her town had only motels, and a door directly onto the outside world was a nonstarter. I had never been comfortable driving, even when I'd been in practice. But I was relieved to find that once I got behind the wheel, the habit came back to me, though every second put me on edge.

I checked into the hotel without incident but also without grace. Unused to eye contact, I mostly stared down at my credit card, my hands, my suitcase. I hated the sound of the words "Caroline Morrow" as I choked them out. Ten years of it, and it still didn't ring true to my ears. And it had never seemed fair that he had been able to rob me of my identity in such a profound way.

Once in my room, I locked both locks, which I couldn't help noticing were made by a cheap manufacturer. I berated myself out loud for being such a freak. Nevertheless, my first move was to find the hotel guide and memorize the locations of all emergency exits. I studied the map on the back of the door and picked up the phone handset to check for a dial tone. I took out my cell phone to charge it, even though it was nearly at full power. You could never be too careful.

I had thought a lot about what I would say to Sylvia, and I ran over it all in my head again as I unpacked my clothes and laid them out on the bed to make sure, once more, that I hadn't forgotten anything. Of course I hadn't, so I showered quickly and set out on my journey. I wanted to make an initial run at it today and get back to the hotel before dark.

I found Sylvia's house without any trouble. A small, nondescript, brick ranch house in a quiet residential area. At first glance, it looked deserted. There were heavy curtains on the windows, all closed.

I pulled into the empty driveway and quickly surveyed the premises. The garage doors in front of me looked as if they were sealed shut. I peered into their windows and saw that the space was neat as a pin. No car there, either. Along one wall, a wide assortment of household tools hung from a row of evenly spaced nails, their outlines traced carefully in marker. A bike in the corner had an obvious flat.

All this way, and she wasn't home.

I walked around to the front door and rang the bell, just in case. I tried three times before I was convinced no one was there. I went back to the mailbox and, out of the corner of my eye, checked for signs of interfering neighbors before I opened it up. It was jammed full. I hesitated for only a second before pulling out a few pieces of mail. Already here I was, day one of this journey, breaking federal law. But at least I could tell I had the right place.

The mailbox contained mostly bills and advertising flyers. I reached underneath the pile and checked the postmark of the phone bill on the very bottom. It was dated three weeks ago. Strange that she hadn't had the post office hold her mail if she had expected to be gone so long. But then, maybe I was the only one who planned ahead like that.

After flipping through the stack to make sure there was nothing from the penitentiary, I shoved it all back in and returned to my car, unsure of my next steps. I sat there for a few minutes, thinking. Since I'd made this trip to Keeler, I might as well explore every avenue, so I decided to stop off at the coffee shop I had passed on my way here. This was a small town—maybe they knew her.

It was a quaint silver train car diner, bright and welcoming inside, right on the little town green. I chose the counter instead of one of the empty booths and ordered a coffee, trying my best to look friendly. I forced a smile.

I could see my face reflected in the mirror behind the counter. My eyes were bloodshot from the flight, my hair disheveled. Yep, total freak, I thought. I stopped smiling. When the waitress came over to refill my cup, I almost lunged across the bar at her. Awkwardness personified. I was clearly out of practice when it came to human contact.

"Do you know Sylvia Dunham, by any chance?" I asked in my best casual voice, which couldn't have sounded less so. I was cursing my ineptitude inside, but the waitress didn't even look up from pouring.

"Sure, I know her." Her cool response made me realize there might be a lot of crime tourists who came in here curious about Sylvia Dunham. She had to be famous in this town. And there were people weirder than I was, I knew. Voyeuristic types who planned their vacations around crime scene destinations. I had to come up with something to distinguish myself from that particular brand of crazy. Yet I hadn't planned to do anything more than confront Sylvia on this trip. I hadn't exactly prepared for snooping this way, and I certainly wasn't ready to announce to the world who I really was, after all these years.

"I'm . . . I'm writing a book," I stuttered.

"Yep." She still didn't look up as she wiped away a tiny drop of coffee I'd spilled earlier. I realized my mistake. I probably wasn't the only person trying to write a book on it either. I knew I was going to have to come up with something a little smoother, if I was going to do this for real.

Finally, she paused and glanced up at me.

"Look, some people like the extra business we get from tourists poking around here about this lady. And some people don't. I have to say I don't. I don't want this guy coming to live here when he gets out. Don't want anything to do with it. Now my husband, he's of a different opinion. He doesn't have much else going on. I'm sure he'd talk your ear off about this subject." She sighed. "He'll be here at five to pick me up, if you want to ask him about it."

I made a quick calculation. If I stayed until five, and talked to him for no more than fifteen minutes, I could still make it back to the hotel before it was fully dark. It was only four-fifteen now, though, so I'd need something to do until then. I thanked the waitress, paid, and told her I'd be back.

To pass the time, I walked around the neat town square, admiring its fresh-cut green lawn and the white-painted benches set out around the perimeter. I stopped in front of the prim white church on the corner. Maybe this was the one. Her church. I walked in and found it empty except for a woman vacuuming in front of the altar, her graying hair pulled up in a wispy, messy bun, her glasses chain swaying with her swift, thorough movements. I waved to her uncertainly, and she immediately switched off the vacuum, wiped her hands on her small apron, and walked briskly over to me.

"Can I help you?" she said, in what I thought was a not-very-churchlike manner. What if I were a little lost lamb looking for redemption? I cleared my throat, not sure what I could say to make me seem like I wasn't the interloper I was.

"Yes, I—my name is Caroline Morrow, and I'm trying to track down an old friend of mine who lives around here." I was fumbling around for the right words. Rambling, I knew. She stood still, waiting for me to spit it out.

"Sylvia Dunham." I finally said it, and before the words were fully out of my mouth, I saw a shadow fall across her face. She knew the name. Everyone here must know the name. I went on.

"She doesn't appear to be home, and I know she is a devout person, so I wondered if by chance someone here might know her. Know where to find her."

She looked at me, coldly I thought, and shook her head.

"Does that mean Sylvia Dunham is not a member of this congregation?" I tried again.

She shuddered slightly, then seemed to remember church doctrine and forced a smile.

"I guess you haven't been in touch with her recently. Sylvia Dunham is definitely not a member here. She is with the Church of the Holy Spirit. A rather interesting little sect, or community, or whatever you want to call it. Well, to each his or her own." Her expression turned dour. Then she looked around at the sanctuary with obvious self-satisfaction, admiring her picture-perfect church with its tall windows yawning up over the shining hardwood pews. "They don't have a church per se." She stopped abruptly, as though she'd said more than she wanted to already.

Her eyes were on the door as she spoke again.

"If you'll excuse me, I need to get things ready before our Wednesday-night Bible study."

"Where can I find someone who is in that congregation?" I asked. I could tell she was planning to take my arm, probably to lead me out of there as fast as possible. Without even thinking, I avoided it by moving quickly in the direction of the exit on my own.

"The only person who can tell you about that congregation is Noah Philben. Probably the only one who will talk to outsiders at all. He's the leader of it, if it isn't blasphemous to call him that. He stays at their . . . compound, but you won't be allowed in there." She looked me up and down, seeming to weigh her next words carefully. She shrugged, but I noticed her tone was softer now.

"They have rented a space though, not far from here—on Route Twenty-two, right in the shopping mall with the Trader Joe's on the way into town. It used to be the community center. I think he keeps an office there. There's a white cross out front. Can't miss it."

"Thank you," I said, rushing to get the last words in as she closed the door in my face. The locks clicked directly in front of me.

I dug in my bag and found the small notebook and pen I had packed. I carefully wrote down Noah Philben's name and the directions she had given to his rented office.

Just before five I wandered back over to the diner, figuring the waitress's husband sounded like my best bet for now. The waitress was already standing out front, a light trench coat wrapped around her tightly, smoking a cigarette. I surprised her.

"Oh, it's you," she said, this time not unfriendly. She gestured to a small wooden bench to the left of the door, and we sat down. She put out her cigarette on the arm of the bench, and I stared at it, transfixed, thinking of the fire hazard, as I watched to make sure each glowing ember burned out completely.

"Gotta quit these." She turned to me, her newly applied lipstick glistening. "Now, why would a nice young lady like you want to write about such an awful story?"

I didn't have a ready answer, of course, and was regretting mentioning a book at all. I could hardly pass for a real journalist and was wishing I could have come up with a better cover story. I'd have to make do, though, so I decided to treat the question as rhetorical, and only smiled in response.

"Haven't there already been some books about this?" she went on.

"Three," I said a little too quickly, a little too bitterly.

"So what's the point? Hasn't that story been told? Or do you have a new angle, as they say?"

"Those other three books were . . . incomplete."

"Really?" Now she seemed intrigued and leaned in a little closer, so close I could smell the cigarette smoke on her clothes. "My husband will be very interested to know that. What was wrong with them?"

I hadn't thought through how to explain this, so I carefully avoided eye contact as I spoke.

"You'll have to read my book, I guess." I put on my best voice of false cheer, which usually didn't work very well. This time was no different, but she didn't seem to notice, or maybe she had only asked the question in the first place to be polite.

"Not me. I can't read that kind of stuff. Life is hard enough without filling your head with all those awful things." She paused. "Those poor girls. I hope they are making it okay. My friend Trisha, she had an abusive maniac for a father. He ruined her life. She started drinking in high school, ran away, eventually started doing meth. She's cleaned her life up now, but she's not over it. Probably never will be."

"I suppose you never get over something like that," I said flatly.

"No," she continued. "You never do. Trisha's doing better though now, from what I hear. She moved to New Orleans last year. She thought the change would do her good. Had a cousin out there. When she was here—she worked here at the diner—I'd catch her looking off into space, staring at the window, and I always thought, she's going off someplace dark in there. Real dark."

At the words *New Orleans,* I bolted upright. Something was ringing a bell. Tracy had been from New Orleans originally, and she'd also had a rough childhood, so maybe that was all it was. I took out my notebook and jotted down a reminder to think about it when I got back to the hotel.

As I slipped the notebook back into my bag, a car pulled up, and the waitress waved to the man in the driver's seat. She turned to me, as he approached us, and said, "I'm Val, by the way. Val Stewart." She extended her hand to shake mine, saying, "Honey, I don't know your name."

I saw her hand coming toward me and froze. I had to respond normally. This would not be the only time someone would want to shake my hand, now that I was corresponding with live people and not just the ghosts in my head. I braced myself, but as she was about to make contact, I lost my nerve. I dropped my notebook and bag, in what I was sure seemed an obvious ploy to avoid her touch. As I bent down to pick up my things, I nodded up at her and told her, in as friendly a tone as I could muster, that my name was Caroline Morrow. She smiled back warmly and pulled out another cigarette. Disaster avoided.

Val's husband, Ray, was a small man, a few inches shorter than she was. He was very trim, in his sixties, with salt-and-pepper hair and a twinkle in his blue eyes. You could see right away what Val meant when she said he could talk your ear off. When he heard from Val that I was writing a book about the Derber story and specifically about Sylvia Dunham, he invited me home for dinner without hesitation. I begged off, even though I wavered. I wanted to go but couldn't bear the thought of driving back to the hotel after dark. Instead, Ray insisted we go into the diner for a quick coffee.

Val rolled her eyes, "See, I told you, sweetie. Listen, I've seen enough of that place today. You two get coffee, and I'm going to run over to Mike's and pick up a few things."

Back inside, we sat at a booth, and as soon as we'd settled in, Ray started talking.

"Sylvia moved here about seven years ago. You probably know she's from the South. Nice girl, but quiet, you know. It was a shame she took up with that Church of the Holy Spirit. It's nothing but a cult, if you ask me."

"Why do you say that?"

He hesitated, his eyes sweeping the room before he went on.

"Well, Noah Philben wasn't always religious, I can tell you that."

"You know him?"

He put his elbows on the table and bent his head toward mine, a conspiratorial look on his face now. "I went to high school with his cousin, so I knew the family. A sorry one, that Noah. He drank a lot, did some drugs. Left town after graduation and was gone for several years. No one knows what went on then. Nearly drove his family crazy, but they didn't like to talk about it. When Noah came back, he seemed a little off. Went back to work at the quarry for a few months but couldn't keep that up. Then he started his 'church,' if you want to call it that." At that moment, he pointed out the window of the diner.

"There they go." I looked over and saw a white van with tinted windows pull around the square. "Church van."

"The lady at the church on the square seemed pretty dismissive of it, to say the least."

"Oh, that woulda been Helen Watson. You met her? Ha. Friendly one, eh? Well, she wouldn't be too happy about anything having to do with Noah, that's for sure. He was her high school boyfriend. She ran off with him when he left. She came back two years later with her tail between her legs. Never talks about those days. She says it's none of anyone's business. Later she married Roy Watson, who became the pastor at that church about ten years ago. People say she pushed him to go to seminary school. She always wanted to be a preacher's wife, I guess. Now she thinks she rules the roost of this town."

Not seeing how the town gossip was getting me any further, I tried to redirect the conversation back to Sylvia.

"I went by Sylvia's house today. There was no one there—doesn't look like anyone has been home for some time." I didn't want to admit I'd riffled through her mailbox, and felt a blush of shame creeping up my neck.

"Come to think of it," he said, "I can't remember when I last saw her. She keeps to herself, but usually comes in to the diner just about now, when I'm picking Val up. Maybe comes in once or twice a week."

"Does she have a job? Anyone else I could check in with?" I felt I was hitting a dead end.

"Not that I know of. Not around here anyway. Guess I'm not as helpful as I thought I'd be."

"What about her family? Did she ever talk about them?" I wasn't used to asking all these questions. The last thing I ever wanted to do was engage people more; usually I wanted interactions to end as quickly as possible. Even my voice sounded strange to me, foreign, remote, like a bad recording of the way I imagined it in my head. I noticed I almost couldn't formulate the right lilt at the end of a question.

"No, that was the strange part too. If I had to guess, I'd say she was running away from something down there, but she never really talked about it. She was from somewhere around Selma, Alabama. Town with a history. Maybe she just wanted out of there."

It was on the drive back under the darkening sky that it hit me. I nearly veered off the road. New Orleans. Where Val's friend had moved. It reminded me of something in Jack's letter. Ignoring the fact that the sun was fading over the horizon, I pulled over onto the shoulder and hit my hazards.

My heart pounding, I pulled the letter out of my bag. The lake. The lake was Lake Pontchartrain. I reread the line. It still made no sense to me, but I knew now it had to be that lake, and if so, then it meant only one thing: this was part of Tracy's story.

I went through the whole letter again. I needed Tracy. I needed her to tell me how this fit in with her past, to tell me what it meant. Somehow I would have to make her talk to me, maybe even meet me face to face, to think with me to see if there was meaning in this madman's words. To figure out if he was leading us somewhere, and whether he meant to or not.

CHAPTER 7

Tracy's story had come out slowly over the years, a little here, a little there. I pieced it together out of small details that slipped out, mostly when she was feeling particularly low, desperate and hopeless down there in the cellar. For the most part, she tried to keep her life locked away from us. Her head was a private area where she could escape from him and from us too, I suppose. She was paranoid about each delicate shred of information she told us being used by Jack to manipulate her mind. That was their battle.

He always had Jennifer to use against me, so he didn't need to rely on my memories, at least not while she was alive. I suppose that was why at the time I didn't understand how high the stakes were for Tracy, how critical it was for her to keep her previous life as a sacred place. It was a mistake that would cost me dearly in those later months of captivity. Nevertheless, we spent so many countless hours together, it was impossible not to get a pretty vivid picture of her life on the outside.

Tracy was born to an eighteen-year-old high school dropout in New Orleans. Her mother was a heroin addict, with all the pain and suffering and horror that comes along with it. Men wandered in and out of their filthy apartment on the first floor of a Creole townhouse on Elysian Fields, one that looked like a crumbling cake that had hardened with age on somebody's countertop.

When Tracy was five her little brother, Ben, was born right in the apartment. Tracy watched his birth from the corner and saw her mother take a massive hit of heroin during labor, an anesthetic so powerful that she barely moved as Ben's head emerged. It was a miracle the child survived, and an even greater one that Child Protective Services managed to forget about this little corner of the world. Apparently the city of New Orleans had chaos enough to deal with elsewhere, and after a brief, perfunctory interview, the social workers had left them alone.

For years that brother was just about all Tracy had in the way of familial love and affection, and she fended for the two of them with all the fierceness I came to know was in her. Her mother provided little if anything for them. She rarely ate, so consumed was she by the drug, and there was never much food in the house, certainly not enough for both kids. So Tracy had gone out onto the streets of New Orleans to build an entirely different sort of life for them. In any other city, that might not have been possible, but in New Orleans, alternative lifestyles took on a new meaning.

Over time Tracy ingratiated herself into the world of street performer culture—would-be life dropouts and buskers looking to get discovered, while making their daily bread in service of the tourists who swamped the streets. Tracy and Ben became their orphaned mascots, and they in turn protected the children from the horrors of nightlife in the city.

Tracy was a clever young girl who learned all the tricks—magic, juggling, acrobatics. She also had a gift for storytelling and charmed tourists and fellow street performers alike with her precocity. The other minstrels built a special dais for her in a back alley of the French Quarter. She would stand and recite poems or tell stories to the gathering crowd. Inevitably, as her audience dispersed, Tracy would overhear the wife in a couple saying they ought to call someone, someone ought to adopt her. Tracy used to dream of that— that some rich tourist would come along, fall in love with her and her brother, and take them away from their pathetic little strain of existence.

Sometimes they would stay out all night in the Quarter, Ben tucked away in an alley on a pile of dirty old blankets, but never out of her eyesight. She'd watch the drunks scuffle home and the prostitutes she mostly knew by name wandering back from their johns. Eventually the city would go quiet in the hour or so before dawn, and only then would she gather Ben up, sleepy-eyed, and trudge back to their grimy apartment. Their mother never asked any questions.

Tracy rarely went to school, and after a while the truant officers, just as overwhelmed as Child Protective Services, didn't even bother her. But she read like a maniac. Autodidact, she would always say, and I've never seen a more perfect example. The owner of a used book store on Bourbon Street would slip her books as long as she returned them quickly. She read everything, from *Jane Eyre* to *The Stranger* to *The Origin of Species,* waiting out the long days on the sidewalks of the city, oblivious to the noise and smells around her.

She and Ben just barely managed to stay alive with the coins they gathered over the course of the day. They supplemented their meager food supply by grabbing scraps of beignets tossed by tourists or stopping in at the transvestite bar around the corner after hours for leftovers. Tracy put up a strong front, seeming to take it all in stride, and even handed over to her mother a share of their money when they had a little extra. That at least kept her quiet and out of their hair.

When Tracy became a teenager, her crowd morphed into the street kids her own age. The Goth kids. They dressed in black and dyed their hair dark shades of red, purple, or black. They wore chunky jewelry dangling from black strips of leather, bold rings with bloodred fake gemstones, and from their piercings hung silver-plated skeletons or crucifixes. Tracy's favorite symbol, ironically, was the ankh, the Egyptian symbol of eternal life.

Some of the kids got into heroin. Tracy wouldn't touch the stuff, associating it with her mother. She drank a little and got into some trouble, but nothing that would get her locked up where she couldn't protect Ben.

By then he had taken up the charge on the performer front. He was a talented acrobat, having befriended one of the Quarter's old-timers who mentored him. Some days he could collect ten full dollars, and then they'd go into a bar and order a giant plate of fries and two half-pints. Those were the good days.

Unfortunately, the bars of New Orleans had everything to offer. Straight, gay, transgender. Dancing, leather, S&M. No one carded. In the strange trajectory of Tracy's life, I suppose it was inevitable that her crowd started gravitating toward the darker side of the city, the parts the bus tourists avoided. Her favorite bar had no sign, just a black door against a black wall throbbing with the beat of industrial music. Nine Inch Nails. My Life with the Thrill Kill Kult. Lords of Acid.

The door creaked opened on its rusty hinge to reveal a dark cavernous interior, like a black hole, with threads of cigarette smoke unwinding out into the night air. That was it. The bouncers, with their slow-healing cuts in the shapes of slave markings, knew Tracy and stepped aside for her to enter.

Later she would admit she'd been naïve. At the time she didn't understand where this life could lead. All she knew was that she felt like a part of something, something secret, something that gave her a sense of belonging. The rich tourists coming through the city had nothing on them. This was an empire. And the angry music that pounded in her head every night almost matched the anger she felt at her mother and at the world. This was a strong empire they'd built, and she felt its strength coursing through her veins, more powerfully than any Class A narcotic ever could.

Tracy spent four years in that scene. On the rare occasions when she talked about that life, I almost grew jealous of it. The freaks and weirdos had all congregated in the church of New Orleans, a privileged spot in the world of outsiders, and they lived together on the streets, in disintegrating rooming houses, in group apartments, all hanging with bright scarves, cheap jewelry, and unclean sequined garters, in a strange community of acceptance.

Nothing really mattered there: age, appearance, gender, preference. It was all one big melting pot of aberration, and the sex and drugs and occasional violence were only small pieces of the picture, pieces that helped them all live through the experience of being misunderstood, used up, and broken but still deeply, unerringly human. There, in that bubble of underground life, judgment was suspended for an hour, a year, a lifetime, while occasionally a shred of self-esteem and even pride would blossom under the folds of gossamer, lace, and leather.

Then something happened to Tracy that caused all that power to drain out of her. She kept the story a secret from us for years. In the cellar, we named it the Disaster, so she wouldn't have to spell out the details of the worst thing that had ever happened to her. The worst thing besides Jack Derber, that is.

And after the Disaster, her mother disappeared again, maybe for good. When she'd been gone for three weeks, Tracy just about decided she wasn't coming back. She figured she could hide that fact from Social Security for a while and could forge her mother's name on the checks long enough to get some savings together, but by then she didn't even care.

She sank deeper into the club scene, sickened, miserable, and alone. Her life was going nowhere, and she was smart enough to know it. Drinking wasn't helping. That night at the bar some stranger offered her a hit. That night she took the needle in the dark, her hands shaking with fear and anticipation. Maybe this was the answer after all: the quick way out of the pain, if only for a little while.

She had seen enough people shooting up to know the drill, and she took the leather strap and fastened it tightly around her arm. The needle found its way into her vein easily, slipping in like destiny. The first rush of the drug filled her with euphoria and wiped away her suffering, sweeping it out like a burst of clean air whipping through the city streets at dawn. At that moment, for the first time ever, she thought she understood her mother and wondered if she hadn't been right about life after all.

Somehow Tracy stumbled out of the club, into the back alley, where she could be alone to savor the pleasure. It was a hot summer night, the air full, so thick with humidity it hit her like a wall as the door slammed closed behind her. The sweat was beading on her forehead, dripping down her chest and into the cheap leather of her hand-me-down bustier. She leaned against the Dumpster out back and slid down into the refuse of a thousand sunken lives—used condoms, cigarette packs, ripped underwear, part of a rusted-out chain. But even then something at the heart of the pleasure of the drug made the tears well up, made her think about everything that had happened, and she'd cried, an animal howl from deep inside, until she slowly lost that final grip on consciousness.

She woke up, probably days later—she couldn't tell—in the cellar, on the cold stone floor, in a pool of her own vomit.

CHAPTER 8

I sat on the bed in my hotel room, looking at my face in the mirror over the empty bureau. I gripped my cell phone, talking myself into making the call I knew I had to make. It was a Monday morning, and I had Tracy's office number scribbled on a piece of paper in my other hand. I took a deep breath and dialed.

After three rings I heard her voice answer hello, and I almost couldn't summon my own to reply.

"Hello!?" she said again, impatient as always.

"Tracy?" She was the only one who hadn't changed her name.

"Yes, who's this? Is this a sales call?" She was already annoyed.

"No, Tracy, it's me, Sarah." I heard a sound of disgust, then a dial tone.

"Well, that went well," I said to my face in the mirror. I dialed again. It rang four times, then she picked up.

"What do you want?" she said angrily. Her voice dripped with disdain.

"Tracy, I know you don't want to talk to me, but please hear me out."

"Is this about the parole hearing? You can save your breath. I'm going. I've talked to McCordy. You and I have nothing to talk about."

"It isn't about that. Well, it is, but it isn't."

"You're not making sense, Sarah. Get it together." She hadn't changed much in the ten years since I'd spoken to her. I could tell I only had about twenty seconds to persuade her not to hang up. I got to the point.

"Tracy, do you get letters?"

A pause. She obviously knew what I meant. Finally, suspiciously, "Yes. Why?"

"I do too, and listen, I think he's telling us something in them."

"I'm sure in his crazy head he is, but they don't make any sense at all. He is *insane*, remember, Sarah. Nutso. Maybe not legally, maybe not enough to get him off the hook. But crazy enough that we should be throwing out his letters unopened."

I gasped. "You don't do that, do you? Throw them out?"

Another pause. And then, quieter this time, with reluctance, "No. I have them."

"Maybe he's crazy, maybe not. But listen, I think I've figured something out. I think he is sending messages to you in my letters, and maybe to Christine as well. I think there might be something in his letters to you that I might understand, and vice versa."

She didn't answer for a long time, but I knew her well enough to know I should wait. She was thinking.

"And how is this going to help us, Sarah? Do you think he's letting us each know how special we are to him? How much he still loves us? Do you think he's going to give us some key to put him in jail longer? He is many things, Sarah, but he is not stupid."

"No, he's not stupid. But he likes to take risks. He likes games, and he might want to give us a fair hand. It would give him a lot of pleasure to think he was telling us something meaningful and we were too stupid to figure it out."

I could sense her mulling this over in the quiet over the line. "You have a point. So what do we do? Send each other our letters?"

I took a deep breath. "I think it's more complicated than that. I think . . . I think we need to meet."

"That seems indescribably unnecessary." Her tone was icy. I could hear her hatred loud and clear.

"Listen, Tracy, I'll be back in New York in two days. Can you drive down and meet me there? I'm sure you have a lot going on right now with your journal and all that, but I don't think we have time to waste. What is your cell number? I can text you when I get in, and we can meet."

"I'll think about it," she replied. And then the line went dead.

CHAPTER 9

After ordering in herbal tea from room service to recover from my contact with Tracy, I drove back out to Keeler, to pay a visit to Noah Philben at his new office. As a rule, I didn't like people with radical ideas, and I had, up until this point, structured my entire life to avoid them. Fanatics, mystics, and extremists all tended toward irrational and unexpected action. Statistics could not protect you from that.

I wanted people to fit squarely within their appropriately delineated demographic category: age, education, income level. These facts should have predictive value, and when they didn't, my ability to interpret and relate to people went askew. As Jennifer and I would always say, at that point, anything can happen, and there were too many categories of "anything" I didn't like.

Even though the tank of my rental car was not even half empty,

I stopped at a gas station on the way down, taking advantage of what appeared to be an unusually pristine BP right outside of town. I noticed with no small satisfaction that the attendant was locked away from me behind unbreakable plexiglass. If only everyone could be like that.

I found the shopping center with no trouble and pulled into a parking space close to the grocery store, where a buzz of shoppers passed in and out, their carts rattling loudly as they crossed the uneven pavement. I sat in the car for a minute, wondering what the hell I was doing here.

I reached into my bag and pulled out my cell phone, checking it out of nervous habit. It was comforting to see the fully charged battery icon and the five signal bars radiating out at me. My shoulders dropped half an inch at that, and I breathed in deeply.

As I considered my next task, however, I felt the urge to bolt, to race back to New York and forget this whole escapade. I could simply testify, the way Jim wanted me to. No way would they let Jack Derber out of jail—the parole hearing was surely just the State of Oregon going through the motions of its administrative process, wasn't it? I didn't need to do this.

But was there a chance?

From what I knew of prison terms, it could happen. The criminal justice system did not dole out that justice fairly and evenly, in proportion to the crimes in question. Someone could spend their whole life in jail over possession of a gram of cocaine, but rapists, kidnappers, and child molesters could end up hardly serving any time at all. Ten years might satisfy the State of Oregon after all. Release was possible, especially if they fell for a religious conversion story, and I knew his behavior in prison had been, naturally, impeccable. I had heard he was even teaching a course in there to the other inmates. Fuck. I had to talk to Noah Philben.

The building looked almost inviting, considering what I'd been expecting anyway. It was still painted in bright colors, with a giant rainbow mural covering the front wall, a relic of its community-center past. Through the glass-fronted door, I could see an office tucked inside to my left. The administrative staff, a young man and woman, each of whom looked to be no more than twenty-five, sat busily sorting papers. They were clean-cut and eager. This didn't seem like a cult at all. More like a YMCA. I felt my anxiety lifting.

Bracing myself, I pulled open the door and walked over to the office. The young man looked up at me and smiled. He seemed perfectly normal, except for a glint of heightened zeal in his eyes that made me a little uncomfortable. I hesitated.

"Welcome to the Church of the Holy Spirit. How can I help you?" he said brightly. Too brightly.

I took a deep breath and explained, as politely as possible, that I wanted to talk to Noah Philben. The boy frowned and furrowed his brows, seeming unsure of what to do. I guessed Noah Philben didn't get a lot of visitors.

"Not sure he's in yet. Um, hold on just a minute." He left me alone with the girl. She smiled at me too, a little less forthrightly than the boy. Then, casting her eyes back down, she returned to her paper shuffling in silence. I knew any normal person would have initiated small talk, said hello, at least brought up the weather, but I didn't know how to do such things anymore. So I just stood there under the bad fluorescent lighting, looking around the room awkwardly.

A few minutes passed before the boy returned, now with a tall man in what must have been his fifties following behind. This had to be Noah Philben, for he was wearing not only a clerical collar but also a priestly black robe that extended down to his ankles. His hair, a scraggly blond fading to gray, just touched his shoulders. His eyes were a piercing blue. His face was perfectly controlled as he came toward me, a mask of impersonal calm.

As he passed the office, however, a lopsided grin broke out on his face when he greeted the girl behind the counter. She looked away shyly, appearing to be uncomfortable with this attention. A cold shiver went down my back. Maximum creepy, I thought to myself, but I forced my own smile as he approached. I tried to take a step toward him, but my legs protested by going wobbly on me.

Just at the moment he reached me, my phone started beeping. Probably Dr. Simmons, since it was my regular appointment day. I ignored it.

Noah Philben looked down toward my hip pocket, in the direction of the sound.

"You need to answer that?" He grinned that same grin at me.

"No, it's fine." I reached into my pocket to shut off the ringer. "Mr. Philben, I—"

"It's actually *Reverend* Philben, Miss . . ." That was clearly my cue, but I stood there for a full three seconds, a little slow on the uptake. He was waiting patiently for me to tell him why I was there.

"I'm Caroline Morrow," I finally forced out. "And I'm so glad you're here. I don't want to disturb your day, but I'm looking for someone, an old friend. Sylvia Dunham? I understand she is a member of your . . . church." I looked over at the girl. Her head was still bent down over the mail. The boy was on the phone in the opposite corner. They didn't appear to be listening.

Noah Philben raised an eyebrow.

"Interesting," he said as he glanced at the front door, considering my words. "Shall we step into my office?"

He aimed his thumb down the hall, toward a door in back. No way was I stepping into some back office down the hall. Not with this guy. Not with anyone. Anything could happen. I tried to smile sweetly, as I pointed over to a bench in the entry hall.

"Oh, I don't mean to take up much of your time. Maybe we could talk for just a moment, right over here?"

He shrugged again and lifted his hand toward the bench, "Whatever you say. After you."

I eased myself slowly onto the seat, never taking my eyes off his face. He remained standing. I immediately regretted sitting, for now he was towering over me. He folded his arms and leaned against the wall, ignoring the bulletin board beside him with the words *Come worship with us* in stenciled, multicolored construction paper that flickered from the air he had stirred.

"How do you know Ms. Dunham?" he asked, with that slow grin still sliding across his face.

"I knew her growing up, and I've been traveling in the area. On business. I heard she was one of your parishioners."

"Yep," he stared straight at me. Clearly he wasn't planning to volunteer anything.

"I'm trying to reach her. She doesn't seem to be home. I thought maybe someone at her church might know where she is." Again, my faux casual voice. I could never have been an actress. I could feel a blush running up my throat as I thought how woefully unsuited I was for this task.

Noah leaned forward. I thought for just an instant that I detected a hint of menace in his eyes, though I told myself it was just in my head. The grin was gone now. I leaned back against the hard bench, almost overpowered by the force of his gaze. Then he stood tall and smiled again. I couldn't tell whether he had noticed the effect he was having on me.

"No idea. Haven't seen her in a few weeks. It's not like her to miss . . . services. Only *the Lord* knows where she is. But, um . . . if you hear from her, let me know, all right? I naturally have a great deal of concern for my parishioners, as you say. I'd love to know where she is." Noah leaned back against the wall again, relaxed and cold as ice.

"Sure, sure, I definitely will. Well, thanks anyway."

Something about the look in his eyes made my stomach clench up, and a cold sweat break out on my skin. I felt the air start to catch in my chest. Something in my body clicked into automatic gear, something all too familiar. I knew where this was headed, and for some reason I was desperate not to let this man see me panic. Almost involuntarily, I shot up from my position and backed toward the door, reaching into my pocket for my car keys.

I had to blink back tears as I smiled timidly, nodding my thanks and waving a halfhearted good-bye as I pushed open the glass door that led out onto the parking lot. The two young people still didn't look up. I wasn't sure if it was my imagination or not, but I thought I heard Noah Philben laugh as I turned and walked away. It was a hard sound. Humorless and raw.

CHAPTER 10

I tried to sleep on the plane back home to stave off a panic attack about flying, but instead I kept going over the Sylvia Dunham disappearance in my head. I wondered if I should talk to Jim, let him take over and figure out where she was. But I knew that legally there wouldn't be any cause for them to look unless someone who was legitimately in her life reported her missing. She could just be out of town, after all.

I had never been happier to see my building, after a six-block walk from the subway. I lugged my suitcase across the threshold and felt my whole body begin to relax. It was only at that moment that I realized how much the stress of this search was wearing on me.

Then I noticed Bob. He was gesticulating to me furiously. He put his finger to his lips and pointed to the back of a woman standing in the corner with a cell phone to her ear. Before I could comprehend what Bob was trying to tell me, she turned around and saw me.

"Sarah?" she said, hesitating as she clicked her cell phone off. I could tell Bob was puzzled by the name.

"Tracy! You came," I replied, stunned.

Bob looked at me, then her, unable to disguise his shock. I'd lived in the building for six years and never had had any visitors other than my parents, my shrink, and Jim McCordy. And here, standing in the lobby of the building, was a petite punk rocker, with dyed black hair streaked with hot pink, a leather-studded jacket, black tights, and black lace-up boots, with tattoos and piercings all over her face. And I knew her.

Seeing Tracy for the first time in a decade made everything come back to me at once. I had to lean against the wall for support. A flood of images flashed in my mind. Tracy's eyes, as she hunched in the corner, recovering from pain. Tracy's eyes, as she laughed quietly during those long hours when we had no one but each other to stimulate and entertain us, when our conversations were the only lifeline to the real world, and we were the only things keeping each other from losing our minds. And then the final image, as always when I thought of her, of Tracy's eyes gleaming with rage when she found out what I'd done.

Was that look there in her eyes now, lost somewhere behind her glassy stare of incomprehension? I imagined she was struggling with her own memories as well, as we stood there in the polished lobby, on a bright May day, in the middle of millions of people oblivious to the monumental event occurring there. In my head, I ran the numbers on how many other great and meaningful reunions were taking place in the city at the same moment. But could anything else matter quite as much?

"Sarah," she finally said again, her eyes slitting, with what kind of energy I could not tell.

I walked up just close enough, but not too close, to her so that Bob couldn't overhear, and said quietly, "Caroline. I'm Caroline now."

Tracy shrugged, threw her cell phone into her bag, and said, as if there were nothing extraordinary going on, "So can we go up?" She tilted her head toward the elevator.

I could sense Bob approaching on my left, ready to take a stand to protect me from what he clearly deemed to be some criminal element. He'd come out from behind the desk braced for battle.

"It's all right, Bob. She's an . . . old friend." I stammered out the word and, without looking, could feel Tracy wince. I led the way to the elevator rather reluctantly. I'd hoped to meet somewhere on neutral ground, but it wasn't working out that way. Bob returned to his post, but I could tell he was not comfortable with the situation. And neither was I.

We stood in silence listening to the old mechanism clink as we slowly rose to the eleventh floor, then Tracy said very quietly, almost to herself I thought at first, "I brought them."

I knew exactly what she meant and felt a quick, sharp pang of regret for asking for them in the first place.

When we reached my apartment, Tracy walked around, looking at everything. Whether she liked it or not, I couldn't tell. She smiled slightly as she dumped her bag on my coffee table.

"Overcompensating much?" she said with a smirk. Then she relented and added without looking at me, "Really it's very nice, Sarah. Very . . . calming."

Without sitting down, I gave her a quick recap of my trip to Oregon and my search for Sylvia. I skipped the fact that it had been my first trip anywhere in years and that I had specifically vowed never to return to that state.

Tracy took it all in stride, as usual. She clearly thought I was being overly dramatic about Sylvia's disappearance.

"She's probably on a trip," she said as soon as I'd finished. "And if you really think she's missing, isn't the correct course of action to go straight to the police?"

"I'm not quite ready to trust my stellar investigative instincts yet, I suppose," I replied.

Tracy smiled a little at that.

We set up in my dining room, each of us spreading out our letters in chronological order on the table. In each instance, the postmarks were only a few days apart. I brought out two empty notebooks and brand-new Uniball Deluxe pens. We sat down and pored over the pages.

At first I was disoriented by the sea of black ink swirling in my pristine white world, but I forced myself to concentrate. Only thinking can save us, I thought automatically, my mantra from the past.

I wrote out columns in my notebook, one for each of us, and we began to categorize the references as best we could. Under Tracy's name I wrote, in the careful block letters Jennifer had always used in those other notebooks, NEW ORLEANS, COSTUMES, LAKE. She glanced over at the page and quickly jerked her head away. I figured the word *lake* must have brought back some painful memories.

I carefully thumbed through Tracy's letters, terrified at what I might find but eager as well. Finally, I came across what was clearly a reference to Jennifer and me: "A crash and then drowning, fast, in a sea of numbers." Under my name I carefully set the words CRASH and SEA OF NUMBERS. Of course. The car accident that killed Jennifer's mother. The journals. He had figured out so much, so easily, while we were his prisoners.

We studied the letters for nearly an hour, until my columns were two pages for each of us, when Tracy finally leaned back and sighed. She looked me in the eye, but without menace this time.

"They make no sense whatsoever. I mean, yes, the letters are about us. Yes, he likes to torment us with how much he knows. It seems like he's spending a lot of time in the slammer rehashing old memories for the thrill. But in terms of interpretive value, I'm going to have to give this a zero."

"It's a puzzle," I said. "It's some sort of word puzzle. I know we can break it, if we just use logic. If we just get these ideas organized. If we just—"

"—*do the math*?" Tracy interrupted with frustration. "Do you think that can really help us? You think all of life can be sorted and arranged and comprehended? That the whole universe is organized in accordance with some inner logic, and with enough statistical analysis, we can solve some sort of philosophical algorithm? Life doesn't work that way, Sarah. I thought you'd learned that already. If three years in a dungeon didn't teach you that, then nothing I can say will. Look what he did to us. Our heads are the puzzle, not these letters. He spent years mixing us up, and now you think you can overcome that, and apply the methods you used as a teenager to decode some hidden message? You think there's invisible ink in there too?" She got up and stormed into my kitchen. I followed.

She opened my cabinets one by one until she found what she was looking for. I stared at her in disbelief. She had a box of cereal in her hands, and she started ripping it open.

"What are you doing?" I thought she'd gone completely mad. I backed away from her, quickly calculating the seconds it would take me to run to the door, flip all the locks, and get to the elevator.

"I'm looking for the decoder ring, Sarah. I'm looking for a secret spy tool that can solve this puzzle for us."

She must have seen the alarm in my eyes, because when she looked at me, she put the box on the counter and took three slow, deliberate breaths. Then she put her hands over her face, her fingertips massaging her scalp. When she dropped them, she looked back at me, dry-eyed, and spoke with a new firmness in her voice.

"We can't be the ones to go through these letters. Send them all back to McCordy, with your little chart. Let him put his agents on it. They have techniques and methods and strategies. We just have a lot of fucked-up memories that are only going to keep us twisted up inside the more we dwell on them."

I stood beside her, staring past her at a small stain on the kitchen floor, the kind you can never get off, the kind you have to renovate your whole kitchen to make go away.

Tracy sat up and stared at me, dejected. "You got my hopes up a little bit, I admit. But this is a waste of my precious time. I gotta get out of here . . . I left the journal in the hands of the deputy editor. I'd better get back to my next issue." She stood up slowly and started gathering her things, looking around the room again. "You know, all this white is actually pretty stifling."

"Wait, wait." My normal human instincts almost kicked in for a minute, and I lifted my hand to reach out for her, but then I recoiled from the thought of touching flesh, pulling my hand back as though from a fire. I wanted her to stay, but I didn't want anything that badly.

"Wait a second—your journal. Your writing. He says to 'study the teachings.' Could that be your journal, your work? Or does he mean the Bible?"

Tracy didn't stop packing up. She didn't sit down but rested a knee on the chair for a minute, her hand holding the notebook paused in midair. I waited, fully prepared for her to ignore me and stomp out the door.

"Not my work," she said slowly, thinking. "Everything else he refers to is in the past, before . . . before, well, you know. I don't believe it's the Bible—his religious conversion is an obvious farce. He wants to tell us something else. But what about his own 'teachings'? He was a professor after all. What if he's talking about his academic work? Something to do with his classes, the university?"

Tracy sat back down, pondering this idea further. "That's interesting, actually. I mean, this is really unrelated to the letters," she said pointedly, "but I just wonder if this has been explored by anyone. It makes some sense if you believe, as I do, that he was testing his own psychological theories on us. We were, after all, regular lab rats, in a medieval scholar kind of way."

I felt renewed hope, if only because this idea might lead to something concrete we could do. It was at that point, when I felt hope stirring in me again, that I knew there was no going back for me. I couldn't rest until I had followed this path to the end. I *had* to do this.

I took up her line of thought. "If we're going back to the university, we need Christine. She was his student, in his own department. She can help us navigate."

Tracy laughed. "As if. Christine is not going to have anything to do with us. Literally nothing. She shut that door years ago. I don't even think we could find her to ask."

"Yes, we can." I remembered what McCordy had said, perhaps indiscreetly.

"How?"

"I know where her kid goes to school."

Tracy looked up, interested. Her wheels were turning now.

"It's Thursday." I looked at the clock. "School lets out in an hour."

"Well, okay then. Let's meet her at pickup."

CHAPTER 11

It was ironic that we were going to find Christine on the Upper East Side, right back where she'd started. After all she'd told us in that cellar, I couldn't understand why she would have returned to it when, if nothing else, she'd had the chance to start her life over. Maybe after all we'd been through, she decided she just wanted something familiar after all. She didn't want to take another chance at transforming her life. She'd tried that before, and it had nearly killed her.

Christine was the only child of a wealthy Manhattan investment banker and his socialite wife. She grew up in the most exclusive of the exclusive prewar Park Avenue buildings, right on top of Carnegie Hill, in a sprawling classic nine co-op apartment that had been handed down from generation to generation. Her family summered in Quogue and went skiing in Aspen during winter breaks.

It was a good life, insular and staid, and Christine, a compliant and dreamy child, had passed her early years contentedly, paying no attention to the world outside her tightly protected enclave.

Until she was sixteen, that is, when everything changed. That was the year Christine figured out how her family maintained its rank in the social and economic hierarchy. The year she learned that all the old money and the gentility that went with it had dwindled away long ago, and that her father had replaced both over time by trading less in high-yield financial instruments than in information. Material, nonpublic information.

He'd been accused of having an inside track on earnings statements for several blue-chip companies days before their release. And the timing of his trades didn't look good.

She believed in her father at first and stood by his side, following the case closely, asking questions, trying to understand the complicated mechanics of sophisticated financial transactions. But the more she learned, the more she began to believe, along with the attorney general and the *New York Post*, that he was guilty. The more she began to see Wall Street as an insiders' club, with its own code of ethics that was very different from what Christine would have ever imagined, had she ever bothered to imagine it before. And what's more, it was dawning on her slowly that her father's illegal activities were par for the course for him and his business associates. And every time he saw her eyes open wide with that realization, he'd tell her to relax, that this is just the way business is done.

But Christine couldn't accept that. Standing on her balcony at night overlooking the placid interior courtyard of their building, she'd cry quietly to herself, understanding that the comfortable lifestyle she'd always taken for granted was built on fraud and dishonesty. She couldn't look at their beautifully appointed apartment, their luxury SUV, or her closet full of designer clothes without thinking about the dirty money that had bought them.

At brunch on Sundays at the Cosmopolitan Club, she sat with her mother in the crowded sunken ballroom, with its sparkling chandeliers, glistening silver service, and clinking crystal. Wearing the pale blue sweater set that matched her eyes, she gazed out at the elegant diners around her, all of them, she knew, listed members of the Social Register. Now she bristled at the way their practiced fingers effortlessly balanced the finest of china teacups and their frosted pink lips poised to form polite, tepid conversation. They presented themselves as so entitled, as if all this luxury were their natural right, but she wondered if they'd all gotten there the same way.

Nevertheless, she had her pride. Each weekday she'd set out for Brearley with her head held high, not saying a word to anyone about her suspicions. She looked straight ahead, unblinking, when she walked past the reporters massed outside their building each morning. But in secret she'd lock herself in her room after school and read the damning newspaper articles they wrote, her eyes burning with tears as she saw the truth printed there in black and white for the world to see.

In the end, as Christine would have anticipated had she had an inkling of how money really worked, her father made it through the experience relatively unscathed. His company paid a hefty fine to the SEC, and his high-priced lawyers managed to find a lower-level employee to serve as a scapegoat, thereby keeping him out of jail. The press coverage eventually died down, and her parents' lives returned to normal, everything snapping automatically back into place. This sort of thing happened often enough in their social circles to be considered a minor nuisance, part of the game of business. A blip. An annoyance. A harmless setback.

But by then it was too late. Christine knew the truth, and she couldn't move past it.

After struggling for weeks with the moral implications of her situation, she made a decision. She had less than a year left at home, and after that she would turn her back on this privileged life. She would start from scratch and make her own way in the world. She would never touch her trust fund or take a dime of her eventual inheritance. She'd pack up all her sweater sets and become someone new.

Christine was proud of her resolution and would lie awake in bed at night thinking what it would mean for her. She knew it would be hard. Painfully hard. She knew that she was giving up a lifetime of comfort in exchange for hard work and uncertainty. But it felt good.

She decided to make it a smooth transition, for her parents' sake. She maintained the facade of the perfect daughter right up until it was time to leave for college, living exactly as she had before, joining the Junior League, attending the Gold and Silver Ball, standing at her parents' side demurely, shaking hands when asked, saying please and thank you, and smiling at appropriate intervals.

They never noticed the change brewing inside her.

When it came time for college, her parents naturally expected Christine to continue the family tradition and go to Yale. But even Yale felt tainted to her. Instead, Christine was determined to make her move. She closed her eyes and drew a line on a map far in the other direction from New York City. She landed on Oregon. It seemed about right to Christine—as far as possible from Park Avenue as she could get without landing in the Pacific Ocean.

Her mother was horrified that her daughter would be at school in a state where no one they knew even had a vacation home. But somehow Christine managed to prevail and even got a full tuition scholarship to the University of Oregon, thanks to the wonders of the Brearley exmissions office. Though her parents relented, they must have secretly hoped that after one semester she'd realize her mistake and transfer to the hallowed halls of Yale, where she belonged.

Once at school in Oregon, however, Christine felt enormous relief. She was exhilarated being on her own. She had managed to extricate herself gracefully from her protected world, and now she was embarking on a journey of total reinvention.

That first semester, though, despite her best intentions, she was forced to dip into her trust fund. She took as little as possible, living frugally, determined to repay it as soon as she could. She looked for her first part-time job. She lived on ramen noodles and canned tomato soup. And all the while, slowly and steadily, she turned herself into just another kid on campus, in jeans and a sweatshirt, living in a dorm room with linens from Target.

There in Oregon she was able to return to the blissfully anonymous state of her youth, before all the trouble broke out. No one there seemed to have read the *Wall Street Journal* articles about her father, or at least they didn't recognize her last name. She never volunteered information about where she'd come from or who she really was. If asked, she said she was from Brooklyn and that her parents owned a retail shop.

It all might have turned out perfectly for Christine had she not developed an interest in psychology in her second year and, in particular, in her brilliant and dynamic psychology professor, Jack Derber. She had enrolled in his class by chance, to satisfy a social science requirement. But after the first day she was hooked.

She would tell us, her voice still bearing traces of that initial awe, how he'd virtually cast a spell over the classroom, how the students would sit rapt with attention, as he made Psych 101 sound like a new religion or at least a profound calling. He was charismatic, in a calm, hypnotic way, his voice soothing everyone into accepting ideas they'd never even considered sane before.

At the start of each class, he'd pace back and forth slowly in the front of the room, his hands clasped behind him, lifted only occasionally to stroke his thick, dark hair, as he formulated his thoughts. The hall was full—visitors sat cross-legged in the aisles, and faculty from other departments stood in back. Several minicassette recorders had been placed near the podium. In any normal lecture, the students would have spent this time chattering, shuffling papers. But for Professor Jack Derber, they sat in a respectful silence, waiting for his smooth, full lips to speak, for his powerful voice to echo in the air. When he finally began, turning to face the crowd as his penetrating crystal-clear blue eyes squinted out above the tiered stadium seating, his words were inevitably polished, succinct, brilliant. His acolytes took notes furiously, not wanting to miss a thing.

Christine, in particular, was thrilled by him, staying after class to ask questions, working on special projects, meeting with him during office hours. She'd pull all-nighters on papers for that course, struggling to bring her text to life, to do justice to the overpowering phenomenon of his lectures.

He, in turn, had noticed Christine right away. She sat in the front row, and even though she'd worked hard to shed the gloss of her luxurious upbringing, something must have made her stand out. Something that revealed her high pedigree, that showed her exceptional breeding and poise. Something that suggested a certain delicacy of feeling from being cosseted her entire life. Something that he wanted to break.

Jack's instincts were finely tuned, indeed, and he must have noticed she was trying too hard, that she was flustered in his presence. He must have felt that she was more vulnerable than even the freshmen. Maybe he could see she didn't fit in with the others, that she was looking for a place in life different from where she'd come. And as a matter of fact, he had just the spot.

So midway through the semester, he offered her a highly coveted position: his research assistant. Christine was elated. Not only would she be working with one of the most admired professors on campus, but the job's stipend meant that she could stop taking her trust fund allowance. She would be financially independent for the first time in her life. It was a huge step for her, and she solemnly cashed the first check, proud she'd gotten this far on her own. She almost couldn't believe it.

It didn't take that long, however, before Jack decided Christine's time had come.

Christine had always been too traumatized to tell us the details of how she went from being Jack's research assistant to being his captive, but there she was before first semester finals, down in that cellar. We had always wondered whether she was the first—whether he had spent months waiting for exactly the right target, and then Christine had come along—or whether it was simply time for him to capture a fresh set of victims.

Either way, she ended up in that cellar, chained to the wall, spending the first hundred and thirty-seven days down there alone in the dark, surely wishing she'd gone to Yale after all.

For that was part of Jack's vision all along—to watch as she tormented herself with her own profound sense of failure. She hadn't been able to live on her own in the end. She hadn't been able to make it outside the protective bubble of the überrich. Once she'd left the rarefied world of the Upper East Side, she had been exposed as weak and defenseless. And she would pay an awfully high price for leaving it.

So she spent the next five years down there, thinking and re-membering and regretting.

It must have been too much for her, because Tracy and I watched her fall apart in that cellar. Bit by bit, the darkness started to over-take her, and there was nothing we could have done, even if we'd wanted to. She had a complete breakdown over those last three years, and it accelerated rapidly toward the end. Her mind deterio-rated before our very eyes.

She had long since stopped making sense when—and this was even more dangerous for her—she stopped taking care of herself. It didn't take long for her to look dirty and disheveled. For her face to be smudged with muck from the cellar floor, for scattered clumps of matted hair to burst out all over her head. For her to smell. And Jack didn't like that.

Some days, though, she scared us as much as he did, as she sat hunched over, mumbling unintelligibly there in the dark. She would huddle up on her mattress, clutching her knees, and rock back and forth, her eyes closed, her voice soft as she whispered to herself for hours.

I didn't try to make out what she was saying. I didn't want to know.

Honestly, it was a relief that she slept so much, because when she was awake, you couldn't help but keep one eye on her at all times. It was exhausting. You never knew when a violent outburst of tears was coming. Or worse. I sometimes thought that even Tracy, her erstwhile protector, seemed a little afraid of what she might do. At any rate, toward the end, we both stayed as far away from her as we could manage in such close quarters.

If you had asked me back then, I would have said that, of the three of us, Christine would be the one who would never recover. That she was the one whose psyche was battered beyond repair. I would have predicted she would be totally devastated from this experience forever, unable to have any semblance of a normal life if we made it out alive.

It just goes to show, you never can tell. I had never been more wrong about anything in my life.

CHAPTER 12

Tracy and I arrived in front of Episcopal, an imposing town house that had been impeccably maintained. A sea of adorable, perfectly turned out children headed out the door, escorted by nannies and emaciated trophy wives. A line of black Town Cars waited outside.

We stood close by, watching, but not so close that we would make the staff uncomfortable. Tracy nevertheless got a few looks, so we crossed the street, pretending to be deep in conversation.

"Do you see her?" I asked, my back turned from the scene of Upper East Side perfection.

"No. She probably has one of her teams of nannies pick up her children," Tracy remarked with irritation.

"She has a team of nannies?"

"I guess that's not fair. I'm speculating. Oh wait, I think that's her coming from a couple of blocks away. Hard to tell because these women all look the same. Hurry, let's intercept her before she gets too close to the school."

We ran down the block, and by the time we got to Christine, we were both winded. We must have looked ridiculous, all red faced and breathing hard. Instinctively, she jumped back from us as we came to a sudden stop in front of her.

Her hair was the most shimmering shade of golden blond I had ever seen, and her face, whose skin had always seemed translucent, now glowed with health. Her teeth were in perfect even rows, and her cornflower-blue eyes looked as though they'd been dyed for effect. She was impossibly slim, and every stitch of her casual clothing looked immaculate, as though she had just stepped out of the display case of a Madison Avenue boutique. I looked down in dismay at my travel clothes from my flight that morning: jeans, T-shirt, and hoodie.

"Christine!" said Tracy triumphantly, seeming almost happy to be reunited after all these years. I felt a pang of what had to be jealousy, which was erased when I saw that Christine definitely did not feel the same way.

Christine pulled herself up tall and said haughtily, "As you know, I don't use that name anymore."

"Oh, right," said Tracy. "I keep forgetting about the cloak-and-dagger names. What is it now? Muffy? Buffy?"

Christine looked Tracy up and down this time, obviously annoyed.

"My friends know me as Charlotte. Really, Tracy, why don't you go back to one of your protests, or whatever, and leave me alone? And *you*"—she turned to me and then, unable to find the words, immediately back to Tracy—"I'm surprised to see you two together."

I decided to get straight to the point. "Jack comes up for parole in four months—"

Christine held up her hand in the air, cutting me off midsentence. "I don't want to hear it. I don't care. I actually really don't. I have told McCordy that that is his problem and let the justice system do what it may. If they can't manage to get a raving madman locked up in a straightjacket in some rubber room, then they are clearly incompetent buffoons, and nothing I can say or do is going to help them. I want nothing to do with it."

"You don't care if he gets out?" Tracy jumped in. "Don't you have daughters? Aren't you worried about them? Haven't you read his letters? The guy is still obsessed with us. What if he makes a beeline for your door when they let him out? I don't think they'd like to see him showing up on the steps of The Episcopal School."

Christine looked at Tracy with a steady gaze, her voice firm.

"No, I most certainly have not read any letters from that monster. I told McCordy he could keep them. You think I would want those in my *home*? And as for my daughters, I will get them each a personal bodyguard if necessary. But I don't think that is a realistic concern. Jack may be crazy, but he is not stupid, and I can't imagine he has enjoyed being locked up. And now, if you will excuse me—" She started to push past us, but Tracy blocked her way.

"Fine, fine, you want nothing to do with it. We get that. But tell us something—if we go back to the university, to talk to people there about his work and his life there, who should we talk to? What should we do there?"

Christine stopped walking. At first I thought she was going to turn in the other direction and run, but she didn't. She looked at each of us in turn, as though she finally recognized us as members of her species. Was she letting herself remember? Surely she couldn't have blocked it all out as completely as she made it seem. She couldn't be that strong, entirely recovered, able to handle anything, including Jack's release. But then Christine had always been a person of extremes—unpredictable in a way that put me ill at ease.

I thought I saw a hint of sadness flicker across her face, and then she shut her eyes for a moment, her lips twitching ever so slightly. When she opened them again, she shrugged with an air of resignation.

"Well, what about that woman who testified at the trial? The one who had been his teaching assistant when we were there? Isn't she a professor there now? Aline? Elaine? Adeline? Something like that."

So Christine had followed the case. She knew a little more about it than she'd let on. Tracy was nodding. I pulled out my notebook and started writing.

Christine paused. "And there is one thing that I have thought about over the years. I suppose now is the time to bring it up. Jack had what I suppose you could call a friend there. I sometimes saw him at the cafeteria with another professor in the department. Professor Stiller. I never took a class with him, but they seemed to hang around together a little bit. I mean, it could be nothing, but—"

"Thanks, C," Tracy said, using the name she'd used sometimes back in the cellar. "That's something. I'm sorry . . . I'm sorry we—"

"Whatever," said Christine. "Just—well, good luck." She seemed to be relenting for a moment. Then she pulled herself upright again and said quietly, "Just please leave me out of it."

As we walked away, I saw Christine rush up to another elegantly dressed mother and give an air-kiss greeting. Then she walked off with her, chatting merrily, as if her dark and hidden past hadn't just collided with her on the sidewalk.

CHAPTER 13

The first time I was allowed upstairs was almost magical. I had been held captive for one year and eighteen days when I was finally selected for that honor. I had begun to think I would die in that cellar without ever seeing any more sunlight than the sliver that sneaked in through the boarded-up window. I almost didn't care why I was being led up those cellar stairs in chains, as I counted off the steps in my head.

I remember my surprise when I had my first look at the living areas of the house. I had imagined, for whatever reason, a run-down 1970s aesthetic. In fact, while the furniture was not new, it was classically nice, some heavy antiques from the Empire period, lots of dark woods and high cathedral-beamed ceilings. Solidly upper middle class. Well designed. Tasteful.

The space had an ethereal glow to me, as a light wind delicately blew through the open windows. It was damp out. A soft rain had just finished falling, and the leaves dripped slightly. I had been through periods without food and evenings filled with electrical shocks. I had been tied up in various unseemly positions for hours, until my muscles ached and burned. But I could almost forget all that for the delicious pleasure of feeling the air on my skin again. I looked at Jack Derber with gratitude. That's what it does to you.

He didn't speak to me for a long time but merely pulled me along through a hallway with several doors. Barely turning my head, for fear of seeming resistant, I peered into the kitchen at the back of the house, an immaculately clean room, cheery even, with a flowered dish towel draped over the edge of the sink.

That caught my eye for some reason. This dainty little hand towel that he must have used carefully and, I knew, meticulously to dry the dishes . . . he . . . this same person who had made me suffer so much, who had ripped my life out of its socket and put me in this hell also dried his dishes and put them away every night. It seemed to me he lived in accordance with an orderly and regular routine, and our punishment was just a part of it. For him, just an ordinary part of his ordinary day, and then at the end of a weekend, he'd drive back to that bustling college campus and go about his business, as if nothing had happened.

That first time, he led me into the library. The room seemed enormous, with high ceilings and walls lined with expensive-looking oak bookcases, the shelves brimming with volumes. Each one was covered in an off-white binding, so I couldn't tell much from their spines. They were labeled in some way, and even though, over the next several months filled with trips upstairs, I stared at them to take my mind off the pain he was inflicting in that room, I could not decipher their titles. The words were in English, but I seemed to have lost the capacity to comprehend even that.

In the middle of the room, there was a large rack I would later find out was a reproduction of an actual medieval torture device. It was set up to look like a novelty item, a decorative piece, a joke. But it was no joke. When we were upstairs, we would go on the rack.

On a good day, he simply did what he wanted with your body. And you could bite your lip or scream or do what you needed to bear the pain and humiliation.

On a bad day, he talked.

There was something about his voice, something about the way he modulated his tones for you, that made you almost believe for the first instant that he was filled with empathy and warmth for your plight. That he really hated to have to do all of these distasteful things to us, but he really had no choice. He had to keep on, for the sake of science, for his studies. Or sometimes it was for our sake, so we could understand something beyond the physical world.

Maybe I wasn't smart enough at the time, or hadn't read enough to understand what he was talking about, but now I know some of the references he made, in his long, rambling speeches: Nietzsche, Bataille, Foucault. He talked a lot about freedom, a word that made me cry when he said it, even on days when I swore to myself he couldn't do anything to get me to shed a tear. I am stronger than this, I told myself. Most days I wasn't very strong. But in the end, I think I was.

Over time I got the sense that he wasn't driven by uncontrollable urges. Torture was simply fascinating to him. He was in awe of what it did to us and how it made us respond. As we writhed there before him, he studied, yes, studied, how long we could fight back tears. He was interested in why we so badly didn't want him to see us cry. He'd ask us about it. He'd probe. And yet we were afraid to tell him the truth about anything.

He knew how arbitrary shifts would disarm us and fill us with fear. And he liked to see the fear. He would change roles in an instant, from father confessor to maniacal devil. He laughed sometimes, out loud, with sheer glee, when he'd see the fear seeping into our eyes.

And it was impossible to hide everything all the time. He figured out quickly how much I was suffering over Jennifer. Not knowing what was going on in her head all those days in the box. I wanted to ask him how she was holding up, but I didn't want to reveal just how much she mattered to me, so I said nothing for months. He knew, of course. He knew how close we were, that we were not random co-eds sharing a cab home that night. Maybe he had gotten Jennifer to reveal some details, or maybe she called out for me to help her when she was on the rack. I would never know.

But he knew enough to use her against me. He would ask me, as if he wanted me to make a noble choice, if I could take just a little more pain, a little deeper cut, if it would help her. And I did. I took as much as I could, squeezing my eyes shut tight each time the blade approached my barely-healed skin. When I eventually begged for mercy, he looked at me with disappointment, as though I were admitting that I didn't love her enough, that I wasn't able to protect her from what he was, quite unfortunately, going to have to do to her now.

I started hating myself for my weakness. I hated my body for what it couldn't handle. I hated myself for begging and bringing myself low before this man. I dreamed at night of smashing his face, of rising up like a banshee, screaming, hysterical, full of strength.

But then, inevitably, when, after days of starving me, he would come and feed me little bits of food from his own hands, I would suck it off his fingers like an animal, greedy, thankful and pathetic—a supplicant again.

CHAPTER 14

In the end, I flew to Portland alone, for the second time in as many weeks. Tracy had lost faith in the project once again or was maybe losing her nerve. Either way, she'd made an excuse about her work and had ended up driving back up to Northampton the same night. Maybe at the end of the day I was the only one strong enough to revisit those memories. The thought almost cheered me, as each day I was feeling slightly more up to the task, slightly more determined, even though I was no closer than I had been at the very beginning.

There was something about this search that gave me a sense of purpose and made me feel that, for the first time in ten years, I wasn't abandoning Jennifer. I knew that if I could find her body and put her to rest in that quaint little churchyard in Ohio with her ancestors, the whole experience wouldn't seem quite as appalling.

People died young all the time. I could almost accept the simple fact of her death, but I could not accept the way I'd lost her. And now finding her was the only way I could truly leave that cellar behind.

I stayed at the same hotel in Portland as before. I had been impressed with their security last time, and they were very obliging when I asked for a room on the top floor. The concierge remembered me and knew to cancel housekeeping during my stay. The last thing I wanted was someone knocking on my door, coming into my room, touching my things.

I drove to the university the next morning. I had done my Internet research and knew more or less where to find the two people I needed.

Her name was actually Adele Hinton. I'm sure Christine remembered that with great precision, though she would never admit to that kind of familiarity with the trial.

Though both had been psychology majors, Adele had been a sophomore when Christine would have been a senior, so Christine was in Jack's cellar before Adele enrolled. Adele went on to the graduate school program, and was Jack Derber's research assistant for two years, until the day he was arrested and hauled off by the FBI in the middle of a lecture to three hundred co-eds. Naturally, it was very shocking to the students, and the university had to do quite a bit of damage control in the press and on campus. It was, among other things for other people, a PR disaster.

I remembered from the trial that the prosecutors were surprised, and maybe even a little impressed, that Adele had not only continued on in the program—the other female graduate students in the department had transferred out immediately—but she barely missed any of her other classes during the time of her testimony.

Then several years later she accepted the very chaired professorship that Jack Derber had once held and that no one had taken since. I found it a little strange at the time, but I had other things to worry about in those days. Now I wondered what it was about this woman that allowed her to be so impervious to the horror of those events. She hadn't seemed afraid back then, according to what I'd overheard the lawyers say. She hadn't seemed to register her brush with death, working so closely with him on his research and spending late nights in the lab with him, as she surely must have done.

And even now her career seemed to be built on the same kinds of sick perversions she had learned about through Jack Derber. From the university Web site, I discovered she specialized in abnormal psychology. She studied people with deviant behavioral issues, who had atypical mental development. In other words, people who did horrible things to other people—that was the cohort that interested her.

As I walked toward the psychology department, I saw her leaving the building across the quad carrying a small stack of books. I recognized her from her bio page, though she was prettier in person. Stunning in fact. Tall, with long brown hair loosely flowing down her back, she still looked more like a student than a professor. She carried herself with enormous confidence, hips swaying purposefully, chin jutting slightly forward, almost defiantly. She was moving so quickly, I had to run to catch up to her.

"Excuse me. Are you Adele Hinton?"

She kept walking, maybe thinking I was a student. If so, she was clearly not interested in a student-teacher conference here on the lawn. This woman was busy.

"*Professor* Hinton, yes."

This time I had prepared a story. I had put in my time online at the hotel and felt ready. I took a step closer and began.

"My name is Caroline Morrow, and I'm a doctoral candidate in the sociology department." I rushed the words out. I knew my lines sounded overly rehearsed and that she'd be able to check up on me later if she wanted, but I pushed on, hoping to find out what I needed quickly. Adele was still walking. I knew how to get her attention, though.

"I'm writing my dissertation on Jack Derber."

At that, she stopped dead in her tracks and looked at me warily.

"I have nothing to say on that topic. Who is your supervising professor? Whoever it is, he or she should have known not to send you to talk to me about this." She stood and waited expectantly, as if every command she'd ever given had always instantly been obeyed. I hadn't anticipated this response, that his name would be such an anathema to her, considering her fortitude all those years ago.

I had hoped to avoid telling her who I was. I wanted the emotional cover of anonymity. Not to mention that my tragic life story was a distraction, a sideshow, and one I didn't want to be a part of for the millionth time. Nevertheless, Adele's eyes were narrowing suspiciously. She either wasn't buying my "research" story, or she was going to march directly into the university president's office to put an end to my nonexistent project.

I froze. She was waiting for an answer, but I didn't have one. In ten years I hadn't told a single new person who I really was. I hated hiding this way, behind a made-up name, but I felt safe there.

It wasn't going to work with Adele, though. Jack's name touched too deep a nerve with her. I had to come out from behind the mask for Jennifer's sake. I didn't have a Plan B this time.

I took a deep breath.

"Actually, my real name is not Caroline Morrow. And I'm not even a student here. My name is Sarah Farber." I was surprised at how good it felt to say those words out loud, despite the circumstances.

Adele looked stunned, clearly recognizing my name immediately. I could only imagine the sorts of memories it must have conjured for her. She looked uncertain for a moment—but only for a moment—then calmly put her stack of books on the ground and leaned closer to me.

"Prove it," she said testily.

I knew exactly how. I lifted up my shirt and rolled the top of my pants down slightly, so she could see the skin over my left hipbone. There, in red-scarred flesh, was the brand.

When she saw it, Adele swallowed hard, leaned over, and picked up her books quickly. I almost thought I saw a glint of fear in her eyes as they darted right and left. As if I were dragging that past around behind me physically, and Jack might be about to spring from my head, fully formed, like some sort of Greek god.

"Walk with me." She moved fast and didn't say anything for a while, her eyes fixed straight ahead. During my years of seclusion, I had lost some capacity for reading human expression, and I was feeling that loss acutely now. I couldn't even begin to tell what she was thinking. But was it me? Or was there something about this woman that was impenetrable to anyone? Her face might as well have been cut from stone.

"How—how are you?" she finally said rather stiffly, without a single note of actual pity or compassion, as though she had only just remembered that she ought to indicate some small semblance of humanity.

Despite its utter lack of warmth, the question made me smile with relief. I knew this line of questioning by heart. It was really all anyone had asked me for years. I had all my lines memorized.

"Me? Oh, I'm fine. It was nothing ten years of therapy and self-induced seclusion couldn't fix."

"Really?" She turned to face me at that, suddenly interested. "No anxiety? No depression? No flashbacks or night sweats?"

I looked away from her, my pace slower now. "That's not why I'm here. Don't worry, I have a professional support system. I'll live. Unlike Jennifer."

She nodded, not taking her eyes off me, understanding perhaps that I was not fine at all, but not pushing me further.

"So what are you really doing here?"

"I want to find Jennifer's body. I want to prove that Jack killed her, so he doesn't get paroled."

"Paroled? They're going to parole Jack Derber?" For an instant she seemed genuinely shocked, and then she regained her composure.

"Maybe," I replied. "I don't know. I don't want it to be possible. But I guess technically it is."

Adele nodded, even as she looked off in the distance, thinking hard.

"That would be just about the worst thing in the world," she finally said. "I would help you if I could. That man deserves to be locked away forever. But I don't have any new information on him. I told the police what I knew back then."

By now we were at the steps of the psychology building. She paused for a moment, then gestured for me to follow her in. It felt like my first real victory.

We made our way down the hall to her office. She didn't say a word, and I followed obediently.

We sat down, she behind the desk and I on a small worn sofa across from her.

"Actually," I began, "I'm not expecting you to remember anything more about the past. I mostly wanted to talk to you about his academic work. What he was studying at the time, his research. I have this idea that it could lead to something new. And I know you were his research assistant, and that your work now seems somehow . . . relevant."

I wasn't sure how that would go over. By now she was making me nervous. She just stared at me. Maybe she was thinking. Maybe she was willing me out of her office after all.

I glanced around the room to avoid meeting her eyes. The space was impossibly neat and orderly. The shelves were lined with titles in alphabetical order, and her notebooks were stacked and organized with color-coded tabs. It was mesmerizing in a way. Finally, she spoke.

"His research? I don't think you'll find anything there. His work was highly theoretical, and his subjects were varied. He covered a lot of ground, but I suppose he was careful not to study topics that might reveal his dark side. When he was arrested, he was in the process of designing a research study about sleep disorders. I worked with him on his last published paper, 'Insomnia and Aging.'

"My own work is really not related to his at all, except you might say it developed in the direction it has because I've been trying to understand Jack Derber and others like him. I guess I sort of narrowly escaped something, and I want to understand exactly what that something was."

We sat in silence for a few moments after that, while I tried to think of something else to ask and she rubbed her brow, lost in thought. I was disappointed. I'd hoped his published work would be more revealing, that he'd left us a clue there without meaning to. But maybe this was another dead end.

Just as I was beginning to feel hopeless again, she stood up and, with a quick glance out into the hall, closed her office door. She crossed her arms over her chest, almost defensively, I thought, and started talking, this time hesitantly, her back against the door.

"Listen, what I told you before is not entirely true. I might know something helpful." She paused. She seemed to be struggling with her next words. "Through some of my academic research, I found out something about Jack. This may seem a little strange, but I'm wondering, how much do you think you can take?"

"What do you mean, 'take'?" I was afraid of what she meant. I didn't like where this was going.

"I mean, what kind of shape are you really in, and how badly do you want this? Because I do have one thought. I mean, if it will help keep him locked away. There's a place I can show you.

"You see, my research is very field-oriented, based on the observation of subjects in their natural environments. I've been conducting a longitudinal, ethnographically-oriented study at a particular location for several years. And I discovered, quite accidentally, that this place has a connection with Jack Derber from long ago. There are things . . . there are people . . . I don't know . . . it's a long shot. But I suspect, knowing what I know about Jack, you are only looking at long shots."

"True." I was hopeful, despite my apprehensions.

"It's Thursday. Unfortunately, tonight would be the best night. Hope you don't have plans—otherwise you'd have to wait a week." She took out her BlackBerry, her thumbs flying fast on the keypad. "If I give you an address, can you meet me there at midnight tonight? It's a little . . . out of the way. And, frankly"—she looked up at me from behind her thick lashes, studying me as she spoke—"it's going to scare the shit out of you. It might remind you a little of your trauma. But on the plus side," she said brightly, "therapeutically, that might not be the worst thing for you."

"What exactly is this place?" Whatever it was, I knew I wouldn't like it. Plus, I didn't go places at midnight. Period. Much less any place that had the potential to scare the shit out of me.

"It's a club, a very special kind of club. I've been studying the psychological influences and effects of this . . . particular subculture. He used to go there."

I breathed deeply. I could only imagine what sort of place Jack Derber would like. And what kind of subculture Adele would be studying, given her intellectual proclivities.

"Okay. A special club. I get the gist. But that really doesn't seem like a good idea to me, therapeutically or otherwise."

She put her BlackBerry down, leaned over her desk, looked me straight in the eyes, and nodded. She spoke slowly, with her voice pitched a little higher than usual, as if to a child.

"Okay, that's completely fine. Maybe you are just not ready. I imagine it would be a hard place for you to go. I totally understand."

It might have been my imagination, but I was pretty sure her voice had a hint of challenge in it. She was a psychology professor, after all, maybe not on the clinical side, but close enough to know some tricks of the trade. These psych types, they knew how to push your buttons.

My head started reeling. It was like hitting replay on some bad scene from my other life. Could I take a deeper cut, could I take more pain, could I save her? Jack's face flashed in front of my eyes for just a second. Right now, even while he was locked up miles away, he was winning again. Once again I couldn't take the pain, couldn't take the fear. I turned to Adele, meeting her eyes, screwing up my courage even though my heart was pounding madly.

"What do I wear?"

She smiled, seeming almost proud of me. "Good. You've clearly made a lot of progress." She looked me up and down, noting, I was sure, the sad state of my sartorial choices. "I'll bring you something. It's important to blend in there. The last thing we'd want to do is stand out in this crowd. And I guarantee you don't own anything appropriate for this venue."

CHAPTER 15

Late that night I sat in my car in the parking lot of the hotel, regretting my decision to go as powerfully as I'd ever regretted anything in my life. I was talking to myself out loud, fighting down the panic attack I could feel creeping up on me. For one thing, for the first time in years, I would have to drive at night. While it was true that Adele had offered to take me, I never got in the car with strangers. No matter what.

But if the driving in and of itself was not enough to push me over the edge, the "special" destination most surely was. At a minimum, it would be dark and crowded and, from the sound of things, filled with exactly the types of people I had spent my life trying to avoid.

I gripped the steering wheel and banged my head on it gently several times. I couldn't believe Tracy was not here for this. This was exactly why I needed her to come, I told myself. This was her element. She probably went to this kind of place for fun.

I started feeling anger welling up in me. It reminded me of how I'd felt during the time just before my escape. I hadn't examined it much in the cellar, I was so focused on my goal. But now, sitting alone in my rental car in a deserted parking lot, something dawned on me. Tracy had always made me feel guilty for everything I did back then. But really, *I had borne the whole burden*. For all the bossing around she had done, for all her leadership down in that cellar, she had never done anything productive to get us out of there. And I did. I did. And now all I ever felt was guilt about it.

Here I was, having a revelation, and Dr. Simmons was nowhere to be seen. To be fair, I knew she had tried to make that point subtly in sessions for years, but I had dismissed it. Yet here I was, facing perhaps the most terrifying situation I had encountered since my escape, and I was having a psychological breakthrough. Maybe Adele was right: therapeutically, this experience was good for me.

I sat up straight and pulled out of my wallet the photo of Jennifer I'd brought along. I opened the glove compartment, bent the end of the photo, and closed the compartment door on its edge. There. Jennifer before me, like an angel, to keep me going forward. I checked the rearview mirror and turned the key in the ignition. *I am stronger than this*, I told myself. These were the words that had gotten me through my escape, and they would get me through this, too.

I thought of Jennifer, as I looked at her face before me, and of how different everything would be if I could put her to rest. Maybe then I'd even be able to live a normal life, among other humans. Out of my apartment. In the real world.

I drove for nearly an hour along the winding back roads. Plenty of time to tick through the list of all the dangers of the situation. Before I even got to my destination, my car could break down, or I could have an accident here in the middle of nowhere. I checked my cell phone reception no fewer than four times. The bars were all there, but I wasn't sure I could have explained to anyone where I was anyway. I considered pulling over and sending Jim a text, but I didn't want him to know I was on the trail of something yet, if I even was.

Finally, I arrived. I saw a driveway cut into the road, with no signs or markings other than a small, barely noticeable metal post with a yellow reflector, just as Adele had described. I pulled in and drove for about a mile up a hill along a crudely rutted dirt drive. I felt panic rising up inside me again. This activity did not meet my standards for careful behavior. What if this was a trap? What if there was nothing out here but empty woods, where anything could happen? What if somehow this Adele person was in league with Jack Derber? It occurred to me that I knew very little about her and was relying on what I thought of as our shared history together, some kind of bond that she may not have felt at all. And yet I had let her lead me down this path.

When I finally rounded the bend in the road, I saw to my relief a club of some kind, complete with other patrons. Fifteen or twenty cars filled out a gravel lot at the edge of the woods. How likely was it that they were all in league with Jack Derber? Not very, I decided. I pulled into the space farthest from the door, breaking my usual rule. I wanted to keep some distance from this particular destination for a few minutes longer. Three spaces over, in a sporty red Mazda, Adele was waiting for me as she'd said she would be.

At first she didn't notice me, and I thought again that there was time to turn back. I sat still in the driver's seat, an icy chill tingling up my body. I looked out at the darkness, something I usually shut out tightly with the heavy white linen curtains of my apartment. Now it surrounded my car, seeming to penetrate the glass of the windshield, coming in to suffocate me slowly. I was in it, of it. It wouldn't let me go. I was struggling to breathe as I tried to block out the steady pounding reverberating in my head. I couldn't tell if it was the beating of my heart or the music from the club thudding in the background.

Just then Adele noticed me sitting there. She opened her door and made her way over to my window. She looked at me, puzzled, and gestured for me to get out of the car, but I couldn't move. I rolled down the window about an inch instead. The air coming in helped clear my head, and slowly I started breathing again.

"Come on out," she said, looking at me with something approaching concern. I must have looked like hell. "I have something for you to change into."

Adele was wearing a full-body black vinyl catsuit, and her hair was pulled back tightly into a bun. *Dominatrix*, I thought. *How fitting.*

Her voice brought me to my senses at least. She hovered over me, looking at me expectantly. I took a final deep breath and opened the car door, grabbing my cell phone as I got out.

She handed me a rather heavy shopping bag. I could feel through the plastic that these were no ordinary clothes, and my suspicions were confirmed as I peered into the bag at a pile of high-gloss black leather. Even though I had anticipated it, when faced with the reality of entering some kind of fetish bar, my heart pounded violently and my knees went weak.

Adele was studying my face.

"Look, I know you're scared, and I know that, after your experience, this is going to be hard for you. But it will be worth it. I'm going to show you something the cops never knew about." She took a deep breath and continued.

"For years I regretted not telling anyone about Jack's connection to this place. At the time I had convinced myself it wasn't relevant. The truth is, I hadn't wanted to get myself into trouble. I hadn't wanted my parents to know what I was studying in college, since they were footing the bill. And in my mind, I had told the cops all they really needed to know anyway. Everything they asked about at least. He was convicted, after all. No harm, no foul, right? But now, well, you're not the cops, and there's no tuition to pay, and . . . I know how you must have suffered. About your friend. And if it will help keep him in there . . ." she trailed off.

Her words indicated compassion, though I still couldn't read it in her eyes. But on the surface at least, she did seem to want to help me. I could only imagine too that, somewhere in there, she had to be afraid of Jack Derber getting out almost as much as I was. She had his office, after all, and his chaired position. He might not like coming home to that.

"So tell me about this place." I had barely dared to look over at it yet. When I finally got the nerve to glance that way, it didn't exactly set me at ease. It was a low-slung, windowless building, with gritty, bare cinder-block walls and a flat, rusted metal roof. No way did this structure meet fire code. A fluorescent orange sign over the door blinked out the words THE VAULT. Charming.

"Well, for starters," began Adele, "I should explain that it's BDSM. Do you know what that means?"

"BD . . .?"

"Bondage-Discipline, Sado-Masochism. Not as bad as it sounds. Real BDSM has rules. Very, very strict rules. First and foremost it is based on *consent*. Jack never really got that part. He kept breaking the rules. So much so that they banned him from coming here eventually. It simply didn't excite him when he had permission. That's probably why he—he—took you and the others."

"This is not making me feel better about going in there."

"It should. My point is that absolutely nothing will happen to you in that club without your consent. Nothing. No one will even touch you without your explicit permission. I've been coming here for years for my fieldwork, and no one has ever laid a hand on me."

I couldn't help staring at her in her vinyl getup. I could understand why they left her alone. She looked pretty damn intimidating.

"Okay, but if they kicked Jack out of there, why do I need to go in at all? What good will it do me?"

"This is the one place where you can meet people who knew Jack. Really knew him. This is the only way to reach that layer the police never could. Members of this club have been coming here for many years. It's the only one of its kind within a hundred miles; everyone in that circle comes through here eventually."

"I guess that's what scares me—who are these people?" I said it with some disgust, but then stopped myself, wondering if Adele wasn't really one of them after all. How long could you study these types, going in and out among them, dressing like them, immersing yourself in it, without participating in some way? I struggled for the right terminology before asking my next question: "What do they want out of this . . . lifestyle?"

She leaned back against the car and sighed. "My doctoral thesis asked the same question—*Paraphilia and Its Discontents*. Look," she began again, suddenly serious, "they want the same things as everyone else: community, connection, maybe a little thrill. Some people are wired differently, numb to the ordinary. Some are trying to make up for a lack of something, maybe fix something that's broken. Others just have a different mode of self-expression."

I thought about that a second and decided to dare asking what I really wanted to know. "And for you, is this just something you study . . .?"

She smiled wryly at first, but the smile faded almost as quickly as it came. She bit her lip—hard, it seemed to me—then pushed back a stray lock that had come loose, taking both hands to smooth it back into that tight bun, her fingers working like those of a magician, fast and familiar.

"Come on, let's go," she said, ignoring my question. She stood up straight and nodded down toward the bag.

I looked at it, then back at her, realizing the time had come to move forward. Steeling my resolve, I slowly opened it. I took out the clothes and started changing into them, crouching down low beside the car behind the open side door. A black leather vest with some very intricate laces. Vinyl pants with spikes running down the sides. She let me keep my own shoes, which were black slip-on Keds. I looked ridiculous, but Adele simply jerked her head in the direction of the club. No one would even notice me, she said. An appealing thought.

The bouncer was a huge man with a shaved head and arms covered with fine spidery tattoos running all the way down to his wrists. He nodded at Adele. Clearly she came here enough to be recognized. He raised an eyebrow at me, shaking his head. I thought he seemed slightly amused, but he shrugged and let me follow Adele in. As I crossed the threshold, I closed my eyes, trying to beat back the terror inside me.

Once in the building, my body felt enveloped in a mist of darkness and evil. This place was a vision of hell to me, all red and black, packed with a crowd geared out in studded leather who seemed, beyond any other terror, utterly unpredictable. The music was crushingly loud, and the air above the bar heavy with cigarette smoke. "Slaves" hung back behind their masters, heads down, cowering. I had to wonder if they were here voluntarily or if they were just brought out for play.

Along the far wall was a T-shaped stage, and a girl in a full-body leather suit with a ball tied into her mouth was doing something I supposed had a distant relationship to dancing but seemed more like alternating poses of pain and ecstasy.

I realized, from the way I was hunching my shoulders as I followed

Adele, that I must have looked like her slave. For a moment my mind was catapulted back to the reality of that time when I *was* a slave. I started to feel dizzy—another sign of the panic attack I knew my body was harboring.

The place was full, and to me at least, everyone else seemed like a regular in this underground world. They appeared to be moving in slow motion, their faces contorted with rage, some of them following me with their eyes as I passed meekly by. I looked around at the carefully constructed scenes of torment that filled the space: machines, contraptions of agony were in use everywhere, with elaborate ropes and pulleys, chains and spikes, nodes and wires.

I realized I hadn't taken a breath since walking through the door.

Across from what I could only imagine were medieval torture instruments, a row of booths with tables lined one side of the bar. Adele led me over to an empty one, weaving her way through a sea of dark bodies. As we walked deeper into the club, my senses were taken over by the stale smell of the place: the odor of sweat, lubricants, and indeterminate bodily fluids mingled to overpower the underlying scent of commercial-grade disinfectant. My stomach turned, as I imagined microscopic particles of these elements penetrating my body through my nose and mouth and skin.

When we finally reached a table, a decade later it seemed, I started to ease onto the bench across from her, but Adele motioned for me to sit next to her instead. I assumed this was part of the ritual here between master and slave, and I followed it almost mindlessly, slipping into that role with a disturbing sense of familiarity.

I looked at Adele hard. She still had not explained what made someone gravitate toward this particular form of perversity, whether as role player or scholar. Was studying this world as much a twisted fetish as being a part of it? Was it just a form of voyeurism that happened to have the stolid edifice of a university to support it? Or was she, as she claimed, merely trying to understand the near miss of her youth, to plumb to some strange depths to overcome the fear of how close she had come to personal destruction?

"Well? How are you doing?" she said, looking at me curiously.

"Just fine," I managed to mutter, and I looked away, remembering that in real life it wasn't polite to stare like that.

Then I saw a couple approaching us. The man was tall, with a long mustache and beard, and a perfectly bald head, glistening with sweat. In his hand he carried a black leather leash, at the end of which was a thin woman, clad entirely in black leather from head to toe. Only her eyes peered out at us from a slit in her tight-fitted hood. Her mouth was covered by a flap that was zipped closed. She was stooped, shuffling along with irregular footsteps, almost as though she were injured. I squinted in the darkness, trying to determine if there was, in fact, something physically wrong with her.

The man waved pleasantly to Adele. She greeted him equally cheerily, "Hi, Piker."

They hugged, and I could have sworn I saw an air kiss. It was hard for me to accept this benighted place as a locus of some kind of community, even a deviant one.

Adele leaned over and whispered to me, "Perfect."

"Have a seat," she said to him.

He ambled over to the other bench and slid in. The woman waited silently for his command. He ignored her and sat down, leaving her standing there at attention. Adele didn't blink.

He turned calmly to us.

"Who do we have here?" He looked only at Adele, never making eye contact with me. I figured that unless she identified me as someone worthy of speaking to, he would treat me like an object.

"This is . . . Blue, for tonight, anyway." She smiled. "She's doing some research on Jack Derber."

A look of scorn crossed the man's face. "Oh, him." He turned to me then, meeting my eyes for the first time, as he realized I wasn't Adele's slave after all. "I hope you're covering how he set our movement back twenty years. That bastard."

"Movement?"

"BDSM. When that story broke, everyone assumed that he was a BDSM practitioner. That couldn't be further from the truth. I mean, he had been, but we kicked his ass out of here years before he had those girls. I hope you get the truth out there about him. He was not like the rest of us. He never obeyed any rules."

"What kind of rules?"

"Well, for starters, he didn't respect safe words. Just blew past them. None of this"—he waved his arms in a sweeping gesture of pride—"works without safe words. That's what it is all about. This is about love and intimacy too, you know. He never understood the importance of trust. That's the only way to achieve TPE."

Adele turned to me. "Total Power Exchange," she explained, rather inadequately, I thought. "You are in luck, tonight," she continued, "meeting Piker and Raven. Raven was Jack's slave years ago."

Piker winced. "I hate to think what he did to her. It really breaks my heart."

I could see tears welling up in his eyes for real now. He turned to Raven, who was clearly agitated by the discussion, though she stayed perfectly still.

Then some kind of inner force broke through, and a small cry escaped Raven's lips. Piker yelled, sharply and abruptly, "Silence!"

I jumped, the command was so sudden and loud, but Raven simply fell silent, her head bowed down in ultimate servitude. I felt sick to my stomach.

I hated to pursue this topic, but I had to ask the next question.

"What did he do to her?"

I was afraid to hear the answer, because I knew only too well what he was capable of doing to her. Here was this strange woman beside us with whom I shared this awful connection. I wanted to tell her I understood, explain that we shared something unique and terrible. But I sat perfectly still instead, immobilized by fear, over-whelmed, waiting for her to speak.

Piker turned to Raven. "Raven, you may sit."

She moved to the seat of the banquette in an instant. She watched his face carefully, waiting for the next command.

Piker reached over and unzipped the flap covering her mouth. "Speak."

I could tell from the circles around Raven's eyes that she had to be in her forties at least. She had fine lines around her mouth, and one of her front teeth had a silver cap. The other was chipped. Battle injuries, I supposed.

Raven's eyes moved back and forth between Adele and me; she seemed unsettled, whether from being granted permission to speak or because of the subject matter I couldn't tell. But as she began her story, the answer became obvious.

"I met him here in this club. This was over fifteen years ago. We didn't know each other's real names then. No one did." She stopped and turned back to Piker. He nodded for her to go on. He wanted this story out. Jack Derber was bad for the "movement."

"The club was only a few years old, and the members were still nervous about the cops. Even though nothing we did was strictly illegal, we knew they would find a way to shut us down. So we kept it very word of mouth."

She shifted to face Adele as she explained, "This was before the Internet made things easy. Back then there were a few chat rooms and alt.net sites we used to communicate, but all of it was spotty."

Raven paused, took a deep breath, and looked over at Piker again, who lifted his hand in a gesture of impatience, motioning for her to keep going.

"We met here, as I said. He was very charming. He went by the name Dark—we used some of the private rooms in the back."

She pointed in the direction of an unmarked door I hadn't noticed before.

"Eventually, he wanted to take things a little further. He asked me to meet him at his house in the mountains. I said yes. I was young and stupid, but so far he had followed the protocol, so I believed it was all under control. And I was having fun, not realizing how seriously he took it. So I said okay to going off premises. I didn't tell anyone what was going on. Hardly anyone even knew we were getting together."

Then she was quiet, looking up at the ceiling, tapping one finger slowly and rhythmically on the table. When she looked back down, she clenched her hands tightly and settled them in her lap. From then on, the timbre of her voice changed. She spoke quickly and softly, in a monotone, reciting the facts, just as I had done during difficult sessions with Dr. Simmons. I figured that meant this memory hurt.

"I went to his house late one Saturday night. As I drove up that long, winding driveway, I thought it looked haunted. It excited me. I went up to the front door and knocked, timidly, of course. He opened the door, and the first thing I saw was a huge gloved fist coming at my face. He punched me, then dragged me into the room. I was kicking and screaming but still thought this was just a more extreme scene than I was used to. I was confused, though, because we hadn't agreed to this in advance. Then he pummeled me, relentlessly, over and over again. I tried to get out my safe word—it was 'yellow' then—but I couldn't before I passed out from the pain."

Raven stopped for a minute and closed her eyes. I was surprised because I thought this was what the "masochist" part of BDSM would want. This world made no sense to me. Piker rubbed her arm lovingly and told her to take her time.

"I woke up, and I was hog-tied in the middle of this big library."

At this, I had to close my eyes. Images of that room spun in my head. The color. The light. The smell of it hit me suddenly. I gripped the table edge and forced myself to focus.

"I was there for three days. No food, very little water. Lots of pain. And he . . . he . . ."

She couldn't go on.

Piker leaned closer to her, "Don't say it, honey. Just show her."

Raven stood up beside the table and pulled the side of her leather pants down so we could see her hip. There it was, in twisted flesh. A brand. It looked very similar to my own, though it was hard to make out in the dark. I looked away, blinking back tears.

At just that moment, the MC announced the next act. I glanced over and saw three hooded men pushing a large contraption onto the stage. I could not believe my eyes as they slowly and carefully rolled a rack to the center of it. It was different from the one in Jack's library, but the purpose was clearly the same. I felt a wave of nausea rising up inside me. Raven saw it too and turned to Piker, her eyes pleading.

He stood. "Let's get out of here. I don't like this show."

I started to feel my throat constrict. I couldn't get any air. The room was spinning. I saw a door toward the back marked EXIT, and without a word to Adele or the others, I got up and ran toward it, nearly tripping along the way over a man in chaps crawling on the floor behind his master.

I pushed open the exit door and ran over to a secluded spot behind the Dumpster, leaning back against the building, panting for breath. Up above, the sky was filled with stars that to me were whirling ominously. Trying to right the world, I took several more deep breaths, my hands on my knees, and slowly slid down the wall. I thought of how similar this was to Tracy's escape from the club in New Orleans, and a wave of fear washed over me. How had

I gotten myself into this situation? How had I thought I could be ready for this?

I tucked myself into a small indentation in the building, where no one could see me. No hooded men, no zippered women, no leather-clad minions. I wished I could will myself to be invisible and hide out here until morning. I could be still. I could be quiet.

No one need ever know I was here.

CHAPTER 16

It was a warm evening, and I could still hear the thumping of the music through the club's walls. The door creaked open, and Adele called for me, careful to use the name, Blue, that she'd assigned me for the night. When I didn't reply, the door slammed back shut.

I don't know why I didn't answer her at that moment. I just needed a break to clear my head and process, even if only a little, what I'd heard. I'd planned to go back into the club in a few minutes, but it didn't work out that way.

Car headlights shone into the woods behind the building. An engine revved up and then began to idle a little farther away, closer to a second back door about thirty feet to my left.

Two men got out, and I peeked around the corner just enough to see that it was a large van. They were talking in low voices. I couldn't hear their words distinctly, but I thought the low rumbling voice of one of them sounded familiar. I crawled out a few inches from my hiding place, intending to sneak back inside, when I saw the taller of the two pass in front of the van's headlights.

I almost rubbed my eyes in disbelief. It looked like Noah Philben. It couldn't be. I had to get closer, if only to prove to myself I was mistaken. I had to be letting my imagination run wild in the midst of my fear.

There was a cluster of bushes a few yards away, and the low rise of a hill ran along in between. If I could make it over there, I would be able to see what was going on and still be hidden in the dark shadows of the back lot. My pulse was racing, but I had to know if that was Noah Philben or if my mind was playing tricks on me.

I took a deep breath and pushed myself on. *You are stronger than this*, I thought, willing myself to be so. Slowly, I eased down onto my stomach and crept over to the bushes.

The men's voices got louder. They were laughing about something. I heard the door of the van open. There was a little scuffle and a loud thud. Then the door slammed again.

I reached the bushes, which were dense and prickly. I stepped back from them and peered through the leaves. The men were now clearly within sight. The first was of average height, heavyset, with what looked like reddish-blond hair and a goatee. The second man was tall. He walked unhurriedly, at ease, along the side of the van. Then the headlights shone on him just long enough to reveal his face. There was no doubt about it: it was Noah Philben.

I went cold. Why would a religious leader hang out at a remote S&M club in the middle of the night? The very one where Jack Derber used to go, no less. Was Noah looking for Sylvia, the lost lamb from his fold? Or did he have something to do with her disappearance? Whatever it was, this could be it, the lead I was looking for.

It was now two-thirty in the morning. I hadn't been awake this late in years, but I had a feeling this night was far from over.

I sneaked around behind the building in the opposite direction of the van. Crouching down in the parking lot, I ran over to my car to wait for them. As quietly as I could, I opened the door and slid in behind the wheel. I was sweating, but my skin was cold and my mouth had gone dry. This was more than just fear of night driving. This was complete terror.

The van finally pulled around the corner of the club, toward the exit of the parking lot. At that moment my hands felt like lead on the steering wheel.

I was back on the battleground in my head. I wanted to keep going—to follow that van—but my entire body was tensed up against me, and my thoughts were garbled. It was as if I could hear the sixteen-year-old Jennifer whispering in my ear, *Stay away, go home, go back to your fortress.* But the part of me that was searching, that knew this was the only way, countered that the young Jennifer would never have been able to understand the stakes here. She wouldn't have understood how I needed to find her now. That if I was ever going to get past it, I had to put her memory, and my memories, to rest.

Bracing myself, I took a deep breath and started the engine.

As I sat there, hesitating, two latex-clad men exited the club, one calling the other "master" as he followed dutifully behind on his leash. I waited for them to settle into their sedan, the master driving, the submissive one slumping in the backseat; then I carefully maneuvered my car behind theirs toward the exit. The van was ahead of us both as we pulled out onto the road. I pursued them at a safe distance, four car lengths behind.

Baby steps, I thought to myself. Right now I'm just driving in a car on a public road. The doors are locked. My tank is three-quarters full. I have a cell phone and good reception. My bag contains both mace and pepper spray. I can turn around and go back to the hotel at any moment. I am in control.

About ten miles down the road, the other car turned off. There was an SUV behind me. I let it pass, putting it between the van and my car. With one hand on the wheel, I groped around in my bag for my notebook and pen. Giving up on that after a couple of seconds, I took my phone from the inside pocket of the leather vest and dialed all but the last digit of my home number in New York, peering out into the darkness ahead. I was too far away to read the license plate number, so I threw my phone toward the seat beside me. I heard it miss and clatter to the floorboard.

"Damn," I muttered. After another twenty minutes or so, the van turned left onto a dirt road that was almost entirely hidden by trees. I drove past it about a hundred feet, turned off my lights, and made an illegal U-turn.

I followed the van slowly up a hill, as I reached down to the floorboard for my phone. Shit. The battery had fallen out when it hit the floor. I fumbled around in the dark, searching for it futilely.

I stopped the car halfway up that drive, feeling the old familiar dizziness rising up in my head. Cycling through every cognitive therapy trick in the book, I visualized the fear, imagining it as a ball that was separate and distinct from me.

It wasn't working. I knew that, in fact, right now, my anxiety was very real and entirely justified. Eventually I calmed myself just enough to keep from hyperventilating, but my intestines were squeezing up on me. I dug my pepper spray and mace out of my bag, placing both canisters carefully on the seat beside me. I looked at the photo of Jennifer I'd fixed to the dashboard, gathering what strength I could from it. I had to keep going.

I inched the car a little farther down the road, until I got to a clearing in the woods. I was thanking my lucky stars that the rental car was dark gray. I didn't think I could be seen, but I was close enough to make out in the distance, probably fifty yards from me, a small warehouse with one garage door and a small windowless entrance to the right of it. A single floodlight covered the front yard of the building.

As a precaution, I slowly turned the car around, so I could drive out facing forward. I sat perfectly still, my breathing faster than normal. I turned off the engine and twisted myself in my seat so I could see. After that I didn't move. Not even to find my phone.

I could just make out Noah Philben's outline as he walked over to the back of the warehouse and picked up what looked like a large tarp. The other man followed him, and together they covered the van, then turned to go back in. Suddenly Noah paused, walked over to the side of the building, and flipped a switch, killing the floodlights.

I kept as still as possible, holding my breath, as though that would make a difference. I held my keys in the ignition, ready to turn them if he so much as took a step forward. I waited, the seconds feeling like hours. *Go back inside,* I tried to will him. Finally, after an excruciating minute or two, he turned around and trudged back into the warehouse.

I wanted to know what was in that van. Why was there a tarp? What could they be doing in that warehouse? Was this somehow related to his cult?

All I knew about religious cults was taken from headlines. Maybe they were doing something mystical. Or planning a mass suicide. Maybe it was a wedding with plural wives and child brides. Or maybe that's where they kept the cache of weapons they'd need in case the feds invaded. Whatever it was, it was my only connection to Sylvia, and I knew I needed to understand what was going on to make any progress.

I waited for at least half an hour, not moving, barely breathing. I rolled down my window a few inches to let in the cool night air.

I briefly considered getting out of the car to get a better look, to see what was under that tarp, but the very thought of it made me sick. I was stuck here for now.

Finally, I decided nothing more seemed to be happening. Maybe they were staying the night. My heart was heavy as I finally started the engine, knowing it was pointless to wait here any longer and definitely too dangerous.

As I slowly drove back down the driveway, my hands were shaking so hard I could barely grip the wheel. Only when I had put several miles between me and that warehouse did I start breathing regularly again. But as I continued along, the back roads suddenly seemed like a maze, a labyrinth specifically designed to trap me.

I pushed several buttons on the GPS to try to get the route back to the club, but it only told me it was "recalculating." Cursing, I turned it off.

It seemed hours before I happened upon the main road, and by then there was no way I was going anywhere except straight back to the hotel. Adele would have to wait until tomorrow for an explanation.

CHAPTER 17

When I was safe in my hotel room, I decided the time had come to call in Agent Jim McCordy. This search had gotten too dangerous for me; they needed someone without post-traumatic stress disorder to go following vans out of S&M clubs.

Even so, I was feeling proud of myself. A year ago, a month ago even, I would have had to page Dr. Simmons on an emergency basis if I had even thought about something that frightening. Now I felt a little bit stronger, a little more determined, each day out of my apartment. That felt good. And I knew I was on to something here. It was too much of a coincidence that Noah Philben would be there at Jack Derber's old haunt. "What are the odds?" as Jennifer would have said.

It was four a.m., which meant seven a.m. Eastern time. Late enough to call. I dialed Jim's number. As usual, he answered immediately.

"Sarah? Where are you? Dr. Simmons said you'd canceled another appointment."

"You might say that. Jim, look, I need your help. I think I have figured out a strange connection. It might not mean anything, but—"

"Connection? Sarah, what are you doing? Right now you should just be meeting with Dr. Simmons regularly to prepare yourself to face Jack at the parole hearing. That is how you can best help to keep him in prison."

"You're right. Theoretically. But I think I'm on to something."

I took a deep breath.

"Jim, I'm in Oregon." But before he could speak, I hurried on. "Let's talk about that later. More important—Noah Philben. What do you know about him?"

"Sarah, I—"

"I know, Jim. I know what you're going to say. Please. Noah Philben?"

He sighed.

"The pastor?" He paused, perhaps deciding whether to indulge me, but giving in at last. "I did a preliminary workup on him when Jack Derber married Sylvia. No record. Totally clean. Religious zealot who has been running that church since his early twenties. Sketchy operation, and I've got the tax guys monitoring it, but no other suspicious activity."

"Really? Well, here's the thing, Jim. I went to this S&M club where—"

"You did what?" He was incredulous.

"Just hear me out. I'll explain another time. I went to this club where Jack used to go, and I . . . for various reasons I was out back, getting some air . . ."

"I can only imagine."

"And I saw a van and there seemed to be some sort of . . . transaction . . . going on, and it was Noah Philben."

"Sarah, there is nothing illegal about going to an S&M club, and I think if history proves anything, it's that it's not unprecedented for the leaders of small religious organizations to get mixed up in that sort of thing. It's a trope of the genre, as Tracy might say." He laughed at his own joke.

"Tracy? Has she been talking to you about this?"

"She called me yesterday. She thinks you are going a little too far. That you believe you can find Jennifer's body."

"Don't talk to her about me. Please. She is always going to hate me, and I don't want her convincing you I'm crazy. I'm not crazy. Okay, well, I might be a little crazy, but not about this. I am approaching this in the most methodical way humanly possible."

"But of course you are, Sarah. As is your way. But you aren't actually a detective, after all, remember? Listen, I know you think we failed you, but we interviewed every person even remotely connected with Jack Derber, and—"

"Did you talk to Piker and Raven?"

"Who?"

"I don't know their real names, but they go to this club. Did you even go to the club?"

"What club?"

"Exactly. You didn't. It's called The Vault. And I think I have a whole new angle on Jack Derber. I think it should be explored. Can you look into Noah Philben again?"

There was silence on the line, and then finally, "I'll see what I can do." He sounded sincere.

Since I was getting somewhere, I thought I'd push it even further.

"Also, Sylvia is missing."

"Tracy mentioned that. But a full mailbox is hardly enough

evidence to file a missing person report. Sounds like she's on vacation. Like you."

"If that's the case, maybe I'd better wait it out here in Oregon until her return," I countered.

"Listen, Sarah, I'll be frank. This search of yours doesn't worry me any less than your reaction to the last letter. I don't want you putting yourself in harm's way, physically or mentally. Tracy said you'd gone to Oregon, but neither of us expected you to take it this far. What you're doing is dangerous. Please come back, stay safe."

It sounded like sage advice. Except that it would mean giving up entirely.

CHAPTER 18

I hung up from my call with Jim feeling dispirited. Maybe he was right. Sylvia was probably visiting her parents. Noah Philben was probably involved in a tax evasion scam and sex scandal all rolled into one, but that wasn't going to help me find Jennifer's body. Maybe I was wasting my time. Time I should be spending on that victim impact statement.

I checked my plane ticket, thinking maybe I should just get out of here and leave the past behind once and for all. But my flight didn't take off until the following evening. I shrugged and told myself I might as well keep going until then. But if something concrete didn't materialize soon, I would be forced to admit defeat.

Early the next morning, I drove back out to campus to find Adele. She had left a note that she was in the library. I found her at a large wooden table in the back stacks of the third floor. The ceilings were high, and dust from the books penetrated the air. Libraries still made me nervous.

Surrounded by piles of books and papers, Adele was typing furiously on her laptop. She didn't look up until I was standing right beside her. I whispered her name, and she jumped slightly, slamming her computer shut.

Some loose pieces of paper covered with scrawled notes drifted to the floor. She leaned down quickly and picked them up before even looking over at me. As she put them back in order and tucked them neatly into a notebook, she turned to me calmly. I noticed that her right hand rested protectively on a small stack of thick books.

"You startled me." She said it in a neutral voice, but her eyes clearly expressed displeasure.

I mumbled an apology as I glanced surreptitiously at the books on the table. Most of them had scientific-sounding names, but one very simple title caught my eye before Adele could put anything on top of it: *Coercive Persuasion*. When she noticed me studying the spines, without looking, she turned them to face the back of the room. Only then did she seem to relax, motioning for me to take the seat next to her.

"Not the best place to chat." She spoke quietly but not in a whisper, as though the library's rules didn't quite apply to her. "But what happened to you last night? I was worried."

"You know, I just needed some air. That place was a little overwhelming." I tried, unsuccessfully, to force out a laugh.

"Sounds like a panic attack. Do you take anything?"

The look in her eyes was familiar though I hadn't seen it in a while: curiosity and professional interest, masked as actual concern.

That first year out of the cellar I had tried to be helpful to the psychological community while they ostensibly tried to be helpful to me. It had been one long blur of sessions, meetings, and examinations. I knew this look. It was the look of someone piecing together her peer-reviewed article in her head. Here I was again, someone's thesis. And I didn't like it one bit.

"I'm fine. No need to worry. Thanks for taking me there, actually. It was tough, but I think it gave me some good . . . insights."

"You really shouldn't be driving if you feel an attack coming on. I could have given you a ride."

She paused, looking at me with that same penetrating gaze I recognized from Dr. Simmons. Studied, practiced, manipulative. I knew what it signaled. She was about to go in for the kill.

"What are you really doing, Sarah? You don't actually think you are going to find a body, do you? Are you exploring your past? Trying to make sense of what happened to you?"

Her tone was patronizing, and I felt an all-too-familiar surge of resistance building up inside me. I imagined it as a wall forming between us, rising up brick by brick. That's what years of cognitive therapy gets you. There we were in battle, swords drawn, in some centuries-old feud of good versus evil. Subject versus object.

She shifted a bit, leaning forward. She must have thought I wouldn't be able to detect the eagerness in her face. I wanted to see where she was taking this, though, so I decided to play along.

"Look," she began, "I hope this doesn't sound strange, but I've been thinking about something. I wonder if, as long as you are here anyway, you wouldn't mind participating in a study. It really wouldn't take much of your time. It wouldn't interrupt your search. Just a few interview sessions. Your case is unusual, of course, and there has never been much of a sample set for people who have survived your type of ordeal. A few years ago I worked on the design for a victimological study, and—"

"Victimological?"

"Just what it sounds like, the study of victims. To help us understand not only the recovery process but also to learn whether there are specific psychological traits that can be used to develop a victim typology for a specified crime."

"Victim typology? As in, whether I was the 'type' of person to be abducted?"

"Not exactly, but you know, we can study patterns of behavior, activities, locations—that sort of thing—to develop models for characterizing those who might be 'victim-prone,' as they say."

I heard her voice continue to drone on, and I saw her lips moving clearly in front of me, but my mind could no longer make out what she was saying. The phrase "victim-prone" was echoing in my brain, and I thought surely the heat I felt on my face was visible as a red rage. The image of her face swam in front of me. I was appalled, but even then, even with my entire body set against her in that moment, I tried to keep my expression neutral.

So that's what they do here in these big universities, I thought. They sit back and figure out whether you did something unknowingly to nurture catastrophe and disaster. Of course, they aren't *blaming* you. It's just that, you know, you were so careless, you let the evil of the world come crashing down on your head.

She didn't understand what I had done. What we had done. She didn't realize the extremes to which Jennifer and I had gone to insulate ourselves from every form of vulnerability. And it had *still* happened.

Yet even as I stood there, furious, it occurred to me that if she wanted to use me in some way, there might be a way for me to use her as well. Was there more to learn from Adele after all?

She had studied with Jack Derber, working side by side with him for two years. She had already told me that she had hidden from the FBI a large part of his past with BDSM, maybe because she'd had a hand in something even more nefarious. Maybe she was

Jack's partner in all this. Maybe that's why nothing had seemed to faze her back then. My stomach turned at the thought that maybe none of it had been so surprising to her after all.

"I'll think about it," I finally managed to mutter.

"Well, let me know." She pulled a card out of a pocket of her purse and scribbled something on the back. "Here, now you have all my numbers. Texting is good too. Let me know. I can rearrange things if you have a little time. How long are you in town?"

"I'm not sure. I want to talk to some others who knew Jack. Someone told me he was friends with another professor here on campus. A Professor Stiller?"

Adele flinched almost imperceptibly at the name but quickly regained her composure. "Yes, David Stiller. He's here."

"He's in the psychology department as well?"

"Yes, as a matter of fact his office is right next to mine." She didn't sound very pleased about that.

"Not a friend?"

She laughed. "No, more of a rival, I'd say. We were friends long ago, but now I'd say our research is a little too similar, and our conclusions too different. I think the university rather enjoys it because it makes us the stars of the conference circuit. They like to put us on panels together to see us fight. That's academia for you. Anyway, if you talk to him, I wouldn't mention that you've been hanging out with me."

"Okay, thanks. As you said, we probably shouldn't be disturbing others here in the library. I'll leave you to your work." I held up her card. "I'm really going to give it some thought."

She smiled and held out her hand, as if we were about to make some sort of pact. I stared at it probably a few seconds too long—her hand extended there in the air—while I frantically searched for a diversion.

"Wait, I should give you my info." I reached into my bag and pulled out a scrap of paper. After writing my cell number, I handed it over to her, careful to make sure our fingers didn't touch.

I looked back at her as I left the reading room. She sat perfectly still, watching me walk out, her eyes following my progress, her face as indecipherable as ever.

CHAPTER 19

As I crossed back over the campus and passed through the heavy swinging doors of the Greek Revival psychology building, I remembered my own days in college, the days after I had escaped and was starting over, this time at NYU, this time alone.

In retrospect it seemed that I hadn't looked up from the ground the whole time I was there. I had spent three years in virtual solitude, cramming in a degree in record time by taking extra classes at night and during the summers.

That second time through, though, I hadn't had the same desire for a normal college experience as I'd had before. I didn't want to go to parties. I didn't study in the library. In fact, I didn't even want anyone to know who I was. I never spoke to my classmates, never ate at the school cafeterias, never went to a single extracurricular event. The school was large enough to disappear in, and I tried. How I tried.

It was also there that I first started using my new name, a name I would never grow accustomed to. I always had to pause for a second before I signed anything, training myself to write it. I never remembered to look up when professors used it in class. I was sure they thought I was dense. Until I turned in my tests, that is, and they realized I had one gift after all.

I majored in math, taking solace in the reliability of a field that offered nothing but solutions. I loved the way the numbers lined up in neat rows, a problem sometimes taking six or seven pages of my angled script, number after number, symbol after symbol, sine after cosine.

In my room, I kept all my class notebooks within arm's length on the shelf by my bed. If I couldn't sleep at night, I could pull one out and pass my eyes slowly over their ordered magnificence, admiring how these problems at least yielded the same answers every time.

Staying true to Jennifer in my own way, my concentration was in statistics. I finished a master's degree in a year. The professors had begged me to get my Ph.D., but I'd had enough of sitting in classes with other students by then. At that point, the sheer volume of people I had to interact with every day had started to wear on me. My phobias had started to mount. Even the largest lecture halls felt claustrophobic. I could hear, with penetrating clarity, every cough or whisper or pencil dropped in the room, making me jump as the sound echoed in my head.

And when classes ended, there were suddenly too many bodies in motion, bumping into one another needlessly as they put on coats and scarves. I would always sit perfectly still after everyone else left, alone in the auditorium, as I waited for the hallways to clear enough to afford me a wide berth. So my body could float through space and time, untouchable, untouched.

Pulling myself out of the past, I looked down the long corridor of the psychology department. It was dotted with students, standing in groups or pairs, with a few lone stragglers at the margins. They looked so carefree, so alive. Some chatted, while others were wrapped up in their own heads, maybe thinking about their course work or the date they had last night. You couldn't see behind the happiness to the traumas that must have loomed there. I knew statistically they had to exist, but you would never know it just by looking.

But there, with the sun streaming through the skylight in the renovated portion of the building, it didn't seem as though trouble could have ever touched these students with their smooth skin and full-throated laughs. Here they were, almost at the end of the school year, preparing to go on to their internships, summer jobs, grad school. I would never know what they were getting over. Maybe no one would ever know, and maybe that was the way it should be. Maybe that's what well-adjusted people do—they actually adjust. And that's what it means to be young and poised for life—you put your past behind you, whatever it is, and you force yourself to be free.

I wiped a tear from my eye and walked by them all. The security guard at the front desk didn't look up from his newspaper. I shook my head, thinking of all the dangers he could be missing, all the while grateful to be ignored. This time I noticed a small sign with neat type pointing out the direction of the faculty offices, and I followed it back to the hallway I'd been down earlier.

I passed the row of traditional oak doors, the upper half of each a panel of frosted glass marked with a name in black letters. Next to Adele's, as she had said, was Professor David Stiller's. His door was open just slightly, and as I pushed it gently, I could see no one was in there.

It was a large office, with tall windows facing the quad. An enormous oak desk stood in front of the window, and a bookcase covered the wall facing it, filled up and overflowing. I fingered the volumes, mostly psychology books on various arcane topics, and a few standard statistics manuals I recognized.

Then my eye happened to catch a low shelf behind the desk on the floor. The works there looked different, unlike textbooks. I leaned over to get a closer look and read the titles quickly. *100 Days of Sodom, Juliette, Story of the Eye, Nietzsche and the Vicious Circle.* This was Tracy's territory.

Just as I pulled out my notebook to write down the names to show her, the door opened behind me.

"Excuse me? Can I help you?" came a deep voice.

I jumped, dropped my pen, and watched it clatter to the floor and roll under the heavy desk. I turned to face David Stiller. He was tall, one might even say handsome, with brown hair and eyes so black, their pupils were indistinguishable within them. It had a disconcerting effect.

He looked at me expectantly, waiting for an explanation for who I was and what I was doing. Startled, I was having trouble collecting my thoughts, so I dropped to my hands and knees and awkwardly reached for my pen under the desk.

"Oh, hi . . ." I said, stalling as best I could. "I'm Caroline Morrow. I'm doing some research and wondered if you might have some time to talk to me." I grabbed my pen quite easily in the end, so to gain time, I flicked it farther over to the wall.

"Wait," he said, with slight irritation, I thought. "Allow me." He walked over behind the desk, gracefully plucked the pen from the floor, and handed it to me in one swift gesture.

"You were saying?" he pressed.

"Yes, sorry." I smoothed my shirt and pushed my hair out of my face, trying to regain some semblance of composure. "I was saying that I am Caroline Morrow." I didn't reach out my hand, and neither did he. "And I'm in the sociology department." I motioned back toward the opposite end of campus, as though he wouldn't know its physical location. "I'm writing my dissertation on Jack Derber, and I know you were starting out as a junior professor here back when he was arrested."

Unlike Adele's response when I mentioned Jack Derber, David Stiller actually seemed interested. His face broke into a sardonic smile, and he sat down, pointing to the chair across from him.

"Please. Have a seat. No one wants to talk about Jack anymore around here. I'm curious to hear about your project. Kind of surprised the department would sanction that research, but I guess times change. What's your angle?"

"Angle? I don't know about my angle. I just think there are elements of the story that have not been thoroughly explored. And I plan to do some original research, from a purely factual perspective. That's why I picked this topic—you know, it all happened right here." Here I was, vamping. I was impressed with myself. He was nodding encouragingly.

"I understand he was a friend of yours." At this, the smile instantly disappeared from his face.

"Friend? No, no, no. I don't know where you heard that. We were colleagues, but I barely knew the guy. Our work was at opposite ends of the spectrum. We were never even on a panel together. But he was definitely a star in his own right."

"A star?"

"Come on. Surely you know by now that that's how it works in academia. You have to be a star to get anywhere at all. Give a lot of talks, papers, symposia, you know, really make the rounds of the conference circus—I mean, circuit. You're signing up for a demanding life."

"And what about Adele Hinton?"

At that, his face darkened. "Oh, her. Talk about Jack Derber." He shook his head.

"What do you mean?" I prompted.

"Well, after that whole business went down, let's just say her talks were jam-packed. More for her notoriety than for her academic insights, if you ask me. I think everyone was waiting for some juicy tidbit about Jack Derber. Don't quote me, but she owes her career to that case, frankly."

"So she got a lot of attention?"

He laughed.

"I'll say. The *Portland Sun* even did a profile of her back then. Ridiculously fawning. I mean, she is an attractive woman after all, so it's not that surprising the reporter wanted to spend plenty of time with her."

He leaned in a little closer, his eyes narrowing, looking at me to make sure I fully understood what he was suggesting. Then he went on, leaning back in his chair now and swiveling slightly to the left and right, ever so slowly.

"You know, if you really want to do some original research, there's another angle you should consider. Jack worked a lot. He did a lot of research, had a lot of studies. Traveled constantly. His office was brimming full of papers. Files, binders. And he was incredibly protective of them. Only *Adele* had access to them. I know the FBI put a lockdown on all of that work pretty fast after they hauled him off. But I'm sure she got hold of something. I *know* it."

He turned his chair to face the window and gazed out for a minute, thinking to himself.

Finally, he spoke, more to himself, it seemed, than to me, "Well, this has never been enough for her, of course. She wants Ivy League, doesn't she? It only makes sense. She has a lot to live up to."

He turned back to me.

"You probably don't know this, but her father is one of the most prominent surgeons in Seattle. Very successful." He smirked and shook his head, shifting forward in his seat.

"But I digress. Back to your paper. I can't prove it, but I'm sure she's using Jack Derber's ideas and research. She's the one you should talk to. There have to be a few facts there that haven't been unearthed. I'd help you with *that* research in a second, if I could. Let me know if there's anything I can do."

He was barely trying to hide his jealousy of, and—it seemed to me—contempt for, Adele.

After a few more fruitless tries to get him back to Jack Derber, I stood up to leave, nearly falling over the chair as I backed out. Exiting as gracefully as I entered, I thought.

CHAPTER 20

I called Tracy several times that day but got no answer. Clearly, she was avoiding me. There was no way I could piece together what I had without her, so I decided to pay her a surprise visit, just as she had done to me.

I changed my flight that afternoon and flew into Boston rather than New York. It was good to be back on the East Coast, even if only for a few days. My real plans would take me even farther afield.

From Boston, I rented another car and took the scenic route to Northampton. I was impressed with myself for so much driving. I was no longer overtaken by debilitating panic when behind the wheel, only mildly discomfited.

I drove straight to Tracy's apartment, whose address I had Googled earlier that day. If she could show up on my doorstep, I could show up on hers.

She lived in an old white clapboard house on a quiet, well-tended block that looked incredibly bourgeois for someone of her ilk. There were two doorbells, each with the names carefully typed out. Hers was on top. I noticed there were bars on the window of the door. Maybe Tracy didn't feel as secure as she pretended to be.

I wondered if I would have to wait on her narrow front porch as she had waited for me, but after a minute I heard footsteps on the stairs inside. Tracy peered out at me through the window, and then the curtain flopped back into place. She hadn't exactly looked pleased to see me, but after a brief pause I heard the lock click. An excellent lock. She opened the door quickly but not all the way.

"Now what?" she said, hand on her hip. She didn't have makeup on and looked tired. If I hadn't known better, I might have thought she'd been crying.

"I have to talk to you. I've been back out to Oregon, and I have more information."

"Well, if it isn't the girl detective." She shrugged her shoulders and invited me in, sounding resigned. I followed her up the stairs.

The first floor of the house was cheery, with the palest yellow on the walls and an old dark wood-framed mirror in the entryway. But as we ascended to Tracy's apartment, the wall color shifted to a dull, muted gray. At the top of the landing I came face-to-face with a framed photograph of a man in chains. That prepared me a little for what waited on the other side of the door.

Tracy's apartment was the antithesis of my own. The walls, which were high because the attic floor had been removed to create a huge cathedral ceiling, were painted the same gray as the stairs. They were covered in black-and-white photography and etchings. All the images were ones that would have given me nightmares if I looked at them too long. The overwhelming drabness made it seem as if Tracy had tried to make her apartment into a prison cell. And it worked. I felt trapped.

If it hadn't been for the signs of homey disorder and the smell of brewing coffee, I might have turned to leave. One entire wall was covered with built-in bookshelves, crammed full all the way to the top, the larger hardcovers shoved in horizontally, the smaller paperbacks double-shelved. The volumes were so numerous, they spilled out onto the floor, on tabletops, in chairs, some of them open and turned upside down. Some had their places held with gnawed pencils, broken points jutting out of them.

The apartment was a single large open room, with a loft at one end for her bedroom. I could see the tip of her unmade bed from where I was, the black comforter spilling out a bit over the ledge. She had clearly been working, because in the front corner, her laptop was buzzing on the desk, and what looked like draft manuscript pages were scattered all around.

"Now you see why I was so stunned by your apartment. Have a seat," she said.

She pointed to a chair next to her desk, which held a stack of books precariously leaning against the back of it. She walked over, lifted the pile all in one armload, and tossed it onto the plush couch. They slid across the velvet cushion, half of them landing on the floor. Tracy gestured again to the chair.

I sat down and launched into an update on my activities in Oregon. I was nervous. I wanted to sound as compelling as possible, since I hadn't inspired much interest from Jim. Suddenly, winning Tracy over to my quest seemed like the most important thing I'd done in my life. I didn't know if I could keep at it alone, and if she also dismissed the things I had found, I didn't know if I had the heart to pursue the plan I'd formulated on the plane ride back.

Tracy listened quietly, raising her eyebrows with surprise when I told her about the S&M club, her eyes opening wide and her jaw dropping when I explained how I had followed the van to the warehouse. I couldn't tell if she was surprised by what I had seen or by what I had done. Probably the latter. Finally, I told her about the books in David Stiller's office. She shrugged that off.

"Everyone in academia reads those writers. It's *de rigueur*. Foucault changed academic life forever. He gave everyone a new perspective to write about. Look, I have a whole section of my own library devoted to him. The indelible mark of too many years spent in grad school."

She pointed to an area in the middle. I walked over. "Bataille too. I mean, he writes about sex and death. That's all academics care about. Really all anyone cares about, as a matter of fact."

"But doesn't that directly tie into what Jack did to us?"

"I'm sure he used it to justify his actions, like so many other men who want to subjugate women, while simultaneously giving it all an intellectual spin. I can easily see how he would have cottoned on to the idea of having a 'limit-experience,' living a life outside societal rules, et cetera. Foucault, Nietzsche, all of them. Excuse-mongers."

I had gotten up and was perusing Tracy's shelves as she spoke, and I found one filled with Bataille's books. Her collection was even more extensive than David's. I pulled out a few but froze when I saw one called *The Bataille Reader*.

I couldn't believe it. There on the cover, in a white setting framed with a black border, was a drawing of a headless man. In one hand he held what looked like a heart with flames coming out of it, in the other a short knife. He had a skeleton drawn over his crotch, and his nipples were little stars. I took it over to Tracy, my hands shaking.

"Tracy, doesn't this look like, isn't this . . ."

She looked at me questioningly, clearly not seeing what I was seeing.

Finally, I spat the words out, "The brand. Isn't this the *brand*?"

I pulled down the side of my jeans and underwear enough so

that she could see it clearly on my hip. She looked at the picture and back at my scarred flesh. Admittedly, it was a little hard to tell, because the scar tissue had grown over the original mark, but the outline was definitely the same.

Tracy stared in silence for a moment before finally looking up to meet my eyes.

"I think you might be right. I never noticed it before. Maybe because I try to avoid looking at the goddamn thing—it's not exactly a memento I treasure. But also, my brand is incomplete. I twisted hard to the right when the iron touched my skin, so my mark is only partially there. It makes it look very different."

She stood up and showed me hers, in roughly the same place on her hip, though a little farther toward the back. I could see what she meant about it—half of the torso and one of the legs was missing entirely—but I also noticed that on her the imprint was a little more distinct on the upper right. I could clearly make out the knife held in the headless man's hand.

"What does it mean?" I asked her.

Tracy sat down, and I did too, my hands clutching *The Bataille Reader*.

"It was an image created for a publication that Bataille was involved with, but as I recall, it was also the symbol for some sort of secret society. A bunch of these intellectuals back in the thirties formed this group just before the war. They were all looking for a mystical ecstatic experience or something. I'm not sure, I only took one class on surrealism, but I vaguely remember it had something to do with human sacrifice. I think it disbanded pretty quickly. We'll have to look it up."

"I may not be up to date on the literary crowd from the thirties, Tracy, but I do know something about math. And 'society' implies more than one. Do you think this means Jack created some sort of secret society at the university, maybe based on this group? Maybe with David Stiller?" I flipped through the pages of the Bataille books, stopping here and there to read passages. It made no sense to me whatsoever. And it was sick.

I looked back up at Tracy, "What is wrong with these people? 'Horror,' 'desire,' 'corpses,' 'filth,' 'sacrifice'. . . Jesus. Was Jennifer *sacrificed*?"

I put the book down slowly and gripped the sides of the chair, the images of debauchery and mayhem from those pages spinning in my head.

Tracy looked alarmed, but I think it had more to do with the color draining from my face than from our discovery.

"Whoa, whoa, you're jumping the gun here, aren't you? So Jack had a thing for some dead philosophers with a perverted social club. Most psychopaths have some strange interests, to say the least."

"But there's something weird about these three. The venom David Stiller directs at Adele is pretty intense."

"Welcome to academia. You have no idea. It's such a circus."

"Circus?" Something was tugging at my brain. "David Stiller used that term, and so did Jack . . . in a letter."

"It's actually a pretty generic metaphor," Tracy said wryly.

"David Stiller misspoke when he said it though. He said . . ." I thought a minute. "He said the conference circus, and then corrected himself to say circuit."

"That's actually kind of funny. It is a conference circus."

"What do you mean?"

"Some people see it as one of the perks of academic life. You know, the university pays for your trip. The conferences are usually held in decent places. There are some lectures, some panels, and then everyone goes out and eats and drinks like they're senators of the Roman Empire. Lots of affairs. Plenty of academic intrigue. Alliances form and break off, that sort of thing. It is a bit of a traveling circus, I suppose—of highbrow, know-it-all intellectuals."

I pulled Jack's letters out of my bag and carefully started unfolding them, spreading them out on Tracy's desk. She sighed and cleared some space for me. I looked through the letters, and finally, in the third one he sent, I saw it.

"There," I pointed at it triumphantly.

Tracy picked up the letter and read it out loud.

"'And I met you while on the circus train. Two sideshows. More travelers.'"

"'I met you' . . .Tracy, do you think he was in town for an academic conference when he abducted Jennifer and me? And what about you? Would Jim have these details? We need to call him."

Tracy looked at me hard, thinking. Finally, she nodded, picked up her phone, switched it to speaker, and dialed. By heart, I noticed. As always, Jim picked up at once.

"Jim?" Tracy began, taking the lead as usual. "I'm here with Sarah."

Jim was silent for a moment. I was sure he couldn't believe what he was hearing.

"That's . . . wonderful," he finally said.

I jumped in. "Jim, at the time of my . . . abduction, was Jack at an academic conference?"

Jim paused as he always did before giving us any new information about our case. I didn't know if he was worried about our mental states or about breaching his confidentiality obligations. Finally, he spoke. "Yes, actually he was."

"And what about when I was abducted?" Tracy asked.

"That we aren't sure of. There was an academic conference at Tulane the week before, but it wasn't his field. And if he was in town for that, there is no definitive record of it."

"What was the conference?" I said, realizing that I was holding my breath. I looked at Tracy and saw she was too.

"It was a literary conference."

"Do you remember the topic?" Tracy said. We knew now that Jack's interests were broader than psychology.

"Hold on a sec. I'll pull it up." We waited, hearing the click of his keyboard over the line. "Looks like . . . the conference title was *Myth and Magic in Surrealist Literature*."

Tracy and I exhaled simultaneously. There was something here, whether Jim knew it or not. We looked at each other, and Tracy nodded at me to start.

"Jim. I know you have massive databases and minions to troll through all that information. I want you to do something for us. I know you think everything I am doing is far-fetched, but if you do this for me, I promise I will show up at the hearing and cry my eyes out before that parole board."

"I have to hear what it is first, obviously."

"Can you have someone do an analysis of Jack Derber's attendance at academic conferences for his whole career? I mean, I don't know how you can do it, but you can—maybe it's his credit card receipts, maybe it's through the university . . ."

Tracy took up the cue. "Have the university turn over his expense reports. Maybe they still have the records."

"And then," I continued excitedly, "can you cross-reference that list with the missing persons reports for the same areas at that time?"

Jim went silent for a long time. Finally, he said, "You think there are others? Ladies, there's no evidence he ever had other captives. We've gone through every inch of that house using every forensic tool available, sniffers, UV lights, luminol. We've done extensive serological and DNA testing . . ."

I didn't want to let Jim on to what else I was thinking, and maybe what Tracy was thinking too, because he would surely think we had gone off the rails.

"Please, Jim. Please. Will you just run the report?"

"I won't be able to give it to you, even if I do that. You realize that, don't you? You two are not, contrary to what you may think, credentialed FBI agents."

Tracy started to say something, but I held up my hand, recognizing victory when I saw it.

"Fine. You'll do it then?"

"I'll see what I can do. You know, it isn't easy to get projects staffed these days. We've had even more funding cuts for our division. All the money goes to the antiterrorism group now."

I pulled out my trump card. "You owe it to us, Jim, don't you think? After that trial?" I almost felt guilty throwing it back in his face, knowing what a sore spot it was for him.

He was quiet for a moment, then, very softly, said, "I'll get it done. Now why don't you guys get back to mending fences? I'm glad to hear that you're seeing each other. It does an agent's heart good." He chuckled warmly.

Tracy and I looked away from each other at that. We both mumbled our thanks and hurried off the phone. Only when we hung up were we able to look at each other again. Neither of us could bear to articulate our feelings, so I changed the subject back to the original reason for my visit.

"I have a proposition for you."

"What?"

"I'm in way over my head with this stuff: literature about sex and death, S&M clubs, academic politics. I need your help, Tracy. You know what all these different things mean. Will you take some time off from the journal, just a few weeks, and come with me? "

Tracy frowned at me. "You think there are things the FBI missed?"

"I know it sounds crazy, but yes. I want to go down south, to see what I can learn about Sylvia's past. Talk to her family. I think there's a lot more we need to learn. About Noah Philben, about Adele, about David Stiller. A lot of things happened back then, and the FBI didn't even scratch the surface. I think there are answers to our questions, Tracy. We just have to find them."

At the end of my speech, I took a breath and looked at her with anticipation. I had surprised myself too. I hadn't asked another person for help since my escape, and I certainly hadn't wanted anyone to get any closer to me, literally or figuratively. And Tracy would have been the last person I thought I had the courage to ask. Maybe deep down I felt that if we went through this together, she could finally see that I wasn't the awful human being she thought I was. Or that I thought I was.

With near-perfect timing, as always, when Tracy was about to answer, my phone buzzed. I picked it up only to see a text from, naturally, Dr. Simmons. I pressed the off button.

"Our shrink," I said with a slightly embarrassed smile.

Tracy laughed. "She seems like a better shrink than we probably give her credit for. Maybe she's psychic too." We were both smiling now.

"Will you, Tracy?"

She looked at her computer, then around the room at her books, and sighed. She walked over to her desk and calmly shut her laptop.

"All right. I'll go. On one condition."

"Yes?"

"We need to take a little detour down to New Orleans. I have to make a visit."

CHAPTER 21

Because Tracy couldn't leave for a few days, I booked a hotel nearby. Neither of us mentioned the possibility of my staying with her. After all those nights next to each other in the cellar, we knew that kind of proximity would bring back too many memories.

That night I had trouble falling asleep. When I finally drifted off, I had my recurring dream, if you could even call it a dream. It was more like a tormenting memory that haunted my sleep.

I was upstairs in Jack's house, and he was testing me. Finally giving me the chance I had wanted and had been working toward, carefully and methodically.

Without warning and in complete silence, he guided me off the rack, out of the library, and over to the front door of the house. Almost instinctively, I turned back from where I had come, looking back in through the door of the library, taking one, almost mournful last glance at the rack, hoping the memory of the pain would inspire me in this moment.

The wood seemed to shine, almost to glow. The sunlight burning through the window over it gave it a magical gloss. I turned my head slowly to look forward again at the door to the outside. I had never seen it open before. My feet must have moved, but in the dream I glided over, unable to stop, unable to control my own movements. A ghost, a chimera, I was nothing but air.

Jack pointed forward, saying, "You want to see her, right?"

He had told me before, taunting me I thought, that one day he would dig up Jennifer's body, just for me, one day when he finally believed I had reached the level where I could be trusted. Trusted to see it. Touch it if I wanted to. Lie down next to it.

I couldn't tell if he was threatening me with the same death, however gruesome it might have been, that he offered her.

I looked through the door, almost afraid of the open space it harbored, after all this time. I had spent months building up Jack's trust in me, making him believe that I was accepting my "fate," that I would never run away. I had built up that trust at a high cost, and I wasn't about to lose everything I had put into it now.

But was this the moment it had all been leading up to? One false move, and I could be dead. Dead or free. There were no other options, and there was a chance they were one and the same. Either way, nothing would be the same after this. This was a turning point. My heart felt as though it might burst.

The opportunity had arrived unexpectedly. I hadn't thought it would come this soon, so even though I had been planning, I hadn't planned this far. I didn't know if the time was right. I hadn't eaten in two days, so my brain could hardly calculate the odds, as if there were enough data points in this situation to run any numbers. It didn't help that I was fully naked and still in pain. I was utterly vulnerable, yet utterly determined.

I had believed my mind was strong, but I knew in my heart I had wavered. That there had been times over these last months when I thought maybe I should give in and accept that this was the rest of my life. That I would stay here as Jack's faithful servant until the day he decided to kill me. That if I didn't fight back, even in my head, he would be merciful at least on the physical punishments. Then I could live happily with the little bit of release I had earned.

Through the open door, I saw a small porch and beyond it a dirt driveway with a large red barn at the end. The barn was tall and run-down, with peeling paint showing the worn boards beneath it. Its door was cracked open about two feet, but all I could see was darkness within.

I didn't immediately notice the body. But eventually my eyes, unaccustomed to taking in such a large depth of field, made their way there. On the ground, to the left of the open door, was a blue tarp, carefully wrapped around a human figure.

My heart nearly stopped when I saw that the discolored and bloated object jutting out at the end of the tarp was a foot. It was almost unrecognizable as part of a human body. It was dirty, the earth caked around the swollen ankles and toes. He had clearly buried her without a casket of any sort.

He pushed me through the open door, and I started to walk slowly toward the body. Even though I had known for many months that he had killed Jennifer, and I thought I had mourned her, somehow seeing her there escalated my grief and fear, compounded it by a power of ten. And yet pushing back wave after wave of regret and pain, I drew my focus back to myself. Was this the moment? Should I run? Should I look at her? My sweet Jennifer.

As I always did at that moment in the dream, I woke up in a cold sweat, Jack's laughter echoing in my head. I sat up, went into the small, antiseptic bathroom of the hotel, and drank glass after glass of cold water. I went back to the bed and sat down, not turning on the lights.

Eventually my eyes adjusted to the darkness of the room, and I could vaguely make out the shapes of the furniture. I stared at the mirror across from me, my outline a visible but darkened shadow. A familiar friend, my only friend. I could pretend my reflection was Jennifer's ghost. I often talked to her, though she never answered, just like the years in the box.

Tonight I just looked at her for a long time, until I finally got up and walked over to the mirror, where I traced her image with my fingertip. The only other human I would dare touch. Who was the lucky one here? I wondered. Jennifer didn't have to be alone anymore, while I was here, locked in my own box, a solitary figure unable to let anyone in. Sealed up as tight as a drum, with nothing but phobias and paranoia to guide me. Broken. Unfixable. Trapped.

CHAPTER 22

A few days later Tracy and I flew into Birmingham. From there we rented a car and drove for hours down a four-lane highway, until we exited into the heart of small-town America, with its disjointed mix of farmers' co-ops, half-deserted strip malls, and VFW posts. Tracy seemed relaxed, happy to be back in the South on her home turf.

Maybe it was her good mood that enabled her to tolerate my many eccentricities. The way I jumped when she slammed the trunk of the car shut. The methodical process by which I counted my bags, checked for my phone, double-checked the credit cards in my wallet, secured my seat belt, and pulled it three times to confirm it was working properly. The way I was a backseat driver, nervously eyeing all the other drivers as though we were in a derby race and they were out to knock us off the road.

I was grateful she chose to find it amusing, because I could only imagine how annoying it must be to travel with me. But I knew if I didn't use those coping mechanisms, as Dr. Simmons would call them, my anxiety would ratchet up, then look for a place to land. I needed to calm myself by running through my lists. The oven is off, the front door is locked, the alarm is set.

June in Alabama was more than I had bargained for. It was hot and humid, of course. That much I had expected. But the weight of the humidity pressed down on you so hard, you wanted to burrow into the earth to escape it. I cranked the car's air-conditioning to high, just as Tracy turned up the volume on the radio, I supposed to avoid talking to me.

Our plan was to drive directly to Sylvia's parents' house. They lived in the small town of Cypress Junction, in the southeast corner of the state, near Selma.

When we finally reached the town, we could tell it was dying. The main street was lined with quaintly faded redbrick Depression-era buildings, which had nothing but To Lease signs in the windows. There was one bank in the center of town, and we passed a post office, the town hall, and a single chain drugstore. No parking lot had more than two cars in it. A small restaurant displayed a placard declaring it was "open," but through the windows you could see chairs flipped over onto tables. The lights were out.

"What do people here do for a living?" I said, as I stared out at the empty buildings.

"The ambitious ones make meth. The others take it. Or maybe work at the fast-food joints in the 'new' part of town. Welcome to the rest of America."

We turned a corner and drove out onto a large bypass. It was deserted, but Tracy assured me it would be busy on Fridays because it led straight down to the Gulf Coast beaches.

We followed our GPS's directions until we reached a brick ranch house in the middle of rolling fields, a mix of cotton and grazing.

We pulled into the driveway, which was nothing more than a red-dish, sandy dirt path. As I stepped out of the car, the sun blazed down on me again, and I wished I'd worn something even lighter than my gray cotton pants and white linen button-down.

Before I took the first step, Tracy shouted, "Watch out!" I looked down and saw an anthill seven times bigger than any I had ever seen in my life. It was a foot high. I leaned over to study the swarm-ing insects, frantic with their communal life, some carrying little white bits, some stopping to connect with their peers with a swift touch before moving on.

"Fire ants," said Tracy. I grimaced and stepped carefully around the hill.

We hadn't called ahead, so we didn't know if Sylvia's parents would be home. We knew they were farmers, though, and as Tracy said, in the South, farmers had to quit working early because of the heat.

It was four o'clock now, the hottest part of the day.

We knocked and heard someone calling from inside. A man in his early sixties opened the door, which I noticed hadn't been locked. He looked as if he'd just woken up from a nap, as he stood before us in jeans and a white T-shirt, no shoes. I hoped he would invite us inside, where I could feel the air-conditioning so crisp and cold, my skin drew toward it involuntarily.

"Can I help you?" the man said in a friendly and polite, if not welcoming, voice. He must have thought we were selling some-thing, but there was no trace of rudeness. And he didn't seem to notice or object to Tracy's unorthodox appearance, even as her facial piercings glinted in the bright sun.

Tracy took the lead. "Mr. Dunham, we are here about your daughter."

Instantly, a look of dazed dread passed across his face. I realized he must have thought we were here to tell him she was dead, so I quickly jumped in.

"She is fine, sir." His face relaxed instantly. "Well, at least we hope she is. We don't really know her, but we want to get in touch with her. We need to ask her a few questions."

"Is she in any trouble?" he asked, clearly pained. My heart was breaking already.

"No . . . no, sir, not that we know of. She just might be a . . . witness to something."

"Something that husband of hers has done?" His voice was gruff, and I could see the muscles in his neck tense. I thought he might cry.

"It's related to him," I said, "but we're not at liberty to discuss the details right now." It was almost the truth.

"You're with the police?" he asked, squinting at Tracy.

"No, not exactly," she replied, "but they're . . . aware of our investigation."

He peered at us, sizing us up. For the first time I thought he noticed Tracy's partially shaved head, because he leaned in closely to see her. Nevertheless, he paused only for a split second before inviting us in.

"Erline," he called out in his lilting accent, "we've got some visitors." He smiled at us warmly then, even though we must have been stirring up his pain. I liked him instinctively. How had any daughter of this man ended up married to Jack Derber?

His wife came out to the entryway to greet us, wiping her hands on her apron as she stepped toward us. We introduced ourselves, but didn't use our real names.

"What, Dan's got you standing out there in that heat? Come on in, girls! Have a seat."

We went into their bright living room and sank into the broad floral-patterned sofas. Wall-to-wall carpeting gave the space an almost womblike feel, and the perfectly controlled climate turned it into its own little biosphere. It was immaculately clean, smelling a little of the fake freshness of powdered room deodorizers.

I was puzzled. I had assumed Sylvia came from a broken or abusive home. Someplace where her self-esteem had been shattered early on, making her vulnerable to someone like Jack. Not this cozy little outpost in the backwoods of America.

Dan Dunham turned to his wife, who was looking at him expectantly.

I wished suddenly we hadn't come here to disturb this sweet couple who were clearly grieving for their daughter who was as lost to them as I had been to my parents all those years ago. I looked over at Tracy. I could see she was feeling something too. These two people were also victims of Jack Derber. Victims in a different way, but victims nonetheless.

Dan began. "Erline, they are here about Sylvia. She's not hurt," he said quickly, "but they'd like to find her to ask her some questions. They think she may be a witness to something."

"Well," Erline said, drawing herself up tall and looking off into the distance, "we wouldn't be able to help you much on that front. She doesn't have much to do with us these days."

Dan continued for her. "It's been over seven years, as a matter of fact, since she left here to join that religious group. I don't know why she had to go so far away. We've got plenty of them right around here. It's the Bible Belt, after all."

"How did . . . how did Sylvia manage to get involved with one so far away?"

He sighed. "It was all on those computers. We don't have one here at the house, but she would spend hours at the library in town."

"She found the group online?" I asked, surprised.

He nodded. "There was no stopping Sylvia once she got something in her head. She was twenty when she left, so it was hard for us to tell her what to do." He shook his head. "I'd hoped she'd at least finish up at the junior college first, though."

"What was she studying?" asked Tracy.

Erline sighed, "Religion. It was all she cared about then. I could see it was taking over her, and it didn't seem healthy for a girl her age. But you know, everyone has to find their own way. You can't live their lives for them."

"But it was too much," Dan continued. "Praying all the time, going to religious revivals, church lock-ins, all that stuff. At first I thought maybe she was in love with the young preacher over at Sweetwater. He was a good enough man, despite his profession." He tried to muster a laugh. "But then he up and married Sue Teneval, over from Andalusia."

Dan and Erline stared off in different directions, reflecting on their daughter, I supposed. I wondered exactly what she had found at those terminals in the public library.

Then Erline pulled herself back from her thoughts and said, "But I'm being so rude. You ladies must have come pretty far from civilization to make it all the way out here. Can I invite you to supper?"

Tracy nodded almost imperceptibly at me as I thanked Erline for her hospitality.

While Erline prepared dinner, Dan gave us a little tour of the farm. We stepped out into the still-sweltering heat to explore the land where Sylvia had been raised. I somehow hoped I would be able to sense a kinship with her, seeing these fields where she'd spent her youth, where she'd dreamed of her future.

As Tracy and I looked out over the rolling hills, Dan took out a small pocketknife and picked up a stick. He started whittling it, his head down, ignoring the gorgeous sunset that was starting off on the horizon. Finally, he spoke.

"She was a bright girl, our Sylvia. The school said they'd never seen a student score so high on those standardized tests they gave. And she was a delight to be around, warm and helpful and full of love. It all changed when she hit her teens. People always said it would. We didn't believe them. We figured she'd go off to some fancy college, and maybe she'd even live someplace like New York City, or even Europe. That we would have been able to handle, even if it meant not seeing her all the time. That's what we expected. But we never expected the way things turned out."

"How did it all begin, Mr. Dunham?" I asked.

He went quiet for a moment, holding the stick up close to his face, examining his handiwork.

"The religion thing started her senior year of high school. She would talk to us about it at first—wanting to have deep, philosophical conversations. It really wasn't my sort of thing, I told her. But I realized if I didn't discuss it with her, she would shut me out forever. So I went to the library and checked out a bunch of books. I fell asleep most nights trying to get through all of it.

"I only started to worry when she got on the Internet. Soon she was telling us about her 'religious leader.' I didn't know what was really at the root of it. Was it some sort of scam? Were they trying to get money? But she didn't have any money, and neither did we."

He tossed aside the first stick, its point now fine, and picked up another.

"She drifted further and further away from us. Barely talking at the dinner table, which had always been the heart of our family life.

"By the time she physically left, she'd really been gone for quite a while. She finally did pack up her bags, though. Told us she was meeting her leader down at the depot in town, and not to worry, she would stay in touch. We tried to go with her, but she wouldn't have it. She seemed panicked at the suggestion. So we let her go."

"She left us with only her e-mail address. I set up an account that day, with the librarian's help. She did e-mail us back a few times, but they trailed off very quickly."

"Did she . . . did she write to you when she got married?" I asked tentatively, sure that would touch a nerve but hoping he knew something specific.

He shook his head.

"We hadn't heard anything from her for two years, and then, when we did, it wasn't from her. It was in the newspaper. Saying she had been writing these letters to a man in jail, and that she was marrying him. When we looked into it and found out who this man was, Erline just crumpled up in my arms. She cried, and I am not too ashamed to admit that so did I. So did I." At that he lifted his head up, put his knife in his pocket, and looked out over the hills.

"It's hard to explain it. Picturing the little girl you raised up out here, on the same land farmed by her grandparents and their parents before them, ending up in the arms of a sick and twisted man. A man who would hurt other girls. Almost anything would be better than thinking your daughter chose a life like that over the life you offered her."

I saw tears welling up in Dan's eyes, and I had to turn and walk a few steps away. I wasn't prepared for this much emotion, and I certainly wasn't equipped to see the same kind of anguish I had imagined my own parents going through, all those nights I spent in that dungeon. All the nights wishing I could tell them that I was okay. Well, not okay exactly, but alive, and thinking of them.

Tracy kept her eyes on the ground. Here was this man showing an outpouring of love such as she had never known from a parent. I could only imagine it must have hurt her to think it was wasted on this girl who walked away from it all, voluntarily, into the arms of the devil.

But Dan stood upright and wiped his eyes. "Well, there's nothing I can do about it now, I suppose. She's an adult and can make her own decisions."

I turned around and walked back over to Dan.

"Mr. Dunham, I know this might be a hard question, but do you happen to have those e-mails she sent you all those years ago?"

Dan pulled himself back to reality. "Well, I know we printed them out back in the day. We can probably dig them up, but I don't think you'll find them to be very useful."

After baked ham and several kinds of deep-fried vegetables, we cleared the table and Dan brought out his old box of files. Marked on a thick folder toward the back was one word: *Sylvia*. He pulled it out, and her life until the age of twenty spilled out before us: her birth certificate, immunization cards, school reports, and class photos tucked in a small pink envelope.

I picked up a photograph.

She was a pretty girl, with sandy blond hair, blue eyes, and a forthright smile. She looked confident, appealing. Dan told me it was the photo from her junior year.

In the next one, she had the same haircut and was only barely older, but her smile was tight and her eyes appeared to be settling on something far away. Dan didn't have to say a word, but he lingered on that photo for a while before putting it back into the envelope with a sigh.

Erline didn't leave the kitchen as we sifted through these old memories. I pictured her in that kitchen alone, standing before the darkened window with a pained expression, vigorously scrubbing pot after pot, her hands red and scalded from the dishwater, as we pored over the life of her child reflected in official records.

Finally, Dan thumbed through the last pages at the end of the file, the printed e-mails. Tracy and I looked through them but couldn't find anything meaningful. They reminded me of Jack's letters, poetic but nonsensical. But they were also optimistic, idealizing her new life with her leader.

The last e-mail didn't sound as if it would be the last one. It sounded like an enthusiastic fourteen-year-old, writing home from camp about finally swimming across the lake. She was thrilled to be "enveloped in this mystical and divine experience," to have her "dreams made manifest through a true and living miracle."

I wished it were a letter from camp. A letter with a postmark so we could know where she went from there.

Tracy and I declined Dan and Erline's offer to stay the night, and instead we drove for more than an hour before finally coming to a brightly lit motel on the side of the highway. Tracy glanced over at me, and I shook my head. I couldn't do it. She continued on, looking for something bigger and safer. We ended up driving the entire two hours back to Birmingham, where we found the sturdy edifice of a historic hotel in the center of downtown. With valet parking no less.

I felt relieved to be ensconced in the fortlike structure of the hotel, as I dropped my bags onto the soft cream-colored carpet. The room felt like a sanctuary. The sheets of the bed were taut and crisp, the duvet thick. And the paper case of my room keycard had the passcode for the hotel's Wi-Fi. I was in heaven.

I picked up the remote, turned on the television, and flipped open my laptop. I ran a search on Sylvia Dunham and discovered in seconds that it was a common name. The first hits were the Sylvia Dunham in question, though: the news stories in the small local papers in Oregon and a couple of the Web sites of the bigger news outlets, all articles about her marriage to Jack Derber. The angle most of the stories took was how this evil beast had found love through the mail. They would have been human interest stories, if they had been about an actual human.

One was even written with a humorous slant, filled with crass, silly jokes—calling him "Professor Pain" in the headline—as though Jack had been little more than a comic book villain. When I read it, I slammed my laptop shut so hard, I had to open it back up again to check the screen, to make sure it hadn't shattered. I grabbed the remote and turned off the television. I sat in the silence, staring at myself reflected in its blank display.

I didn't know what I was looking to find in those news stories. I guess I'd wanted to see a more recent picture of her, to see which face of hers was looking back at me—the girl from junior or senior year. But of course there were only pictures of Jack, the star of the story, staring out with his own creepy half-smile.

Could Sylvia really have found that happiness of her junior year being bound to a man like Jack?

I could certainly understand her appeal—that smiling exuberance bursting from that stiff school picture pose. From what I knew of Jack, it must have been enticing for him to meet someone so young, vulnerable, full of life. I could only imagine how he would have treasured her enthusiasm, her naïve ideals. And mostly, how he would have enjoyed putting out that special light of hers with a brutality few could understand as well as I.

CHAPTER 23

The next day Tracy and I set out on our detour to New Orleans. I felt even more anxious than usual because I was impatient to get back out to Oregon to investigate. All the threads of this story were coming together—I could feel it—though in what way I couldn't yet see. This trip was Tracy's one condition, though, so I knew we had to go. I wondered where she was taking me, but I didn't ask any questions, for fear of invading her privacy.

We finally reached New Orleans in the late afternoon. I found myself strangely excited to see it, remembering vividly all the stories Tracy had told us over the years in the cellar. It had sounded so magical.

The French Quarter was indeed beautiful, both stately and ramshackle at once. But as Tracy drove me up and down the streets, she pointed out the gritty landmarks of her childhood: a street corner of panhandlers, a run-down deli, a creepy back alley.

"Not exactly from the tourist brochure, right?" she said, smiling as she parallel parked in front of a seedy diner.

It was only when we returned to the car after a quick bite that I noticed how serious she had become.

"Okay, let's go."

I had no idea where we were going, but I nodded. I was always nodding to Tracy, as I did all those years ago when she ruled my life almost as much as Jack Derber had. I noticed she never expected me to do anything other than follow her every command. She never asked me now—as she had never asked me back then—what I thought. I felt a small revolt happening somewhere deep inside, but I stifled it. I owed Tracy at least that much, since she had joined me on this wild journey.

Tracy turned the car around and drove in the opposite direction from downtown New Orleans. I looked up at the rearview mirror, only to see it receding into the distance.

"Tracy," I said, somewhat timidly, "aren't we going in the wrong direction?"

"Not exactly," she said. "We're not going far outside the city."

I didn't say another word, even when we pulled off the highway onto a dirt road no one seemed to have been on in years. The ground was muddy and soft, and the car tires sank in a little too deep, I thought, to be entirely safe. Tracy rode the car hard, shifting into low gear and gunning the engine. I suddenly felt unsure of what was happening. The look of determination on Tracy's face frightened me a little.

"Tracy," I began again, this time almost in a whisper, "where are we going?" I swallowed hard. I wasn't sure I wanted to know the answer. Suddenly it all flashed before me—maybe she still really did hate me. Now she would finally take her revenge. Maybe that had been the motive for this trip all along. And now I was at her mercy. She knew these forgotten roads like the back of her hand, and there was no one around. She could do anything to me. Anything.

I felt the panic surge up from my stomach, penetrating my rib cage, filling my head. I started to feel dizzy, all the familiar signs. How could I, after all my precautions, have fallen for something so obvious? She had told me once, years ago, in the cellar, that no matter where I went, no matter what I did, if we ever got out of there, one day she would kill me. I had been shutting her out then, knowing I had to keep my focus, but now, now she was my focus. And I was riveted.

I tried desperately to read her eyes. She was going much faster down this dirt road than the economy-class rental car seemed capable of handling. She'd specifically requested a stick shift, so even if I could somehow disable her, I'd be stuck, never having learned to handle a clutch.

Her eyes stayed trained on the road. She didn't answer me. She seemed transformed from the person I had been traveling with—that woman who had kept me at a distance, a space in which I felt very comfortable. I had thought the deep anger had dissipated, supplanted only by a vague but pervasive disdain. I had clearly been wrong.

The car bumped along the road so hard, I thought my head might hit the roof.

"Tracy," I stammered, "Tracy, I'm sorry, really. I don't—"

"Shut up," she said tersely, steering hard to the right to avoid a gaping pothole. "Not right now."

I shut up. I gripped the door handle and considered whether to jump out of the car. I thought about how fast I could run and where I could run to. Not very far, but at least I had my bag with all my ID and credit cards. I grabbed it and wrapped its strap around my wrist several times, so it would stay with me if I got up the courage. There was high brush on the side of the road, but I thought if I held up my arms, I could avoid most damage to my face, and I could roll on my back into the weeds.

I was afraid to jump, but I was more afraid of the look on Tracy's face.

Finally, I forced myself to pull once, gently, on the metal door handle just enough to unlock the door. I closed my eyes, and started to count. One, two, three . . .

I didn't have the nerve to do it the first time.

I checked the speedometer. It felt as if we were going eighty miles per hour, but we were barely touching forty-five.

I looked out at the road. There was a spot of soft-looking grass up ahead. That was my chance. I would open, jump, and roll.

On three, two, one . . . I took a deep breath and popped open the door, propelling myself outward as far as I could. It felt as if the wind whipped me back, but I knew it was just the feeling of the car's trajectory moving forward.

I heard Tracy yell, "For chrissakes!" as she slammed on the brakes.

The car rambled on for several more feet, and the brakes emitted an ungodly wail as she slowed to a halt. Tracy jumped out of the car, and I could hear her running toward me.

It took me longer to get up than I had anticipated. I didn't think I was hurt, but the fall had disoriented me. Slowly I made it to my feet and started running as hard as I could down the dirt road. Tracy was fast, though. Much faster than I was. Within four or five strides, she was right behind me.

I could hear myself screaming, but it felt unconnected to my actual body. As if it were coming from someone else entirely. I was still clutching my bag. Even in my fear I was rational enough to know I'd need that when I got to town. Tracy was yelling something at me, but I couldn't make it out over the din of my own screams. We were both panting loudly, almost in sync. After no more than a couple of minutes, I knew I couldn't run much farther, but to my relief she dropped off even before I did. I kept walking as fast as I could, trying to catch my breath and think of what to do next.

"What the *fuck*? What the FUCK?" was all Tracy was saying, I realized, over and over.

"Please don't hurt me. Please don't hurt me," I said. I was almost delirious. Tracy was closing in on me. Her fingers were inches from my arms when my eyes fully focused on her. I screamed again—this time it was more of a howl of fear—and she shuddered and stepped back. She stood stock-still in front of me, not moving an inch in either direction.

She spoke calmly. "Sarah. Sarah, stop it. I am not going to hurt you. I'm not sure what you're thinking, but whatever it is, you are wrong."

I was crying as hard as I ever had before. Snot was running out of my nose and down my face. I sobbed so hard I couldn't catch my breath.

Tracy still didn't step toward me; she just said reassuringly, "I am not going to hurt you. I would never do that, Sarah. Just calm down."

I could see the fear on Tracy's face. I wasn't sure why she was the one who was afraid now. She had probably never seen me this way, not since the cellar anyway. Maybe it was bringing it all back to her.

She didn't take her eyes off mine. Then she closed hers to prepare for what she was going to say. She inhaled deeply.

"Listen, I know years ago I said a lot of crazy things. Let's face it, we were all crazy back then." She paused. She seemed to want to say this exactly right. "And I know that, even now, my feelings about you are not one hundred percent rational. That might not ever change, but I want you to know I am not the same person I was down there. I do understand, on some level at least, why you did what you did. For the most part. I'm not saying we can be best friends or anything, but . . ."

I didn't know what to say. She paused again, shading her eyes from the sun to see me better, waiting for a response I could not give.

I was starting to breathe normally, and I wiped my nose on my sleeve. I dropped to the ground on the side of the road, rubbing my eyes, thinking about what she said. Tracy hung back, still watching me, keeping her distance.

I wanted to say something to her, but I couldn't find the words. I wanted to say I was sorry, that I was a different person now, too. But I wasn't sure if that was really the case. Instead, I just nodded slowly. All I could really feel sure of was that she wasn't going to kill me. That I had gotten carried away with my own fears and was once again misreading the signs around me. Would I ever be normal?

Without another word, we started walking down the road back to the car, which was still running. Once inside it, Tracy put the car in gear and stepped on the gas. She looked sadder than I'd ever seen her, lost in her own thoughts. I just looked straight ahead, still sniffling.

Tracy drove carefully as she turned down another dirt road, no more than a path really, barely wide enough for a car. Tree limbs brushed the top and sides of the car as we passed through. Finally, the road ended in a patch of grass, and she pulled off to the side.

"We walk from here." She turned off the engine and got out. I followed, holding on to my purse, the strap still wrapped tightly around my wrist. I stumbled as I stepped out onto the grass, then walked forward about fifty yards.

I could see water sparkling in the distance, and I realized we were at an abandoned campsite of some sort. The grass had grown up around the old fire pit, and the open areas were strewn with garbage. I checked my cell, noticing that it was getting late. The sun would be going down soon.

I looked around. It was beautiful, if you could look past the scattered debris. The trees were luscious and green as they are only in the Deep South or the tropics. The air was not as oppressive as it had been in the city. The breezes over the lake had broken the humidity.

We were quiet for a few moments, looking across the lake at the setting sun, and finally I had to ask.

"Tracy?"

"Yeah?"

"What are we doing here?"

There was a long pause before she answered.

"This is where my life changed."

I waited patiently for her to continue. I knew Tracy had to tell stories in her own good time. Finally, she motioned for me to follow her, and we walked down to the edge of the water. The sky was streaked with orange and pink, colors that were reflected from the lake, hitting the water and glistening up at us.

"Right out there." She pointed.

Again, I waited.

"That's where he did it. Where the Disaster happened. Where Ben died."

Of course. I put my hand to my mouth. I wanted to comfort her, but that was not a skill I had developed in all my solitude. I realized I had let my own incapacity to recover from my past shrink my world so that it was big enough for only me. It was hitting me now, really for the first time, how being fucked up can turn into a form of narcissism. So that I barely even acknowledged that others might need something from me.

With what I knew was a wholly insufficient gesture, I took a step toward her, but she waved me off.

"He walked into the lake somewhere along here." She pointed to a small beachlike area about twenty feet from us. "They found some shoeprints in this direction; his tent was back in those trees. He'd been living out here with a couple of our friends who were homeless. He stayed out here with them, drinking beer. One of them had a guitar. I used to come out here too, a couple of nights at a time. It was quite a party.

"And then one night, late, after the other guys had gone to sleep—or passed out, more likely—he got up and headed into the lake. Just went in and kept going. One of his friends heard a splash and tried to run out to save him.

"But there was no saving him. Ben just went right under and didn't come back up. They dredged the next day and found his body. He had weighted himself down with some iron chains he'd found. No doubt about it. He meant it.

"I come out here every couple of years. I try to talk to him. Try to ask him why he did it. It's hard, but I feel closest to him here." She stepped into the water a few inches, then walked in deeper, slowly putting one foot in front of the other. For a second I wondered if she too was going to keep going. She seemed defeated in that moment, her shoulders slumped, eyes downcast, mouth slack.

"I shouldn't have left him alone. I shouldn't ever have left him alone. At that time I was so deep into the club scene, looking for an escape. But it didn't help. And then I wasn't around, and I lost Ben. The only one I ever loved."

I said nothing. I knew from experience there isn't anything anyone can really say to help you through your grief. You just have to let the pain wash over you over and over again, until the tide of it drifts back and away, slowly and gradually. I stood there quietly, looking out over Lake Pontchartrain and the sunset dazzling before us.

I also knew, without her saying it, that the chain of events that started here ended for her in Jack's cellar. If Tracy's grief hadn't driven her to take that hit of heroin, would she have ended up as Jack's prey? Seeing her now, I wondered which was worse—all that Jack had inflicted on her, or this?

We stood there for a long time, until it got late enough for me to get nervous. It was getting hard to see clearly in the dusk.

Then something nearby stirred. It wasn't much more than a crackling twig, but suddenly all my nerve endings were prickling. I looked at Tracy, who was still lost in thought, sitting on the ground now, hugging her knees.

There was the sound again. This time I could tell Tracy heard it. I was startled by how familiar all her bodily signals were to me. As if we were still down there. We listened, without any sign to each other, but I knew we both knew. Just like when we were in the cellar and our bodies tensed when we heard Jack's car approaching from the bottom of the driveway. The way the muscles in the back of our necks and the set of our jaws tightened almost imperceptibly when he entered the house. We both waited, alert, listening for it again.

"Tracy," I whispered. "Can we go?" I looked at my phone, automatically making my usual check. Tracy nodded and got up, fast. As soon as we got into the car, she hit the button to power-lock the doors. I hadn't even had to ask. She turned on the lights, and we drove, slowly at first, then eventually faster and faster, out of the camp.

There, up ahead of us on the road, we saw the shadowy figure of a man. Tracy hit the brakes, and we both uttered a sharp cry at once. He was wearing a plaid shirt, unbuttoned, with a white T-shirt underneath. He had long hair and a goatee. He spread his arms wide—I couldn't tell whether it was a sign of surrender or attack—and started moving toward the car.

I double-checked that the car doors were all securely locked and quickly looked around to make sure there was no one else out there. Out of the corner of my eye, I saw something move and watched in horror as another man rushed out of the shadows. He ran straight to the car door on my side and pulled on the handle.

Tracy and I screamed in unison, and she gunned it, her foot pushing the gas pedal all the way to the floor. The man in the plaid shirt dove into the bushes on the side to avoid being plowed down. Tracy drove faster, even long after we'd lost sight of the men in the rearview mirror. The car bounced hard as the tires hit every bump in the uneven surface. I closed my eyes and took deep, measured breaths, counting quietly to myself.

Tracy didn't slow down until we were within the city limits. We stopped under the glaring lights of a Chevron station to refuel, and then she drove on until she spotted a Waffle House. We took a booth in the corner and ordered coffee, sitting in silence, as we waited for our hearts to stop pounding and our heads to clear.

CHAPTER 24

Two days later Tracy and I got off the plane together in Portland. I was beginning to feel like a seasoned traveler. No panic attacks. I'd learned to cope. I bought a little rolling suitcase I only allowed to be gate-checked. I wore a smaller bag crosswise over my chest. I kept my valuables in its zippered interior pocket that I checked every half hour on the dot. My physical belongings, at least, were safe with me.

Tracy and I had hardly spoken since New Orleans, though I didn't understand why. I wondered if she was embarrassed by what she had told me, regretting it now that we were away from the site of her painful past. Or maybe she had been looking for more of a response from me—understanding or commiseration, something I didn't know how to show. And maybe, no matter what she said, she still couldn't disentangle the past from the present any more than I could.

At any rate I was not, I told myself, eager to rekindle some relationship with Tracy. Yet even as I thought this, I knew I really didn't believe it. I couldn't stay in my bubble anymore, and oddly, I didn't want to.

Still, it was surreal being with her, out in the world like this, without any walls to contain us. Yet here she was, here I was, and we were in Oregon. We never would have believed that anything could make us come back to this part of the world.

I pulled out my phone to do my check, to distract myself. I saw I had another message from Dr. Simmons and thought a busy public area would be as good as any place to call her back.

She answered right away. "Sarah. Where are you?"

"I'm taking a vacation, Dr. Simmons."

"Sarah, Jim and I have spoken. Where are you? Is everything okay?"

"I'm fine. Listen, you've been enormously helpful. Really. But I have to figure out a few things on my own. And then we can discuss them. At length. In elaborate detail."

"I understand. I just want to tell you that it's not all on you. It's not all your responsibility. Remember that."

I stopped. The wheels of my suitcase glided to a slow halt on the smooth floor of the airport. Dr. Simmons always did manage to touch a nerve.

"What do you mean?" I asked.

"Just that. Just that I know you put a lot of pressure on yourself. And in this case, there are a lot of other people bearing the burden of keeping Jack Derber in jail. It's not all on you."

"Well, of course I know that," I said, perhaps a bit too quickly.

"Okay, then. That's all I wanted to tell you. Have a great trip. Call me when you get back. Or sooner if you need me."

I hung up, staring off at the illuminated sign of a barbecue place. Dr. Simmons was right. I didn't have to bear the whole burden, but that wasn't the whole story. Even if I hadn't been responsible for everyone else's pain, I did have a duty to Jennifer. I owed her something more.

My thoughts drifted back over the familiar territory of our abduction. If only I hadn't persuaded her to go with me to the party that night. She'd had an exam to study for, but I had pushed her to go out. I can still picture her face as she hesitated, then relented for my sake. If only I hadn't pushed. Where would we both be now?

I was doing it again, I told myself, as I shook my head to clear my thoughts.

Tracy glanced at me out of the corner of her eye, as she headed straight for the exit. "Dr. Simmons?"

"Yes."

"I don't know why you still see her. She's basically an instrument of the state."

"You mean, because she works with Jim so much?"

"I mean, because doesn't the State of Oregon still pay her? And because she saw all three of us at the beginning. Come on, Sarah. They are keeping tabs on us. To make sure we don't go before the legislature again to demand compensation. I started seeing a private shrink immediately. I only see Dr. Simmons once a year to keep Jim off my back. A check-in, he likes to say. Which is, I'm sure, exactly right. I'm sure he checks in. I'm sure it is a total passthrough situation."

"What do you mean?"

"Come on, Sarah. I'm sure she tells the FBI everything, and they have put us into some massive database of theirs. One day, you can rest assured, they'll be calling on you to be a secret trained assassin. They've probably planted some kind of microchip in our brains. Whatever Jack Derber couldn't achieve, they probably can."

I couldn't tell if this was Tracy's attempt at dark humor, or if the world truly did hold more horrors that I hadn't considered. I needed to think about that one later, I decided, and shelved it in some inner recess of my brain.

Our first stop was Keeler, Sylvia's town. I wanted to see if she'd been home, or at least what was filling up her mailbox.

We drove slowly down the street past Sylvia's house. Nothing had changed. The mailbox was jammed full. The postman had tried to close it, but it would shut only halfway. We pulled up close, and I jumped out, looking around to make sure no one saw me.

I pulled out a slip of paper from the top. A notice that Sylvia's mail was being held at the post office going forward. I dug in a little bit farther but found only more junk mail. No letters from Jack, which suggested to me that maybe he knew where she was. Or at least where she wasn't.

"Okay, go!" I practically shouted to Tracy as I got back in the car.

"Is someone after us again?" she said. I couldn't tell if she was teasing me or not.

"No, but I need to get away from here. That place creeps me out."

Tracy obligingly sped away, and we made our way to visit Val and Ray on the other side of town. I'd arranged for us to have dinner with them, and as we pulled into the driveway of their tidy bungalow, I told Tracy that while we were here, her name would be Lily. She made a face at the name and asked if she could pick it next time.

Ray was waiting for us in the rocking chair on their front porch. He waved us in. Their house was cheerful and bright, decorated in a soothing palette of soft colors. A pot of stew must have been cooking somewhere in the house, its delicious aroma reminding us we hadn't eaten anything since the pathetic boxed lunch on the plane.

I introduced Tracy as Lily, relieved when she didn't dispute it. Ray made a little joke about how her piercings must have hurt, and she nodded and smiled indulgently. She was on her best behavior at least, I thought, as Val joined us.

"It was good to hear from you, Caroline," Val began. I started at the name my body still rejected. She shook hands with Tracy. "And how long have you been working as Caroline's researcher?"

When she was sure no one was looking, Tracy rolled her eyes at me and muttered a pointed "not long" under her breath.

"And I'm delighted that you can stay for dinner," continued Val, barely stopping for a beat. "Ray has some things he'd like to show you afterward."

After dessert Ray excused himself and returned a few minutes later with a large photograph album in hand. He set it down in front of us with an air of triumph.

Val giggled. "Oh, he's wanted to show this to someone for so long. I won't have anything to do with it. Usually I won't let him share it with anyone else, in case they think he's a real weirdo. But we figured you'd be interested."

Tracy reached over to the album and flipped it open to the first page. Instead of photos, though, it was filled with carefully preserved newspaper clippings. Next to each one was an index card covered in a fine handwriting that slanted hard to the left.

"My notes," said Ray, noticing where our attention had gone. "I took notes based on the TV news reports and then added my own thoughts on the story. I always believed there was more to it. You know, the press only found out so much."

I looked over at Tracy. She was transfixed. I had known at the time that the press was covering our story, but I hadn't seen any reports, mostly because I hadn't been allowed to read the newspapers or watch television then. My parents had me cocooned at home, sheltered from the media frenzy. All I remember from those days was eating myself sick with the endless plates of food my mother made or that the neighbors brought over in steaming casserole dishes.

Looking back, I realized I had been almost a prisoner at my parents' house, patiently lying still on the couch as they stared at me in delighted disbelief for hours on end, offering to get me anything I wanted. New slippers, a cup of lemon ginger tea, any and all my favorite childhood desserts.

But my favorites weren't my favorites anymore. My very taste buds had been transformed from the experience. In fact, I began to wonder if my mother suspected I wasn't really her daughter at all afterward, I was so changed. She wanted to know everything that had happened to us, but I told her only the most carefully edited bits and pieces. I doled it out in small measured doses, hoping never to let her feel the full impact of the truth. I believed that only I could gauge how much she could take, and I needed to protect her from what I knew she would be unable to live with.

When I returned, the whole world seemed hazy and bright and unreal. I had been living only in my own head for so long, pushing everything else out, that I found it hard to be present. So despite my mother's best efforts, we were still separated.

It was a gap I would never figure out how to bridge. My mother's deepest sadness was that I could hardly bear to have her cradle me in her arms, when all she wanted to do was hold me. But for me, all my circuits were cut. I had lost all connections except to a dead girl in the ground somewhere in Oregon.

My mother was sad, of course, about Jennifer, but her happiness to have me alive and with her again dwarfed her grief for this other lost child. I thought—I *knew*—that Jennifer deserved more. She deserved a real grief, all her own, and even then I felt I was the only one who could adequately provide it.

We were still in high school when Jennifer had finally stopped speaking to her father, and he never made much of an attempt to connect with her again. He left that part out when he spoke to the press about his deep and abiding loss, of course. I watched him warily when he came to visit me, and I saw behind his eyes that all he really wanted was attention. To me, his tears didn't really count.

So here I was, in this comfortable kitchen in Keeler, with the smell of our after-dinner coffee lingering in the air, poring over the press clippings of another lifetime. I looked them over, reading a few paragraphs here and there, noticing the shift in tone as the story developed, day by day. I detected in those words the familiar aura of professional excitement, this time from the journalists realizing the thrill factor of the unfolding story.

Then I noticed that the byline on most of the articles was the same: Scott Weber. That must be the journalist David Stiller had mentioned, the one who had been mooning away over Adele. I wondered aloud to Tracy whether we should meet with him, and she replied, "Definitely," without looking up from the articles. Her eyes glistened. Even for her this was hard. Even for her.

"Ray," asked Tracy, without looking up from the pages, "why did you take such an interest in this particular case?"

Ray smiled broadly. "Oh, not just this particular case, though this was definitely one of the more dramatic stories. And then when Sylvia moved to the area, it did become a bit of an obsession."

I looked up at him. "What do you mean?"

"Well, girls, come with me." We followed him down the hall to a door at the rear of the house. I hung back, suddenly feeling closed in, too close to other people's bodies. I didn't like going down narrow hallways, even in cheerful homes like this one.

I was a couple of steps behind them as we went into Ray's small study, and I gasped when I turned the corner. The walls were covered in sheets of newsprint, filled with headlines and photographs of the most gruesome crimes. Framed copies of historic documents, all relating to famous murders, were set up on the desk, balanced against the wall. He'd obviously gone to great lengths creating this elaborate and macabre gallery of horrors, dug deep into the past to accumulate an archive of the ways human beings make other human beings suffer.

A long shelf along one wall was filled with photo albums, nearly identical to the one he'd shown us, each labeled with a different proper name. I didn't know if they were those of the victims or the perpetrators, though, I thought bitterly, usually it was the perpetrators' names everyone remembered.

I looked back at Ray and saw him beaming with pride. He felt no shame about his obsession. And why should he? These were just stories to him. Did he even think of the victims as real people? Did he understand the tragedy, the horror those volumes contained? People's lives destroyed forever, and here it was, his hobby. Like stamp collecting.

I could sense without looking at her that Tracy too was repelled. Neither of us could even speak. I was unable to comprehend how someone could be so drawn to the things I was trying so hard to shut out. Ray looked at our astonished faces and started to try to explain.

"I know what you're thinking. That this is a bit, well, strange. Please don't misunderstand me. For a long time I wondered whether there was something wrong with me. But I think . . . I think . . . I just want to understand. I want to understand why people do these things, how it happens.

"So many times people get carried away by passion, do things they never thought they'd do, and their whole lives change in an instant. Sometimes people are simply insane—mentally ill—and it isn't their fault. But occasionally, just occasionally, there seems to be evil at work. Real evil. Like Jack Derber."

"You don't think he is mentally ill, Ray?" Tracy perked up. She suddenly seemed interested. For the first time it occurred to me she was still looking for answers. I thought she had it all neatly analyzed and had moved past it. She always seemed to know everything, but maybe she still had her questions, her doubts. Just like me.

"No, I don't think he was ill. He—he was so calculating. Everything he did required such careful planning, such controlled action. I asked Sylvia about him."

He paused. I didn't think he was going to continue. He looked away.

"Please, go on," I said. "It would . . . it would help us understand."

"Well, she only talked about him that once, when I asked. And afterward she begged me—begged me, I'm telling you—not to let anyone know she had spoken about him. I can't betray that poor girl. I could never let her see her words in a book." He pinched the bridge of his nose, squinting his eyes shut, possibly to push away tears.

"I won't . . . I promise I won't put anything in the book. But it might help us find her."

Tracy jumped in. "Yes, Ray. Maybe, without realizing it, you know something that could make a difference."

"Really? You think something she said so long ago could be useful? I do worry about where she is."

"Please, Ray. We just want to help her too."

Ray looked thoughtfully out the window and sat down in a recliner in the corner. We sat down on a small sofa along the opposite wall, shoving aside a pile of recent newspaper clippings about another missing girl.

"Sylvia told me Jack was a genius. That's why she married him. Because according to her, he had a vision of how the world could be something special and rare. Something only a few could understand, those who would let themselves be open to the true possibilities of experience. But it was more than what she said—it was the way she seemed at once so joyful and so terrified by it. I have never seen an expression like that before. Her face seemed . . . illuminated."

I looked at Tracy, trying to get a read on her. She was thinking hard, I could see. I wondered if, like me, she thought this didn't sound like someone who had been entirely reformed. Someone who just wanted to get out of prison and live a quiet, ordinary life on a quiet, ordinary street. This sounded like a man with a mission. A terrible mission.

As Tracy drove us back to the hotel that evening, she switched off the radio, her constant emotional cover, and we sat in silence for a moment.

"So what do you think, Miss Rational Mind?" she finally asked.

"About what? Kind of a lot to digest in there."

"I guess I mean the big question. Is Jack mentally ill? Or is he evil?"

"What mental illness could he have?"

"Well, at a minimum, the DSM-IV would tell you he is a 'sociopath with narcissistic personality disorder.' But what that means in terms of moral responsibility, I don't know. Is he ill? Someone to be pitied, not feared? I think it makes a difference. A critical difference. In terms of, you know, 'moving on,' as they say."

"Moving on?" I didn't even know what those words meant. And I wasn't ready to explain to Tracy that the whole purpose of this journey was to find that out.

"Yes, moving on. Not feeling those feelings anymore. Not being hardwired with whatever it was he did to us in there. Living a normal life. That kind of moving on."

She paused and glanced over at me quickly before shifting her eyes back to the road. We sat in silence for a few moments.

Then she began again, more hesitantly this time, "Don't you feel as if we have . . . almost an obligation . . . to understand this? To work through it? If we don't, he's still here, you know. Still in us. Still in control."

The conversation was hitting a little close to home. I felt myself shutting down, just like I had with Dr. Simmons. I didn't want to get into this.

"I guess I don't have many expectations in that regard. And I don't really see how what I think about Jack matters to that equation."

Tracy shook her head. "You are really not even out of the gate."

She pressed her foot harder on the pedal, and as the car surged forward on the deserted road, she switched the radio back on and fiddled with the dial until she found something hard and fast and loud. We rode the rest of the way like that, the silence between us more deafening than the punk rock blasting from the speakers.

CHAPTER 25

The next day I decided to show up at the offices of the *Portland Sun*, in search of Scott Weber. I had put Tracy in touch with Adele, and they were going to meet later that day. I was hoping they might speak the same language, or at least be capable of translating each other's academic jargon, and Tracy would learn something I couldn't.

When I arrived at the newspaper offices, a chipper young man in his early twenties stopped me at the security checkpoint.

"Can I help you?" he said brightly, but with enough edge to make it plain I wasn't getting through that gate without someone authorizing it.

"I'd like to see Scott Weber."

"Do you have an appointment?"

"Not per se. But I—I have some information that might be interesting to him," I said, hitting upon a sudden inspiration.

"Really. Hmm . . . well, unfortunately, he's not here." Then he winked at me. "But I will tell you that he just left the building about three seconds ago." I guess I looked innocent enough.

I all but sprinted out of the building, and sure enough, a man with sandy blond hair and a ruddy complexion was crossing the parking lot. He looked about the right age and was disheveled, as if he'd been up all night to meet a deadline.

I followed him. "Excuse me, Mr. Weber?"

He turned at his name. We met in the middle of the lot. "Yes, that's me. Can I help you?"

"Hi, my name is Caroline Morrow." Again that name, though I managed to say it without grimacing this time. I was getting better. He looked at me expectantly. "I'm in the sociology department over at the University of Oregon, and I'm writing a dissertation on Jack Derber. I thought you would be a great resource for . . ."

Scott starting walking away, his hand held up as if to ward me off. "I'm sorry, but I can't help you with that."

I pulled out what I hoped would be my trump card. A little white lie that might help me get his attention.

"One of my advisers, Adele Hinton, sent me. Said she knew you." He stopped dead in his tracks but didn't turn around. I wondered how far Adele's name was going to get me, or if it was a mistake trying to fake it. I waited to see if he would turn around, counting to myself, one, two, three . . .

On seven, he turned around.

"Adele Hinton?" he seemed surprised. "Adele Hinton sent you to me?"

"Yes, remember her? Derber's teaching assistant? You wrote a profile of her."

He stood still, looking puzzled. "Yes, yes, of course, I *remember* her. Adele." He looked down at his watch. "Why don't we take a walk?"

He motioned toward a park directly across the road and pulled out his cell phone. Holding up a finger indicating for me to wait, he walked a few steps away and made a call. I could just make out that he was rescheduling another meeting. Adele was a bigger draw than I'd expected. He must've had it bad.

We walked along a neatly tended path over to an area with a half-dozen picnic tables. Scott sat down at one across from me. He seemed nervous.

"So, Adele. How is she? I haven't heard from her in quite some time."

"Oh, she's great. Just great. You know she got tenure, right?"

"Yes, I heard that." He blushed at his admission. So he kept tabs on her. "I guess she's had a change of heart?"

"What do you mean?"

"I mean, about the Jack Derber situation. At first she seemed to like the attention it brought her, but then it became more or less forbidden territory. But that was a long time ago. I guess by now it's all water under the bridge."

This was getting interesting.

"'At first'? So you had an ongoing relationship with her back then?"

He blushed again and seemed agitated. "She didn't mention that?"

"No, she didn't." He looked disappointed. "Yes, we, um, dated for a bit. After that piece I wrote. Just a few months, but, well, she is quite an extraordinary woman."

Yes, quite extraordinary, I was thinking. I wondered if Adele had had some ulterior motive with this relationship. She was becoming more fascinating by the minute.

"So that must have been a strange dynamic. You writing about it, and she being such a part of the story."

He shook his head. "What can I say? It was my beat. But once he was convicted, we were just running background stories anyway—you know, scraping the barrel for ancillary material to keep it alive. Interviewing his junior high school teachers, profiling the architect of his house, looking at his conference papers, that kind of thing. Just to keep it going. Portrait-of-the-villain-type stories."

"His papers?"

"Yes, the last thing I was working on was a piece about his academic research." He paused, looking uncomfortable.

"I don't remember that one. Did it ever run?" I pressed, sensing he was hiding something.

"N-no. But it wasn't a big deal. Not front page or anything."

"It caused some trouble with Adele maybe?"

He shrugged.

"I see." So apparently Adele thought Jack's research *was* relevant to something. Relevant enough to keep people away from it.

He went on. "Anyway, it's too bad it didn't work out. She had a lot going on, especially with that group she was in." He was obviously trying to change the subject.

"What group?" Now I was really interested. A group, I thought to myself, or a secret society?

"I don't really know. Some kind of Skull and Bones–type of thing at the school. Mysterious, but that's how she was. Maybe that was the appeal. The challenge." He seemed to be getting lost in his self-revelatory moment, his look drifting off behind me into the distance.

"What do you mean?" I asked, loudly enough to get his attention again.

He snapped back into the present. He looked at me, apparently trying to decide whether to go on, perhaps realizing that confiding in me might not be his fastest track back into her heart.

Finally, he shrugged and continued. "I mean, I'd ask questions about her family, her past, even simple things like where she'd grown up, where she'd gone to school, but she always managed to deflect me."

He shifted in his seat, and his face reddened the way only a ruddy complexion can. I wondered exactly what he was remembering about Adele Hinton, especially because there was surely plenty to recall.

"Any idea who else was in that group of hers?"

"I don't know. All I know is they met at odd times—all hours of the night, and sometimes on short notice. She took it very seriously, and if she had a meeting of that club, there was nothing I could do to keep her from it. That was her top priority."

I thanked him and stood up to leave. Once again he looked confused.

"But wait, we only talked about Adele. Don't you want to talk more about Jack Derber? For your paper?"

I had what I needed from him already.

"Let's set up a call. I'm late for class right now, but I really appreciate this," I uttered awkwardly as I eased away backward, waving to him.

"Oh, okay. Well, say hi to Adele for me. And, you know, if she wanted to get together . . . we could talk about your research or something. I can probably dig up some old notes . . ."

"Yes, I definitely will," I called out as I walked quickly over to my car.

Of one thing I was now certain. Adele was a crucial piece of the puzzle. She was right there in it. And she knew more than she was letting on.

CHAPTER 26

I had been in the cellar nearly one thousand days when Jennifer went upstairs for the last time.

During each of the days she was there, I had spent hours just staring at that box, trying to imagine what she was going through. She maintained her absolute silence to the end, even though she was not gagged all the time, and even when he was not around. His control over her was total and absolute, her terror complete.

Early on I had listened for her, thinking that eventually she would try to communicate with me again secretly, as she had in those first days. I'd thought that somehow, surely she would break free of his control enough to try again, if only for the sake of her sanity.

When I'd hear her scratching inside the box, like a trapped animal, I'd listen for patterns, for anything that sounded remotely like a code. I'd drive myself insane wondering why I couldn't make sense of the random noises that would occasionally emanate from in there.

And I kept listening for a long time. If the rest of us were quiet, I could sometimes hear her chewing her food, slowly savoring whatever scraps he'd left for her that day. I would even wake up at night if she shifted suddenly in her sleep. Once I thought I heard her sigh, and I sat still as a stone for an hour afterward, waiting for her to repeat it.

But she never did.

In a way, she might have been better equipped than most for such solitude and reflection. She had always been pensive, hard to read, withdrawn. Always thinking and daydreaming, never focused. She had hardly ever paid attention in high school, her gaze drifting out the window to the clouds above, her mind floating somewhere out there with them, thinking God knows what. But we managed to make it through our classes together, just as we'd made it through everything else. At the end of each day she would copy my class notes down into her own impossibly neat script, and we'd use her version for studying.

I yearned for those days, when we had not been separated by ten feet of cold cellar space, a wooden box, and whatever impenetrable psychological force Jack held over her. Now I wondered if she even had enough good memories left to sustain her, or if, like mine, her very imagination had been invaded by the horrors we were living through, and her mind could produce only nightmares. I wondered if she sometimes wished she had died in that car accident along with her mother, all those years ago. I know I often wished I had.

It must have been that same day—at least it is in my memory—that Tracy was brought down early in the morning after a full night upstairs with Jack. She seemed to be unconscious as he half-dragged her limp body down the stairs. He threw her up against the wall.

She scowled and opened her eyes briefly, just long enough for me to see them rolling back in her head.

She wasn't dead, anyway.

He leaned over and chained her, careful to check the lock twice, then turned to me and Christine.

I know Christine did the same thing I did. We tried not to look away from him, cowering in fear, as our bodies naturally wanted to do. He hated that. But at the same time we both managed to shrink our thin frames into the tiniest possible space, hoping he wouldn't pick us next. He stood over us, laughing softly, allowing his eyes to soak us in, to absorb the sight of his own private menagerie.

The room was utterly silent. We watched him, our hearts seizing with fear. I was willing him away from me with all my might. *Not me, not me, not me. Please.*

Finally, he turned slowly and stomped back up the stairs, whistling as he reached the top.

He had just been fucking with us this time.

As he left, I counted the steps in my head, the sound of the creaks echoing in the colorless space. Christine whimpered with relief. I let out a deep breath, slowly. Overhead we heard him moving about easily in the kitchen, going about his usual routine apparently. As if he'd just been checking the basement for water after a heavy rain.

Tracy slept most of that day, huddled in a ball, looking enough like a corpse that I had to watch closely to tell if her chest was still rising and falling.

In the early evening, marked for us only by the dimming of our precious crease of light from the window, she woke with a start. Without so much as a glance in my direction, she crawled back to the bathroom, her chain barely reaching, and I heard her retching violently into the toilet.

She stayed gone a long time after that. I listened as hard as I could and thought I heard a muffled sob from her. I nodded to myself, knowingly. Tracy would never let us see her cry. She must've been waiting back there for the tears to stop.

I watched for her, tortured as usual by the slow ticking of time, waiting to see what she would do next.

Looking back, it's shameful that I didn't feel anything for her then. No pity. No concern. It had all been stripped right out of me. The only variables I could register at that point were whether something caused me physical pain, or whether it alleviated the soul-crushing boredom of my day-to-day existence. By then I didn't have much of an emotional range beyond that.

Tracy finally scraped her way back over to her mattress, sprawled out on it, and turned her face to the wall. At first I didn't think she was going to say anything, that she wasn't even aware of my presence just a few feet away.

Christine was asleep again.

"Stop looking at me," Tracy finally said, in a stronger voice than I would have anticipated given how weak she was.

I looked away. Finally, she rolled over. I sat, leaning against the wall, on my own mattress, steadfastly staring in the opposite direction. Despite my fear of her, though, after a few minutes I couldn't keep my eyes from darting over to see what she was doing. I was too curious.

She noticed, of course, and snarled at me viciously like a rabid dog. Instinctively I shrank away, my chain rattling loudly.

Christine stirred, opened one eye for a second, and went back to sleep.

I was always awed by Christine's capacity for sleep. In a way it was the most perfect example of the power of human adaptability. She was able to shut out this experience in a way the rest of us couldn't, and in the end, maybe that saved her. Maybe that was the key to it all. Sleep.

But I could manage it for only ten hours at a stretch, max, no matter how hard I tried. And that was on a good day. Perversely, my regimen of near-total physical inertia resulted in bouts of insomnia. I had to make up the rest of the hours either by losing myself in my imagination or by trying to lure one of the others into conversation. Either way was painful.

But there were times when talking definitely helped. When we all got along, in a manner of speaking. When even Christine pulled herself away from her dark private place and we talked almost like normal people. Times when I supposed the others were every bit as bored as I was, as tired of fighting against their own interior torments, and we were able to put our own issues aside to keep our minds functioning, if only at a bare minimum.

We told each other stories, about our past, both real and embellished, anything to keep time moving forward, though toward what, none of us knew.

That was the kicker. We were waiting. Always waiting. As though we wanted something new to happen. Often wishing it would, because the boredom made you even crazier. But when something new did happen, it usually hurt, and then we ended up taking all our wishes back.

That day, though, Tracy clearly didn't want to talk. She was pale and sweaty, despite the cold of the cellar. She closed her eyes again. She usually didn't sleep so much. Something was wrong.

I waited until her breathing became even and regular, and then, convinced she was truly out, I pulled myself over to her. It must have taken me a full fifteen minutes to make it there without my chains giving me away. I carried as much of the metal strand as I could, carefully placing a few links onto the cold cement a little ahead of me each time, so they wouldn't make a telltale scraping sound when they dragged. When I finally made it to where she lay sleeping, I looked her over, scanning her flesh for some sign of life.

And then I saw them.

There on her arm, faint but distinct, were track marks. Seven small spots in a perfectly even line on her pale skin. I could see where the needle had gone in, and I could even identify today's fresh mark by its slightly reddened outer rim.

He was giving her heroin. Not out of pity. Not as an escape. No, he was punishing her. Making her an addict so he could gain even more control over her.

He would not have chosen this particular form of torture randomly. There was always a method to his madness. Somehow he must have discovered what that drug meant to her, the significance it held in her life. He must have known that almost nothing would be more painful to her than the pleasure and release offered by that particular poison.

But how? Tracy was so steadfastly resolved to keep him away from her memories and out of her mind. He must have pushed her very hard. Had she had a moment of weakness and told him about her mother, about that night at the club?

After I saw the marks, I returned to my spot as fast as I could manage without making noise and waited for her to wake up.

It was several hours before she rose and made her way slowly to the bathroom again. I heard her vomit some more, and then watched her haltingly drag herself back to her mattress. By then she seemed to be feeling a little better. Well enough to glower at me, at least, and tell me to leave her the fuck alone. I said nothing, knowing it was safer to wait and see what she did next.

She sat staring at the box, wrapped up in her own misery, and I wondered if she was telling herself that things could be worse.

I managed to keep from looking at her for a good ten minutes, but then I couldn't help it. I had to catch another glimpse of her arm. That second time she saw me looking, and our eyes met. She immediately turned her arm away, covering the marks with her hands.

To my surprise, I felt my eyes fill with tears then, for the first time in months. Even though at that moment, as much as any other since I'd been down there, I felt overwhelmed by the unbearable state of our existence, as I wiped my tears away I felt relief.

Because I was crying for Tracy.

These tears were proof that my emotions could still penetrate the hard shell I'd grown in here. I had thought they were gone forever. But maybe I was not yet an animal. I was still a human being somewhere in there after all.

CHAPTER 27

The morning after I spoke to Scott Weber, Tracy and I met at the hotel restaurant. It was a beautiful June day, and it almost seemed possible to forget why we were here as we ate scrambled eggs and compared notes.

"So. In re the matter of Adele Hinton," Tracy began, "I am ready with my analysis. Wanna hear it?"

I nodded.

"Classic frustrated academic. Always the best in her class in high school, thought she was going to take the intellectual world by storm. She thinks she is a genius with a capital G. And yet here she is, stuck at a crappy state school in the middle of nowhere."

"It's not a bad school, is it?"

Tracy shook her head. "Her words. Anyway, she let it slip that she's working on some big project for a conference a year from now. She was pretty cagey about it, but that's normal in academia. Whatever it is, she clearly thinks it's her ticket to a better appointment. You know, she seems so confident, but I think underneath it all, she feels like as long as she's here, she's a loser."

"Mmmm . . . that makes sense," I muttered as I swallowed a mouthful of eggs. "And what do you make of the S&M bit?"

"Who knows? Maybe, as she told you, she really wants to understand Jack. But somehow I suspect it's just her way to be subversive, to get attention in scholarly circles by going to extremes." Tracy was about to continue when my phone rang. I held up a finger and answered.

"Hello?" I recognized Jim's number, but he didn't speak right away when I picked up.

"Jim, are you there?" Tracy looked over at me, curious, but went back to spreading butter on her toast.

"I'm here. Listen, I have something for you."

"Did you finish your research assignment?" I smiled a little, despite myself.

"Sarah. It's hard to say really, but there . . . there does seem to be a pattern. We looked at the university's files and Jack's personal finances, expense reports, that sort of thing. And we think we have a pretty reliable record of where he was over a large time period, both before you were in captivity and during. And there does seem to be a correspondence. It looks like there were young women who disappeared in each city he went to for each academic conference. I have a list."

"How many names?"

A pause. I tried again, my voice softer this time.

"I want to know how many names."

Tracy held her knife poised in midair, looking at me. Tension filled her eyes.

"Jim, we deserve to know. We need to know."

He sighed. "Fifty-eight. Including the four of you."

Tracy saw the expression on my face and started furiously buttering her toast. When it was dripping, she put it down, swallowed hard, then stared off into the distance.

I took a deep breath. "I want that list, Jim."

As I said it, I could almost picture Jim putting his hand over his face.

"Sarah, you know I can't do that."

"Why not?"

"Technically, it's confidential information. But more important, it's probably not a good idea for you to see it yet. Let me look into it some more. I want to see what kind of connections we can establish."

"Has anyone else on that list been found? Any bodies been identified?"

He paused again.

"Only the three of you."

"Are all those cases open? Are there active searches going on?"

"Sarah, you have to keep in mind that over eight hundred thousand people go missing every year in the United States. This type of case goes cold fast. And some of these cases are more than fifteen years old."

"Right, so if some of those other girls are alive, they'd be just a little older than I am. I'd still want to be found, Jim."

"The chances that—"

"I understand the statistics perfectly well."

Jim was silent.

"Where are you, Sarah? Let's start there. I will come to you."

"That's a lot of families still waiting for their daughters, Jim. I want to see their names."

"Where are you?" he asked again.

I hesitated. "I'm still in Portland. With Tracy. Bring the list."

I hung up and looked over at Tracy.

She was still staring out over her breakfast. "How many?"

"Fifty-eight. Including us."

Tracy's jaw dropped. "I have to tell Christine," she said, putting down her fork and leaning forward. "She needs to understand the scope of this. This is more than just finding Jennifer."

"And it could be more than Jack."

"What do you mean?"

"Fifty-eight girls. Could Jack have really been acting alone? If there was some sort of secret society, one involved with human sacrifice like that Bataille group, for chrissakes . . . couldn't that have something to do with it?"

Tracy was still staring off into the distance. "The warehouse. We have to go back there. We have to see what it was used for, or still is," she said.

My stomach plummeted. "Why don't we wait until Jim is out here? Let's let him explore the dark old warehouse that might be a temple of human sacrifice," I suggested hopefully.

"Sarah, the FBI doesn't want to open up these cold cases, even if Jim is willing. There isn't any pressure on them. There's no press. Things need to be stirred up—that's how it works. Trust me, it's what I do. We need to give them something more to go on, something that will force them to look deeper and do it *now*."

"But Jim says he just needs a little more time," I said pleadingly.

"They've had years to look into this. I'm beginning to believe you're right, and if so, we need to act now. We can't wait for some government agency to get its ducks in a row. There has to be a connection between Noah Philben and Jack. There's something strange about Sylvia joining his church, then hooking up with Jack through that, and then Noah Philben being at that S&M club. That's Noah's warehouse. We need to know what's in it."

CHAPTER 28

"I can't do it," I said to Tracy an hour later, as she opened the door of her hotel room for me. She motioned for me to come in. The room was a disaster, her dark clothes and violent jewelry strewn around like the aftermath of some strange Gothic weather event. I cleared a few things away from the chair by the window and sat down, my back straight and chin lifted, determined to deliver the speech I'd been rehearsing in my own room since she'd come up with this insane idea.

Tracy sat down on the edge of the bed, cross-legged, her elbows resting on her knees and her hands clasped in front of her. She waited expectantly, as though she had known this was coming.

"I've been thinking about it more, and I just don't think I can do it," I began.

"You mean, you can't find Jennifer?"

"I mean, I can't go out to a warehouse in the middle of the night. Without the police."

"The police? Excuse me, but does it seem to you there is probable cause? They don't even think there is a crime. And for that matter, maybe there isn't one. This is trespassing, pure and simple. And maybe, if we get really brave, breaking and entering."

"Even more reason why we shouldn't do it," I countered.

"Do you have any other ideas for leads?"

I didn't answer.

"Yeah, thought so. So where does that leave us then? You want to give up? What's worse? Looking through the windows of a warehouse, or having Jack Derber show up at your door a free man?"

I shivered. "I obviously don't want that."

"Look, I'm not psyched about this either. But I keep thinking about those other girls. The other fifty-four. If there's a chance we could find even one—"

"Can't we at least go during the day?"

"You mean, when anyone there could see us in plain sight? Come on, I don't think I have to tell you how much more dangerous that is. We need the cover of darkness."

I could feel my shoulders begin to shake, but I fought back the tears. I didn't want Tracy to see me cry again. But I couldn't face the idea of going back there.

I needed some air. The hotel windows didn't open, so I picked up the laminated room service menu and started fanning myself with it. Tracy watched me, but I had given up trying to read her emotions, so I didn't bother checking her expression.

"Come on, Sarah," she finally coaxed. "You gotta get there. Look how far you've come already. A month ago you couldn't go to the laundromat. I know none of this is easy for you. It's not easy for me either. But remember, you won't be going out there alone this time."

Tracy went into the bathroom and came out with a wad of toilet paper.

"Here," she said, handing it to me rather unceremoniously. "Go ahead and cry. You'll feel better. Then clean yourself up, and let's take a look at Google Earth." She paused before continuing, "And if you really can't do it, then fine. I'll go out there by myself."

I gasped. "You wouldn't!"

"I would, and I will. You know my theory. Plunge in. Face the fear head-on. Stay on the offense."

Just what I need, I thought. Another body on my conscience. I was the one who had gotten her out here, dragged her back into the nightmare of these memories. I couldn't let her go out there on her own. If something happened to her, I would never recover from the guilt. I had to pull myself together and go. I sat there hating her and, even more, hating myself for starting this whole thing. If I hadn't pushed this forward, I'd still be sitting in my peaceful white haven eleven stories up, ordering in Thai food and watching films on Turner Classic Movies I'd seen a hundred times by myself.

Goddammit, I had to do this.

That night at ten p.m., dressed in black and wearing our most comfortable shoes, we pulled out of the hotel parking lot. Part of me was hoping I couldn't find the warehouse again. That somehow the earth had swallowed it whole, along with whatever perverse rituals were going on within it.

On the drive Tracy told me she'd reached Christine that morning, after somehow persuading Jim to give her the number.

"And how did *that* go?" I asked.

"Of course, it was a miracle she didn't hang up on me immediately, but she heard me out. She didn't have too much to say about it, though. In fact, she was silent for so long, I thought we'd been disconnected. But then she oh-so-calmly thanked me for the 'update,' as she called it. The *update*. And that was pretty much it. She said she had to go catch a plane and hung up."

I could tell Tracy was upset by Christine's indifference, but she didn't want to let me see it. For my own part, I hadn't expected much to come of it, so I shrugged in the darkness of the passenger seat as I adjusted my black gloves and cap.

After a couple of false starts, we found the road to The Vault, which we only confirmed by driving all the way up to its entrance. We pulled into the parking lot and killed our lights. We had to take things slowly, after all. In the darkness, Tracy peered over at a lone man, standing by his car as he pulled a fringed black leather jacket up over his well-muscled shoulders.

"Your kind of place, huh, Tracy?" I finally said.

She laughed quietly.

"It doesn't . . . it doesn't remind you . . ." I trailed off.

Tracy just stared into the doorway of the club. "Yes. Yes, it does. But it gives me control of it."

We sat silently in the dark car for a few more minutes, then pulled back onto the road. While Tracy focused on the winding drive, I looked out into the trees, studying each dirt driveway on the left to find our turnoff. I had been so afraid that other night that I couldn't remember if I had driven for twenty minutes or forty-five.

Finally, I saw it. I was sure it was the right one, if nothing else because of the way my skin crawled just seeing it. We drove past it a few hundred yards, searching for a place to tuck the car. We found a small road where the weeds had grown up, and Tracy eased in as far as she could. She backed it in slowly so we could pull out fast if we needed to. I made Tracy check twice to make sure we wouldn't get stuck in the mud and the grass wasn't high enough to impede our exit. I wanted to be prepared to leave in a hurry.

This time I was fully equipped at least. I had my cell phone strapped to my waist, as well as a backup prepaid phone. One on each side. Tracy shook her head, but I could tell she was scared too and therefore was probably secretly happy I had them. We each had a flashlight, and I had brought a small camera and a can of mace. I carried Jennifer's picture in my pocket to bolster my nerves.

We stood face-to-face, looking at each other, bracing our shoulders as we each took a long deep breath. And then, without a word, we started out. Almost as soon as we were out on the road, we heard a car engine gunning and jumped down into a ditch until it went past.

"Why do I feel like the criminal in this picture?" Tracy asked.

We continued slowly on until we reached the driveway, then crept along in the woods. At the top of the hill, we could see clearly down to the warehouse. It looked totally deserted. No van, no cars, no men. Nothing.

I breathed a small sigh of relief as we got closer. Maybe it had been abandoned. Maybe we had been foiled in our amateur sleuthing after all. It was a welcome thought, and I clung to it.

A single caged bulb on the side of the warehouse formed a large half-circle of light on the ground in front of the door. With a slight jerk of her body, Tracy signaled to me to follow her, and I stayed right behind her as we made our way around the building, dipping into the shadows to stay hidden.

The woods were deadly quiet, except for the vague rustle of leaves as the summer wind shuffled delicately through them. There was just a hint of cool in the air. Back home in my apartment, I might have even cracked open a window on a night like this.

After walking around the full perimeter of the building, assuring ourselves nothing was parked on the far side, we made our way over to the windows of the garage door and peeked in. But it was too dark. We couldn't see a thing. Tracy nodded in the direction of the door, and before I could stop her, she twisted the doorknob. Locked.

Trying another approach, Tracy returned to the garage door, leaned down, and yanked up on the handle. I whispered for her to stop. To my relief, it didn't budge, but she whispered back that she thought with enough force it might give way. She gestured for me to take the other handle at the end of the door. I shook my head vigorously.

"No way," I whispered back to her.

Tracy stood still, looking me in the eye there in the darkness. "This is for Jennifer," she said.

I looked all around at the empty space surrounding us. I took a deep breath and gave in. I positioned myself at the other end of the door and grasped its handle. Tracy held up her fist and counted off with her fingers, one, two, three, and we pulled with all our combined strength. I felt it give a little, and we leaned in again and pulled harder. It was stuck, but we were able to hoist it up about a foot and a half off the ground. With that, Tracy lay down on her stomach and started to slide under.

"What are you doing?" I said, almost out loud.

"How else are we supposed to find out what's going on?"

My breath got faster, and my pulse was racing.

"I'll wait out here for you," I said, all the while wondering if that really felt any safer.

"Suit yourself."

I watched her slide under, out of sight, and started pacing around, counting off the steps to the woods, calculating how fast she could get back out, how long it would take us to be hidden in the dense trees once again. Then I heard a violent clank and turned back to the warehouse. The garage door had slammed shut. If anyone was in there, they would certainly be aware of our presence now.

I walked fearfully back to the windows and, in a state of half-shock, looked in. The light flicked on. A face stared back at me, inches from mine through the glass. I screamed and jumped back before realizing it was Tracy. She smiled and pointed to the door. She met me there and let me in.

"See, nothing to it. No one's here."

The warehouse seemed much larger from the inside, almost cavernous. And yet even so, the walls felt as if they were closing in on me. I looked back at the door nervously, to make sure we'd left it ajar.

The building was empty except for rows of stainless-steel stalls that lined the walls, each about four feet across, perhaps for some sort of livestock, I thought. At the end of each stall was a metal stand bolted to the floor, with a clipboard filled with blank pages, a pen dangling from a small chain on each one.

In each stall, rubber hoses with spray nozzles hung loosely from the ceiling, and small hooks were attached in four places to the back wall. A row of dim bulbs hanging from cords above barely lit up the space, casting bumping shadows as they swayed slightly overhead.

Tracy was standing in one of the stalls, bent over the drain in the middle of the floor. She got down on her knees, staring at something very small. I crouched down next to her. She reached out her gloved hand, took the object between her fingers, and lifted it up into the faint light. I shrank from it in disgust: a human fingernail, in its entirety, with a tattered bit of dried-up flesh clinging to it. Tracy looked at it solemnly, and then carefully put it back down on the floor where she found it. We were both horrified, sitting back on our heels, trying to figure out what this bit of human detritus could possibly mean.

My back was to the door, and that's why Tracy saw the lights first. I saw the panic in her eyes before I realized what was happening. Too late, I heard the whirring of the car motor outside, then a door slam while the engine was left running. We were no longer alone.

There was no time to turn off the lights. The front door lay in the same direction as the noise, so Tracy and I ran over to the garage door, each grabbing a handle to hoist it back up from where it had fallen. When it dropped, though, it had latched. This time it wouldn't budge.

I felt a sharp chill surge through my body. There was no other way out except through that main door. We heard steps approaching and, in a panic, ran over to the farthest stall. We flattened ourselves against the wall, hiding our feet behind a large plastic bucket that mercifully stood there in the corner.

I was cursing myself for the lights. That was my fault. Tracy had turned them on to make it seem safe enough for me. If only we had used the flashlights we'd brought, we would have had a chance.

Just as we ducked into the stall, we heard the footsteps of two or three approaching men. A voice boomed into the dimly lit room. "Relax, relax, we come in peace." A burst of hoarse laughter from the other two.

Tracy and I shifted farther into the corner, all the while knowing that hiding there was no solution. It was only a matter of time before they had us. I carefully pulled my cell phone off of my belt and held it down at my side. I could see my slightest move reflected in shadow, so if I so much as moved my hand, their attention would be drawn to us. Tracy noticed it too, and because she couldn't motion to stop me and couldn't speak, she looked at me with a pleading expression. I hadn't seen one like it since the cellar.

I was caught in a terrible bind. I couldn't get the phone up to my ear without identifying our location, yet if I didn't make a call, if I didn't somehow reach out beyond the walls of this warehouse, anything could happen to us. I looked down as far as I could without moving, selected Jim's name from my contacts, and started to text him with one hand. But what could I tell him? I'm in a warehouse, in Oregon, and I'm not exactly sure where? Useless. I had recognized the voice though, and so I typed slowly, hampered by my forced immobility. Two words: *Noah Philben*. He was the only trail.

Almost as soon as I'd typed the last letter and hit send, the men, who must have signaled one another, started running directly over to our corner. Tracy let out a small scream. I couldn't have made a sound at that moment, I was so paralyzed by fear.

Before I could process what was happening, one of the men grabbed me, gripping both of my arms tightly behind me with one hand, while neatly removing my belt with the other. All my devices clattered to the floor. The other man held Tracy just as firmly, and Noah Philben calmly approached me, leaning over to gather up the cell phones as he did.

"Welcome to the sacristy, Sarah—oh, I'm sorry, what did you *say* your name was before? I really can't remember. But I remember *Sarah*."

He reached out for my chin, rubbing one finger slowly underneath it. My body pulled away from him almost involuntarily. Any human touch was repellent to me, but his in particular, slithery, suggestive, was more than I could bear. I could feel the cold sweat breaking out over my body. When I pulled back, the man holding me tightened his grip and pushed me even closer to Noah Philben.

"Surprised I know your name, Sarah?" He laughed again and stopped to pull out a cigarette. "Mind if I smoke? I didn't think so." He lit it and took a long slow draw, then blew the smoke, predictably, right into my face. I coughed but tried not to show any emotion.

"I knew who you were right from the start, my dear. That first day you came walking into my office. Right to my door! I couldn't believe my good fortune. So, you know, I had you followed. We have tracked you every step of the way. Who do you think that was on your little Girl Scout trip to the lake?"

I looked at Tracy. She was scared. I didn't know whether there was anything to say that could help us here. If I had thought begging for my life would work, I would have begged. But I could see in his eyes that wouldn't get me anything but laughter. It would delight him to see me grovel, but ultimately nothing would change his plans.

"Wondering what we do over here in this nice warehouse? Well, of course, this is where we have our services. Sermons several days a week, right, boys?"

The two men laughed gruffly, and the one holding me slackened his grip a bit. I looked at the door they'd come through. It was open. I could see the white van parked outside in sharp relief against the dark sky. I didn't see anyone out there with it, but could hear the engine humming. A dim hope sparked up inside me.

I glanced over at Tracy to see if she saw this chance too, but her eyes were glazed over from fear and she wouldn't, or couldn't, make eye contact with me. Once again I would have to leave her to make an escape. I hesitated for an instant—a fatal instant, as it turned out, because before I could act, Noah jerked his head toward the door and the men tightened their grips and dragged us toward it.

I fought back, kicking and screaming as loudly as I could. My violent outbreak finally seemed to shock Tracy out of her stupor, and she started yelling as well. I knew, from every warning of my childhood and every experience thereafter, including that most devastating one, that I couldn't let them get us in that vehicle. At that point all would be lost. *Never get in the car.* I'd learned it the hard way.

I summoned every last ounce of strength I had, but my captor squeezed my arms so tight, I thought he might twist the flesh off the bone. It burned. I knew that burn. The pain spurred me on to greater violence. I thrashed, I went limp and then taut again, fighting with all my might. But Noah didn't keep these guys around for their witty conversation. They were strong as hell. And they had us.

CHAPTER 29

Before we could fully register what was happening, the back doors of the van were thrown open, and I saw seven or eight girls, all younger than we were, dressed in identical, thin white robes, with sad eyes and drawn faces, looking back at us without emotion or surprise. We were unceremoniously tossed into the back, almost landing on several of them. They didn't flinch. In fact, they barely acknowledged our presence. New arrivals, apparently, were par for the course.

I looked up in time to see the van doors clanging shut. I heard the front doors open and slam and the engine rev. A solid metal divider formed a barrier between us and the drivers: we couldn't see them, they couldn't see us. A narrow rectangular window ran along each side of the cargo hold. I couldn't quite tell in the dark, but I suspected they were tinted an impenetrable shade of black. The church van.

I banged desperately on the doors until Tracy pulled me away and shoved me into an empty pull-down seat at the front of the van. I noticed there were seat belts, but none of the girls were wearing any. Tracy and I sat next to each other, and I pulled the seat belt around me and clicked it in place with trembling fingers. Even in our desperate situation, Tracy raised her eyebrows at me, but then pulled on hers as well. Might as well not die in a car accident, though perhaps these other girls felt it would be a fate better than anything else they had going.

It was dark in back, but one small light had been left on over-head, so I could see the faces of the girls near us quite clearly. They seemed even younger up close. Some were pretty, or had been be-fore the life had been sucked out of them. Some were not. They all looked half-starved, just as we had all those years ago.

I recognized their self-protective expressions, all of them turn-ing their faces inward somehow, to whatever small safe haven was left inside their minds. The one place far in the back, where no one could touch, where even the body's pain could not reach. I knew that place. I had lived there for about thirteen years now.

The girl across from us must have once had a chic pixie haircut, but now it was as disheveled as she was. She glanced over at us with eyes that were slightly more human, less animal, than the others.

I whispered across to her in the dark, "Who are these guys? Where are they taking us?" I was almost surprised to hear my voice shaking. The shock had—temporarily, at least—conquered my ter-ror. For the moment I was all focus.

A half-smile flickered across her face, then disappeared. I didn't think she was going to answer. When she finally did, I noticed she was missing a couple of teeth.

"Do you really want to know?" she finally said.

"Yes," said Tracy, leaning forward in the dark. "Yes, we really want to know. We have to figure out how to get out of here." I could hear the fear in Tracy's shaking voice, despite her attempt to hide it.

The girl sniffed, "Yeah, good luck with that," hastily adding, "If you do figure that out, let me know. I'm in. In for anything. But I doubt it. You don't know what you're up against."

"Then tell us," I said.

"We've seen some pretty bad stuff ourselves. You'd be surprised," Tracy added.

The girl looked at us straight on. "No. No, I wouldn't."

Her glance drifted away, her eyes lulled into a dead stare at the darkened windows.

"Well, what do you *think* it is?" she finally said in a quiet voice, without shifting her gaze.

I didn't want to think.

Then she faced me directly, "And whatever you *are* thinking? Think worse."

I told myself she didn't know how dark my imagination could go, and I tried to focus on something more productive. Like making an escape.

"Do you think we'll be driving all night?"

"Depends."

"On?" Tracy muttered, her annoyance barely hidden. She didn't like guessing games.

"On the order."

"Order?" I wanted her to get to the point now, too. I wanted to know what was coming.

"You know . . ." She made a typing motion with her fingers. "Whatever the client orders up on the Internet. My advice? Do exactly what they say, and it hurts a lot less overall."

I looked out the back windows to see the highway slipping away behind us, trying not to visualize what she was suggesting.

Tracy leaned over and lifted the limp wrist of the girl next to her, who didn't even seem to notice. "No restraints, anyway."

"Not in the van," the girl replied. "They have to be ready with a story in case we're stopped by the cops. We know the drill. We're part of a religious order." She lifted the arms of her white robe to demonstrate. Then she nodded toward the back doors of the van. "It looks like an ordinary church van, but trust me, they've fixed the door handle on our side. It doesn't connect to anything."

So that was it. Noah Philben's religious organization was cover. Had Sylvia been one of these girls? So eager to get out, she agreed to marry Jack Derber?

I shook my head, pushing away these thoughts. Pointless. None of it mattered if we couldn't get out of this situation alive. At that moment my mind was utterly clear. Even through my fear I felt energized. Just as I had during my escape.

It was as though the only time I could feel calm was when the worst had actually, finally happened. Now I could focus. This is what I had prepared for. And now I just had to think. Only thinking could save us.

"What happens when you arrive at a new location? Tell me exactly," I said.

The girl smiled wryly and shook her head, covering her mouth with her hand this time.

"That really depends. Sometimes we have special instructions. Sometimes, you know, we have to get all . . . dressed up somewhere first." She nodded toward a corner of the van, where a large wooden chest stood, secured with two heavy metal padlocks.

"If we don't have an appointment, they take us to one of their buildings to get locked up for the night. They seem to have a lot of . . . facilities, I'll say that."

"Are you ever left alone?" Tracy asked, sounding desperate.

"Only when they're convinced you're finally brainwashed into total submission. When they know you are so scared you wouldn't dare make a move. When you believe the stories they tell you."

"What stories?" I was dreading the answer even as I asked.

"About the white slavery network. That there's a huge organization that will hunt you down and kill you if you try to escape. And kill your family. If you still have one."

The van's engine revved, and we made a hard right turn.

"How did you end up here?" Tracy asked after a few minutes of silence, while we took in the girl's words, trying to process the impossible.

"I was pretty stupid. Got myself into this mess. I ran away with my boyfriend when I was fourteen, and we hitched our way to Portland. We both wanted to get out of some sticky situations at home."

She wiped her nose with the back of her hand.

"We should've known better," she continued, "but when you're young, you think you're going to beat the odds. You know, whatever, we were just kids back then."

I held my tongue, thinking how very much she was still just a kid.

Tracy shifted forward, "Let me guess. Drugs. What was it? Heroin? Ecstasy? Special K?"

The girl looked at her blankly at first but finally nodded. "Heroin. That was Sammy's thing. So . . . you know the story—he had to pay for the drugs, so he had to sell the drugs. He didn't exactly have an MBA, so you know, funds got low. Especially because he ended up using half of his own shit."

She was shaking her head, clearly more disgusted at Sammy's business acumen than at the fact that he was a heroin dealer and user. "So he got into it with these very gentleman chauffeuring us at the moment. He had to pay off his debts somehow." She shrugged.

"With . . . with you?" I asked, revolted.

"Well . . . Oh, I should have known something was up. He begged me to go with him for a pickup. He got down on his knees and cried, saying he couldn't do it without me. He was convincing. I guess anyone can turn out to be a hell of an actor when their life is at stake."

She paused and stared at the ceiling. I couldn't read her expression.

"Look, I know he loved me. And I know it nearly killed him to do it, but you know, it was him or me. Only one of us was going to live at that point. And he picked himself." She pursed her lips. "Fair enough.

"He took me out to this warehouse in the middle of fucking nowhere, see. I have played this scene over in my head like a zillion times. *Obviously* this was a bad idea. *Obviously* it could not end well. Who knows? Maybe it was a form of suicide walking into that building that day. At any rate, we did it. We walked in, two kids in the middle of one big shitstorm of a life. And there were these three guys"—she jerked her thumb in the direction of our drivers—"sitting at a tiny little fold-out table in the center of the room. It was comical, really. They were really . . . big you see." She held up her hands in the air, far apart. "And the table," she laughed, "it was so small there in front of them." She held her hands close together, showing us the proportions.

She couldn't go on, she was cracking herself up so much. We waited silently, frankly not seeing the humor in it at all.

Finally, she continued. "I didn't suspect it right away, but I was pretty creeped out when I saw the looks on their faces. Grinning from ear to ear. Looking back, I guess they thought they knew an earner when they saw one. At the time I was afraid they were going to rape me. Ha." She looked off in the distance and swallowed hard. But there were no tears.

"That was pretty naïve. I thought a little gang rape was about the worst thing on earth." She laughed, but it was humorless this time. She wiped a strand of brown hair out of her eyes, pushing it back behind her ear.

All three of us shifted uneasily and stared down at our knees. As though we couldn't even look at each other and see our shared shame in one another's eyes. I looked up at the row of girls next to us. If they were listening, they hid it well. Each seemed wrapped up in her own thoughts, or the total lack thereof. Finally, the girl started talking again.

"Anyway, they grabbed me and dragged me away. Sammy was crying and yelling out how much he loved me. But I could see that shifty look on his face and knew he was in on it. Sure he cried, but he was crying for himself. Poor Sammy, losing his girlfriend like this. When they told him to beat it, he turned and ran as fast as he could out the door. He was smart, I suppose. Set me up, then got the hell out. I know it just killed him, though. Well, maybe it was even enough for him to sober up. I hope so anyway." She sighed.

I was amazed at this girl's capacity for what sounded like forgiveness.

"Aren't you—don't you hate him?"

"Oh, what for?" She sighed again, more deeply this time, and looked up at the dim light above us. "He was really just following his fate. No point in using up my hatred on him. It is what it is. I got dealt this hand—no use suffering regret as well as pain. Right now I just have to figure out each morning if and how I am going to survive the day. I don't mean, like, psychologically. I mean literally. Will. I. Live. Through. The. Day. Some girls don't come back."

"Maybe they escape," I said hopefully.

"No way. Like I said. Look at these girls." She gestured broadly at the girls in the van without turning to face them. "They look like they're plotting an escape? They all believe in the network, don't you girls?" She kept her eyes locked on us as she said it. "And you know, maybe they're right. We're marked, after all."

"Marked how?" Tracy sat up straight at that.

"They *brand* us." She said it leaning forward, almost spitting out the words. And then she sat back smugly to watch our reactions.

Neither of us batted an eyelash. "Explain. Details," Tracy ordered in a flat voice.

The girl pointed to her hip. "A brand. Right there. They say that everyone out there in the 'network'—in the underworld, I guess you'd call it—knows their mark. Like cattle herders. And if we get caught by anyone out there, we'll be returned to our rightful owners."

"What does it look like?" I asked, terrified because I had an idea I knew the answer.

"Hard to say. I don't like to look at it too much. They rarely heal just right, so on some girls it just looks like a little lump of twisted flesh. I guess those in the network have special skills at reading scar tissue. I suppose you could say it looks maybe like a bull's head, except the horns kinda go straight out and then up." She held her hands above her head, with index fingers pointed out, to demonstrate.

"Could it be . . . is it possible that it's a headless man with his arms out? You know, with a body sort of like that Leonardo da Vinci drawing?"

She shrugged, whether at the concept of the headless man or the reference to Da Vinci I couldn't tell. "I don't know. Maybe."

I half stood up, nearly hitting my head on the roof of the van, and shifted sideways a bit, unbuttoned my pants, and pulled my jeans down just past my hip. I pointed to my mark, my own little lump of twisted flesh.

"Does it look like this?" I almost shouted, choking out the words.

The girl put her fingers to her lips and whispered to me angrily, "Shut up! You don't want them to have to stop the van to see what's going on."

She leaned closer, and I pushed my hip forward to move it more directly under the light. She studied it carefully, then shrugged again.

"Yeah, that could be it. Like I said, hard to say." She gulped and suddenly looked afraid. "Wait a minute. Does this mean you were in the network when you were young, and you escaped, and you've . . . you've been brought back? So they aren't just bullshitting? And that's why you're, like, so old?"

I felt Tracy shudder beside me. Was she right? We were both thinking it. Had we been led back into the "network" after all this time, back to our *rightful owners*? Were the ten years in between the fantasy, and now we were back to reality?

"So," she continued, leaning back and eyeing us, "so I don't need to tell you what you're in for? You know?"

Tracy leaned forward toward her. Their faces were almost touching there in the near dark, under the soft glow of the single light overhead.

"Listen, what we lived through was something much worse. I was held captive in a goddamn cellar by a goddamn psychopath for five years, chained to a wall, brought upstairs only for torture." She leaned back, expecting the shock to register on the girl's face. Instead she shrugged.

"Sounds a hell of a lot easier than this. Sounds to me like you just had one john. One john is easier than hundreds of johns. Simple math. With one john, I don't care how psycho he is, you can figure him out a little bit. Understand how he works. Plan ahead. Manipulate. Not a lot. But enough to make it hurt a little less. When you've got new johns all the time, who the hell knows."

Tracy said, "You have no idea what you're talking about. At least you're out in the world."

"*Out in the world?*" the girl scoffed. "Is that what you think this is? Unless basements and padded rooms and purpose-built cells and—"

She suddenly shut up, bit her lower lip, and looked away.

When she turned back to us, her eyes were veiled and dark. Her tough-girl stance disappeared for a split second, and I saw only fear and hurt on her face.

I didn't like the images that were suddenly flooding into my head. I didn't want to know what could have caused the pain I saw in her expression.

"Why don't we focus on what we're going to do here? It doesn't matter who has suffered more so far. Let's focus on how to keep us all from suffering *going forward*." I turned toward the dronelike faces beside me in the van. "Girls, there are more of us than them."

The girl with the pixie cut turned back to me, this time anger glinting in her eyes. She whispered fiercely, her lips twitching.

"Shut *up*! If you try to incite a revolution, they will tell on you in six seconds flat. They are *dying* to inform. Then they get an entire day off. An *entire day* without anyone touching them at all. So shut the fuck up."

I looked at the girl in disbelief, and then at Tracy, hoping she would take this point to heart. I had never done anything that bad. I wanted her to understand: this is what suffering can do to you. But Tracy's face was as impassive as a statue's.

The girl abruptly stopped talking.

In the silence, as the van rumbled through the night, I thought about what this girl had told us, and my calm started to evaporate. My heart was pounding so hard, I thought it would beat right out of my body.

After a few more hours, when the dawn was just breaking, the van made a sharp turn and bumped hard along what must have been a dirt road. The van swayed side to side, creaking noisily until it slowly pulled to a halt. Tracy and I jerked to attention, and Tracy poked the girl's leg to wake her up. She slowly shook her head to pull herself out of her haze. She looked bewildered at first, but then, recognizing us, she nodded.

Tracy bent toward her, whispering, "By the way, what's your name?"

"Huh?" the girl muttered, seeming confused. I wondered if she'd forgotten it in all this.

"What's your name?" Tracy asked again.

"Oh, yeah, that." She smiled at us, gaps and all. "No one's asked me that for a while. My name is Jenny."

Jenny. The name gave me a jolt of courage. I looked at Tracy and saw my own determination reflected back in her face. We braced ourselves for the moment the door would open.

CHAPTER 30

We sat for a long time as the van idled, our seats vibrating slightly beneath us. The engine went dead. The front doors opened and slammed shut. Then it was quiet. Too quiet. Five minutes went by. Ten.

Our arms taut, we gripped the cold vinyl beneath us, waiting. Someone lifted the exterior handle of the cargo doors once, but nothing happened. Then the driver's-side door creaked open one maddening inch at a time. It was as if they were taunting us. We sat perfectly still, listening, and then it came. The sudden, dull click of the lock. They were coming for us.

Jenny whispered, "I don't know who that is. I know all their tics and rhythms. Must be a new guy."

"Good, right?" Tracy said optimistically, though her voice betrayed her fear. "He won't know the routine. We can take him by surprise."

Jenny stood up halfway and made her way over to the doors.

We followed, pushing our way past the knees and feet of the girls next to us, who were trying to sleep while they could.

Then the doors flew open. Instead of leaping forward, ready to push past whatever stood in my way, I froze, rooted to the spot, unable to believe my eyes. A split second later Tracy's shaking voice came from behind me, "Christine?!?!"

I could not understand in that moment how it was possible, but there she stood. Christine, in all her Park Avenue glory, dressed in uniform New York City black, perfectly coiffed and shod for a day hike during peak leaf season. She held open the van doors, looking on in horror at the sight of the human cargo filling that van. Then she pulled herself into action.

"Everybody out! Let's go," she whispered loudly but assuredly, like a suburban mom unloading the junior varsity lacrosse team. All of us clambered out of the van, the girls behind us tearing themselves out of their sleep. Tracy grabbed the stragglers by the arms, throwing them into the breaking daylight. Some were dumbfounded and couldn't process what was happening. *I* couldn't process what was happening. What was Christine doing here?

But there was no time for questions.

Once we were out, Tracy jumped down and looked the girls over as they stood there, dazed. "Girls, don't be idiots. RUN!!!"

I glanced around quickly. The van was parked behind a barn, half-collapsed into an overgrown rye field, across from an equally decrepit farmhouse, dark except for a single lit window. I wasted no more time following Christine's lead but sprinted down the hill, away from the house into the woods. Running like hell.

It must have been a beautiful and ethereal sight in some ways. All those girls, barefoot in flowing white robes, running downhill at top speed between the trees of a wild rural paradise. Like nymphs. Like seraphim.

Time was unrolling in slow motion as if in some fluid, hypervivid dream. The girls' faces reflected their shock, their terror, their total disorientation. I could see flashes of white robes flitting in and out between the branches. Tracy, Christine, and I could easily spot one another as the group fanned out, the only black spots in the pure flow of white streaming down the hill.

All of a sudden I felt elated. I laughed out loud. Loud into the dawning sunlight glinting through the green of the trees. I looked over at Tracy and Christine. They heard me, and somehow my joy, my joy at being free, at having such a close call, of having Christine show up as a savior in the early morning, sent my spirits soaring, and I couldn't stop laughing. They joined me, and soon we were running and stumbling and tripping over ourselves, laughing hysterically, maniacally, desperately, as we moved through those woods.

Eventually we came to a clearing. Christine slowed down to check her phone, then stopped, texting like mad. Several of the girls had stopped running from sheer exhaustion, many of them holding their sides to ease the cramps. We gathered in the clearing and tried to catch our breath, listening to hear whether anyone was chasing us. The woods were completely silent. No dogs, no men, no gunshots. It was eerily quiet.

Christine was smiling through tears. Just as I was about to ask her what we should do, I heard the sound of helicopters. There must have been four or five of them hovering overhead, the collective sound of their spinning blades combining into a single roar in my ears. Christine ran over to us, her arms wide, gesturing for us to get down. The girls in white stared up in awe as one helicopter lowered itself down into the clearing.

As the first one landed, a tall man in a black bulletproof vest and black flight suit jumped to the ground and started walking toward us as he spoke into the microphone pinned to his shoulder.

"Jim!" I said. I almost started to run toward him but slowed up as I realized Tracy and Christine were falling in line beside me.

Jim looked at us and shook his head. Then he smiled.

"Sarah, remember—all I asked you to do was testify at the hearing? And now look what you've gotten yourself into." He almost reached out to hug me but pulled back at the last minute, remembering himself. Tracy fell into his arms instead, and then Christine. They were delirious, thanking him over and over again for coming.

Jim looked out at me from their arms. I could only smile weakly at him. He smiled back, holding my gaze with his eyes, which were filled with pity and a tenderness that caught me by surprise. He is pretty human, I thought to myself as I looked away, feeling suddenly overwhelmed. Especially for an FBI agent.

Slowly they got us all boarded onto the helicopters, and an hour or so later we touched down in the parking lot of a local police station, which I would soon discover was in a small town just outside Portland. The squat brick building had been built in the fifties, and it didn't look like anyone had done any maintenance on it since. Inside, the linoleum tiles on the floor had curled up at the corners, and the paint on the walls was chipped and faded, stained with the dull black sheen that inevitably develops from decade after decade of brushes with human flesh.

It seemed every law enforcement officer from the county had gathered in the building, and every journalist and camera crew in the state was camped outside. Three ambulances, sirens turning, awaited our arrival, and paramedics rushed toward us as we entered the building.

Moments later I sat on some officer's desk, wrapped in a blanket, while he stood off to the side a few feet away, mostly gaping. Someone handed me a cup of coffee, and I took a sip. Christine and Tracy were sitting in wheeled office chairs on either side of me, Christine twisting hers slightly back and forth in a nervous rhythm.

The scene brought me back to a similar one ten years before.

Except now all around me were girls in floor-length robes, some being interviewed by police officers, some drinking their coffee and staring straight ahead, all trying to make sense of this new development. I knew how confused they must feel. To me, though, it was a sort of homecoming.

"Someday, someone is going to need to explain to me what just happened. But right now I'm perfectly content to be sitting on this desk in this funny little precinct, drinking this tar-paper coffee," I said, almost feeling genuinely happy at that moment. Instead of retraumatized, I felt invigorated. This situation felt more like the normal condition of the world. This I could cope with. This was easier than waiting for what might happen.

"Well, it's very simple, really," said Christine. "When Tracy called yesterday morning to tell me about the list—"

"The list?" I said, my mind wiped clean from shock.

"Yes, you know, Jim's list of girls who went missing during Jack Derber's academic conferences." I nodded, and she continued. "When she told me that, something in me snapped, and I knew, somehow, I had to help keep him from getting out. After all, as you pointed out, I do have daughters.

"But it was more than that. Ever since I saw you, I've been thinking about your search. All these years I've tried to forget our past. I was afraid if I went anywhere near that edge, I'd fall off the cliff. But if those other girls are out there . . . I had to."

She took a deep breath.

"So I told my husband that my cousin was sick, and I had to fly that day. He took the girls up to his parents' in Connecticut, because, you know, he has a 'crazy' week next week." We all smiled at that. "Anyway, I booked the next flight and called Jim from the airport. He told me where you were staying."

Tracy nodded. "That was the flight you needed to catch."

"How did Jim . . . ?" I started, but she shrugged before I could finish the question. He had clearly been watching out for us more than he was letting on.

"I pulled into the hotel parking lot late last night," Christine continued, "and then sat in my rental car for what felt like an hour, debating whether I could really do this.

"When I finally persuaded myself to open the car door, I saw you two pass behind me, gunning it out of the lot. I followed you, trying to catch up with you enough to get your attention. You were both pretty oblivious, and now I understand why, given where you were going.

"I lost you for a bit and backtracked until I found your car parked beside the road. Tracy had told me about the warehouse, so at that point, I put two and two together. I pulled into the driveway closest to your car—no way was I getting out to walk it—and as I reached the top of the hill, I saw taillights up ahead.

"I was scared, so I turned off my lights and the engine, wondering what to do next. A minute later I watched as those men threw you into the back of their van. I panicked and immediately called Jim. He told me to go back to the hotel, that he'd handle it. But how could he find one van on these back roads in the middle of nowhere? And I had this horrible notion that they were taking you somewhere to kill you.

"Jim grumbled but stayed on the line with me as I followed from a distance. He said he could track me by my cell phone, but it would take a little time to set it up through the phone company. But there was no time.

"Then I remembered the tracking app on my iPhone—the one I use with my sitter."

She noticed my puzzled expression.

"With this particular app," she explained, "you can share your GPS location with others in real time. Jim used it to track me as I followed the van."

I nodded my head appreciatively. Naturally, Christine had the latest, most advanced technology.

"So why were you the one who got us out of that van, then?" asked Tracy.

"Once we got to the farm, the men went into the house. They'd hidden the van behind the barn, so I figured I could get to it without being seen. Jim was still minutes away, and the last thing I wanted was for those guys to come back and shoot you just before he got there. So I went for it.

"When the cargo doors didn't open, I got into the cab. At first I couldn't figure out how to work the locks. It's not exactly a Lexus," she said.

Tracy rolled her eyes, but Christine just smiled back at her.

"But I found the lever," she went on, "and heard the doors click."

"Jesus, Christine," I said in awe, "I can't believe you did that. I don't know what to say."

She beamed. I would never have expected it, remembering her from our cellar days. Maybe it was true—what she'd told Jim—that she *had* fully recovered. What if, in fact, our horrific past had only made her stronger? I envied her.

Jim's eyes met mine across the room, and I waved him over. He approached Christine first.

"You understand how dangerous that was, don't you? Do you know what could have happened to you?" He sounded genuinely upset.

She answered him calmly, with her crisp Upper East Side enunciation, "Yes, in fact, I *do* know exactly how bad it could have been, Jim. That's why I know better than to wait around for the worst to happen."

Jim nodded slowly, taking her point, then turned to me. He handed me my phone, which they must have recovered from the warehouse.

"You seem to have left this behind." He smiled gently. "How are you holding up, Sarah?"

"I'll live. Again." I smiled back. "Did you get him?"

For a fleeting moment Jim seemed embarrassed, then rallied, putting on his best professional demeanor. "No, we didn't, but we're staking out his compound in Keeler as we speak."

He moved closer, looking at me earnestly. "Sarah, I'm sorry I didn't seem to be taking what you'd found seriously enough. But the truth is I *have* been doing my homework. After we spoke, I did some digging. We checked out The Vault. Their ownership records are pretty complex—lots of shell corporations owning other shell corporations. But our accounting forensics guys figured out that the club owners were partnered with one of Noah Philben's entities. We think they were using it as a distribution hub and running most of their financial operations out of there."

"What about the brand, the headless man? These girls are all branded. And Noah Philben knew who I was. My real name. There *has* to be a connection with Jack Derber. If we can prove that Jack Derber is in on this trafficking ring, he'll stay in jail forever, right?"

Jim hesitated. "To tell you the truth, Sarah, I have a theory that Jack might actually be in control of the whole operation. And that he's using Sylvia as a messenger. I don't have solid proof yet, but I'm getting closer."

I stared at him. Could Jack Derber still be controlling so many lives, even under virtual lockdown? The idea made me sick. But before I could respond, one of Jim's colleagues pulled him away, directing him to a computer screen a few desks over.

I turned, only to see Jenny slowly making her way around the desks and chairs in the room, over to where we stood.

"I just wanted to—to thank you. I'm outta here now, so . . . you know, thanks."

"You're leaving? Don't they need to take your statement? To make sure they have all the evidence they can get?"

Jenny looked around the room at the other girls, some sitting at desks, others standing in corners, all of them looking dazed.

"They've got plenty of stories to go on. I just need to get out of here. This place makes me feel like I'm the one who did something wrong. Who knows, at any minute, they could turn the tables and slap a solicitation charge on us. That's how it goes. Either way, I know I'll never be held prisoner again."

"Where are you going to go?"

"I don't know. Women's shelter for the night? Something. It doesn't matter. I'm free now, and I plan to stay that way." And with that she slipped out the door, without looking back at us.

By now Jim had been called over by another officer, and the two of them were talking to one of the robed girls from the van. Her long matted hair hid her face, but I could tell from her quivering shoulders that she was crying pretty hard while she told her story.

Both men went pale at her words. When she finished, she sat down and put her head on the desk, oblivious to the papers, binders, and three-hole punch lying there. Jim didn't waste a second—he turned to the other officer, rattling off orders, even as he pulled out his cell phone and dialed. The younger officer took notes, writing fast, glancing back up at Jim every few seconds, nodding.

Jim made his way over to us in two strides, barking directions into his phone, clicking it off just as he reached us.

"Listen, we're hearing some pretty disturbing tales from these women. I haven't seen anything like this in my twenty-three years with the Bureau. This wasn't an ordinary prostitution ring." He paused, perhaps thinking we weren't prepared to hear the worst of it. "They sold girls for torture. As slaves. I'm going to Noah's compound now. We're going in."

I felt sick. This sounded like Jack's forte.

Jim turned his back to us to take a call, putting two fingers over his other ear to shut out the noise. Then he stepped back over to us, just as officers rushed past and sirens blared outside.

"I'm arranging for you to go to a different hotel—we'll send someone to pick up your things. And I've assigned you a security detail for protection. We're getting you a new rental car—we've impounded the other one as evidence—and Officer Grunnell here will give you a police escort. Stay in your rooms until I give the word."

We nodded obediently, disoriented by the frenetic activity around us, and watched Jim go out the door.

But despite everything, a tiny part of me didn't feel finished here. I turned to Tracy and Christine.

"So what do you say? Do we go wait it out in the hotel like dutiful little victims?"

Tracy sniffed. "I don't think so. I think we've wasted enough years in that role." She turned to me. "Where do we go from here?"

I thought a minute, happy she felt the same way. "It's time for us to head back to Keeler, too. I think you need to meet Noah's ex."

CHAPTER 31

Fortunately, Officer Grunnell was swamped and didn't put up much of a fight when we told him we could make our way to the hotel on our own. He wrote out the address on the back of his card and said he'd see us there in an hour or so. We nodded solemnly and waved to him as we climbed into our new rental car. I hoped he wouldn't get in too much trouble when Jim found out he'd let us walk out, just like that.

It was starting to show that we hadn't slept all night and were running solely on adrenaline. We all looked more than a bit ragged around the edges. Still, I was determined to speak to Helen Watson, Noah's ex, before she heard the news about him from someone else. I hoped the shock of it might cause her to reveal something more to us, something she might not be willing to tell anyone else.

Maybe it was the edge of exhaustion pushing her on, but Tracy drove faster than usual, certainly faster than I thought strictly necessary. Around every turn I pressed my foot into the floorboard, hitting the imaginary brake on the passenger side of the car. She grinned at me and told me to relax even as she sped up more.

I tried to take my mind off the car accident statistics I wanted to recite by updating Christine about everything we'd learned so far. I could see her turning the facts over in her mind, and they were beginning to have the same impact on her they'd had on us. She was with us now. She called her husband to say her cousin was sicker than she'd thought, and she'd need to stay on a few more days to help out.

As she hung up, my phone buzzed in my pocket. I didn't recognize the number, but it was local. Adele. And she sounded more agitated than I'd heard her before. Shaken almost.

"Have you seen the news?" she asked, her voice quavering.

"No," I replied, "but I can guess."

"Guess? Were you involved? Was this part of your search for Sylvia?"

"You might say that. What was on the news?"

"That this Noah Philben—the pastor at Sylvia's church—is wanted by the FBI. They won't say why exactly, but there's a standoff at his compound right now. It's live on Channel Ten. Are you *there*?"

"Um, no. We're . . . going back to our hotel to wait it out."

"Should I meet you? Which hotel?"

"We won't be there for a while. It's the Hermitage, on—"

"Yes, I know it. Let's say at nine tonight? The bar in the lobby."

Just as I hung up, we pulled into the parking lot of the church and looked at one another with dismay. It was nearly full. We had lost all track of time and only now realized it was Sunday morning. Not the ideal time to make our visit. Nevertheless, we knew it had to be now. We pulled into the last empty space, and as we stepped out of the car, we eyed one another's filthy black attire from the night before.

"Will they even let us in there?" asked Tracy, looking down at the mud caked on her black Converse sneakers.

"Sure," I replied, even as I remembered Helen Watson's less-than-welcoming attitude before. "I don't think they can turn you away from a church service. I think it's the rules. We'll sit in the back."

We heaved open the huge wooden doors of the church. Strains of stately organ music filtered back toward us as we slowly made our way through the vestibule into the main chapel, where we found row after row of decent, normal-looking families listening attentively to the service.

When the last hymn ended, the congregation sat back down, and the minister gave the final benediction. As people started filing out, smiling and nodding as they greeted their friends and neighbors—and even us—I was struck by the general sense of well-being emanating from the crowd, a sense of genuine community.

I looked up at the tall windows of the church, admiring the long streaks of light streaming beatifically through them, and remembered my first visit. I braced myself, thinking Helen Watson's welcome would not be quite as warm.

At last the church was empty except for the minister putting away the prayer book at the altar. We approached him with some apprehension, realizing we weren't exactly wearing our Sunday best. He paused and turned his eyes slowly to us, examining us carefully.

"Can I help you?" he asked, without much enthusiasm, I noted.

"We're looking for Helen Watson. Is she around?"

"Oh, yes," he said, clearly relieved to be able to get rid of us so easily. "She's hosting the coffee and doughnuts over in the reception room. Just through those doors."

We followed his directions and found ourselves at the entrance to a crowded room where Helen Watson stood greeting each family as they entered. When the last parishioner passed through the door, we started walking toward her. But the instant Helen Watson spotted me, her brows knit, and she quickly but gently shut the door to the reception room behind her and motioned for us to follow her down the hall.

She led us to a small side chapel that seemed designed for quiet prayer and reflection. She closed the door of the room behind us, standing over us with arms crossed as she waited for us to sit down.

She began with slow, considered words. "I don't know who you really are, or why you are coming to my church again, but I have already told you I can't help you find this Sylvia Dunham. I don't know her. I've never met her. I have nothing to say. But if you absolutely must speak to me, I would most appreciate it if you would make an appointment. At another time." She added, glancing up at the crucifix on the wall, "And place."

"Excuse me, Mrs. Watson. I do apologize for bothering you here, but it is rather urgent, and we didn't know where else to find you," I said.

She said nothing, waiting expectantly for me to go on.

"Mrs. Watson"—I decided to dive in—"you will soon read in the papers that Noah Philben is wanted by the FBI."

I thought I detected a flash of shock underneath her icy demeanor, but whatever she was feeling, she kept it tightly under wraps.

"What does that have to do with me?"

"Nothing. Except your name is going to come up in some way, eventually, when the police figure out your past with him. It won't take them long." She raised her eyebrows, still not giving anything away. "They're raiding his compound as we speak."

At those words, I noticed that Helen Watson's shoulders dropped the slightest bit, and she took in a quick, sharp breath. She was trying to hide it, but this news was having a visible effect on her. Tracy saw it too.

"You're happy about that?" Tracy asked.

Helen Watson paused, but then answered with some reluctance, "Yes, actually I am. I never . . . I never had a good feeling about . . . that organization."

"Why?" asked Christine, leaning forward.

"To put it simply, I thought it was a cult. I'm not the only one who thinks that. But then, I don't know anything about it." She added hurriedly, "And the last thing I want to do is be involved in any of this."

"Mrs. Watson, I know when you were younger, you moved away with Noah. You were gone for a couple of years. What happened?"

She drew herself up tall, seeming both surprised and offended that we would mention those events to her. I supposed this was the sort of thing people might whisper about in the church parking lot but would never say to her directly. She eyed us carefully and then sat down in a chair. She was certainly taking us more seriously now.

"That's true. And whom do I have to thank for spreading that information around? That was a hard time in my life, and I don't want to relive it."

"What happened, Helen?" Now I was leaning forward. "Please tell us. Listen, if I tell you our own secret, maybe it will help you understand why we need to know." I looked over at Tracy and Christine for permission to proceed, and they both nodded.

"I know I told you before that my name was Caroline Morrow. That isn't true. My name is actually Sarah Farber, and this is Tracy Elwes, and this is Christine McMasters. Do you recognize our names, Mrs. Watson?"

She stared at us in disbelief. It didn't feel good to be so famous. "Are you the girls—the girls who were held in Jack Derber's basement for all those years?"

"I'd call it a cellar really, but yes. That's us."

Tears sprang up in Mrs. Watson's eyes. "I'm so sorry those terrible things happened to you. But what does that have to do with Noah? I mean, he had his own issues, no doubt." She was choosing her words carefully; it was clear she was afraid of Noah Philben. "But he had nothing to do with Jack Derber."

"That's just what we're trying to find out, Mrs. Watson. Did he have something to do with Jack Derber? We think there's a connection," I said.

Tracy added, "And I think when you understand more about what Noah has done, you will see why it is so important for us to find out."

At this, she suddenly seemed alarmed. "What is he . . . what did he do?"

"Human trafficking, Mrs. Watson. He was selling girls. His religious organization, or whatever you want to call it, was just a cover for it. And we think Jack Derber is right in the middle of all of it."

To our surprise, Mrs. Watson's stiff pose disintegrated at those words, and she began to cry softly. She pulled out a handkerchief to dry her eyes, but the harder she tried to swallow back her tears, the harder she sobbed. Tracy and I looked at each other across the room. She knew something. Some kind of guilt had to be behind emotions this intense. We gave her a minute before continuing, none of us quite sure what to do.

"Mrs. Watson," I began, "I know this must be hard for you to realize that someone you . . . once loved . . . and whom you knew from your childhood . . ."

Mrs. Watson shook her head and sat up straight as she covered her mouth with her hand. She stared out the window thoughtfully, and took a deep breath.

"Not childhood. I moved here as a teenager. We started dating when I was sixteen. But we were. . . . Excuse me." She put both hands over her face and then took them away, her expression more composed afterward.

"We were . . . so close . . . I thought—I mean, I was . . . troubled by the religious organization, but I thought—I thought it was just about money. You know, cults make people give them their money and all that. And even so I prayed so hard for Noah. I prayed for him every day. I hoped that he would find respite from those troubling feelings of his."

"What troubling feelings?" Christine asked gently.

Mrs. Watson sat up, still trying to pull herself together. She dabbed her eyes again and sighed.

"He was . . . everyone has their cross to bear. You know, temptations to resist. Noah had a lot of anger in him. His father was a wonderful man—the minister at my church. That's how I met Noah. But as I got to know him more, I realized he hated his father. I couldn't understand it. Maybe it was because his father held so much influence in the community yet didn't take advantage of his role—for financial gain or personal favors or whatever it was that Noah valued. I don't even know what Noah wanted to get out of it, to tell you the truth.

"I noticed this feeling in Noah early on, but I ignored it then. I was young. He was young. I didn't want to believe these feelings were present in the boy I loved. Also, with me, at the beginning, he was all sugar. Honey just melting off of his tongue. I was swept away. So we eloped and moved on to Tollen. There we were in a new town where I knew no one. He kept me completely isolated. It was . . . it was hard." Her eyes filled with tears again as she thought back to that time. It was clear she hadn't talked about these events since they had happened. This story had apparently been bottled up inside her, and once she started telling it, it seemed she needed to get it out. Whether she wanted to or not.

"Mrs. Watson, did he hurt you? What made you leave?" Tracy asked softly.

"I . . ." Mrs. Watson covered her face in her hands and sat there, still for a full minute. We waited. When she finally put her hands down, she had managed again to draw her face back into the firm aspect of an uptight preacher's wife I'd seen before. "I don't really want to talk about it." She wiped away a stray tear.

I stood up and walked over to the window, staring out at the picturesque square.

"Mrs. Watson," I began, not taking my eyes from the window, "those girls in white robes who were riding in vans around town— they were not there voluntarily. They were slaves. Some had been abducted, some had been sold by their boyfriends or families, some had been tricked. But they were all slaves. Having to do unspeakable things against their will. You see, Mrs. Watson, this wasn't ordinary prostitution, as awful as that is. These girls were ordered up for torture. Is there a fate worse than that? Can't you help us understand how that happened?" I turned to her, this time with tears in my eyes.

She looked at each one of us in turn, clearly moved by my words but unsure whether she wanted to take the next step and confide in us.

"Why did you leave?" I echoed Tracy's question, more firmly.

Mrs. Watson sat in silence, every kind of emotion crossing her face. She was not crying now, but I recognized a change in her breathing, faster, desperate. I knew this pattern well. She was about to break down.

"I left because"—her voice became a whisper—"because he told me to do that."

"To do what?" asked Christine, whispering back.

"He wanted me to"—she closed her eyes—"to sell myself."

She opened her eyes again, looking at each one of us to gauge our reactions. When we showed no surprise, only empathy, she went on, her words rushed.

"We had run out of money. He had tried to start a church, but we only had a few parishioners in a little run-down hall he'd rented with the last bit he'd saved up. So he—he asked me to do something for him, for us. I told him no. And when I told him no, he—he beat me, and he locked me in our bedroom.

"That night he went out, and I found a hairpin in my jewelry box. I picked the lock. God, it took me hours. But I did it." I could see her reliving that moment in her mind, the relief of the lock finally releasing. "And when I got out, I just ran. I was too afraid to hitchhike—people did that back then—but I didn't want to risk being alone with any man at that point, much less a stranger. I ran. I slept in the woods. It took me four days to get back home to my parents. My mother was wonderful. She just cried. She didn't ask me what happened. She took me to the courthouse and had the marriage annulled, and then when I . . ."

She looked confused, as if she didn't even see us in the room anymore. Her eyes were glazed over, darting around aimlessly, panicked, and she shook her head, looking out the window, up into the sky beyond the town. Finally, she broke into sobs again, her emotions reaching their crescendo at last. It was hard to make out her next words, her voice was cracking so much.

"And then when I found out I was pregnant, she took me somewhere to take care of that as well. Of course, I deserved not to be able to have children of my own after that. I deserve that. But I just couldn't—I couldn't have that beast's child." She was crying even harder now.

Tracy leaned over and patted her shoulder softly.

"For years I have harbored this guilt. This unrelenting guilt. And I've tried to do everything I could to make up for it. I've worked my fingers to the bone for this church and this community.

And whenever I saw those vans drive by—" She broke off, unable to speak.

That's when I realized it. She knew. Maybe not everything, but just enough to be afraid. Afraid of Noah Philben. He had, after all, gone back to her town and started his operation right under her nose. Maybe to spite her. To punish her. And she kept quiet. She kept quiet.

We all sat in silence, listening to Mrs. Watson's soft sobs. Then she started to ramble.

"I don't know what made Noah like this. I don't understand what created this beast. I honestly don't. His family was so loving. So kind. They used to do things like . . . you know, they worked in soup kitchens, they ran food drives, they took in orphans, for God's sake."

My ears pricked up at this. "Orphans?"

"Yes, you know, they fostered children from around the state."

"Did Noah ever talk about any of these foster kids?"

She only had to think about this a second before nodding thoughtfully.

"Well, there was one I think he got quite close to. Even years later he referred to him as his brother, though of course they weren't blood relatives. I think they stayed in touch after he was legally adopted by someone else. I know they wrote to each other for years. When Noah would get one of those letters, he would go off on his own into the wilderness to—as he put it—ponder and reflect. He would always come back saying he'd renewed his mission, that he was on the right path and couldn't stop now. It was bigger than him. More important than us."

I tried to make eye contact with Tracy, but she was shutting me out, looking straight ahead.

Helen went on. "I think—I mean, I know—I have something from those times. When I was packing my things, I had a drawer with some photographs and letters of mine in it. I shoved them into my purse. Mixed in with them were a couple of things that weren't mine, a photograph and part of an envelope with an address. I—I kept them anyway. I don't really know why. Maybe I thought I'd need to prove something someday."

"Where are they?"

"I keep them here. In the office. I wanted to keep them locked up, and this is the only safe I have," she explained.

"Can we see them?"

She stood up slowly and wiped her eyes. She led us down the hall to a well-kept little office in the corner and stepped into a closet. We heard the soft click of a lock, and then she came out with an envelope and photograph in her hand.

"I'm sure it doesn't mean much, but here is what I have."

She put the items on the desk. The three of us nearly bumped heads bending down low over the photograph. On the right was a youthful Noah Philben, about fourteen years old. He was laughing at what the other boy in the photo was saying, looking up at the sky. The other boy had been turning his head when the picture was snapped, so it was blurred.

"What do you think?" I said, turning to Tracy and Christine.

"Could be," said Christine, "but not really definitive."

"Yes, I mean, the hair is much lighter, but that could be age." Tracy leaned down even closer. "I can't tell about the nose."

We turned to the envelope. It was addressed to a Tom Philben at a post office box in River Bend. It could easily have been a pseudonym. We needed to find out who owned that box—that was Jim's jurisdiction.

"May we keep these? Just for a while. We'll return them. It's very important, Mrs. Watson."

She hesitated but eventually nodded yes. We said our good-byes, thanking her over and over, and went out to our car. I took one last look back at this broken woman, finally released from her secret, sitting alone in that tiny room, looking small and helpless there against the wood-paneled wall, under the crucifix.

We got into the car and sat still in the parking lot for a few minutes. No one spoke.

"She's lying," Tracy finally said.

"What?" said Christine. "About what?"

"Tracy's right," I said. "She's lying. She definitely turned tricks. She didn't know whose baby that was."

"Why would you say that? Isn't what she told us bad enough?" Christine seemed genuinely shocked.

"Yes, but there is some reason she kept her mouth shut completely about Noah Philben all these years. Even though she obviously had the feeling those girls in the vans were not just worshipping in the woods. Why else did she keep that stuff in a safe? She knew. And she did nothing. And she carried all that guilt around with her. For only one reason—he knew she'd been a prostitute and that she'd aborted some john's baby. He must have had some proof he was holding over her head all these years."

Tracy nodded. "That's exactly right. But let's just get out of here. None of that matters now."

"Yes, it does," I said quietly. "What if something she said to someone all those years ago could have prevented what happened to us? What if it revealed some criminal connection that Jack and Noah had fifteen years ago? Something that would have landed them in jail before Jack had had the chance to abduct us. Then what?"

"Come on, Sarah, that's not fair. It's not fair to put the blame on her. *Jack* did those things to us. He's responsible. He's the culpable one. Not her." Christine leaned back in the seat, staring up at the roof of the car, thinking. "I mean, you can trace that blame all the way back down the chain. What about Jack's mother? The one who adopted him? She probably had some indication that her son was a little off. He was probably one of those kids who set fire to small animals or something. But she isn't responsible for this either."

"That's different. And at the very least Helen Watson knew someone was suffering at Noah's hands. Maybe she didn't know about us, but she saw these girls riding through town all the time. She lived with it in front of her. And she was probably the only one who knew what was going on. The only other person besides the perpetrators and their clients. And she didn't do anything. Just so she could keep her own dark secret."

Tracy started the car and pulled out of the lot. "Let's go get some sleep. Then we'll see about who owned that post office box."

CHAPTER 32

We spent the rest of the morning asleep in our new hotel rooms, missing the media frenzy over the Noah Philben story.

I woke up later that afternoon feeling uneasy. I surveyed the room, but nothing seemed out of the ordinary—the hotel air conditioner hummed quietly, and my folded clothes lay on the dresser in neat, ordered piles.

On my way into the bathroom, I saw an envelope slipped under my door. I assumed it was a note from the front desk, though I thought it strange that they didn't use the creamy white stationery, stamped with the hotel's logo, that was on my bedside table. I leaned down and picked it up, before I noticed the handwriting. At the sight of that familiar script, something inside me collapsed. I didn't open it. I couldn't bring myself to look at it alone, so I ran down the hall to Tracy's room. It took several knocks to wake her up. Finally, she opened the door.

"Did you get one too?"

"What?" she said groggily.

"A letter. From Jack. Here at the hotel." My voice was breaking. I felt frantic now. The old panic was back, rising inside me. "He knows where we are. How can he know that? Noah Philben's men must have followed us, and now they are acting as couriers for Jack."

I pointed at Tracy's floor, just inside the doorway. There it was. *Her* letter. Tracy's face seemed paler than ever as she stared at it, unmoving.

"Let's get out of here. Go get your bags. I'll get Christine."

I ran back to my room and hastily threw my things into my suitcase. I told our security guard that we'd decided to go back to New York and were racing to catch a flight. He looked confused and made a phone call. Whoever was on the other line clearly needed him freed up for other duties, because we got the go-ahead.

I met Tracy and Christine in the lobby. As shaken as we were, somehow we managed to check out and run to the car, Tracy slipping behind the wheel. The tires spun out beneath us as we pulled out of the parking lot.

In the backseat, Christine was showing the first sign of nerves. "Do you think they're still following us? Where do we go? Another hotel? Jesus, why did I get myself involved with this again?" She ran her hands along the inside of the car door. Even as we built up speed, I had a vision of her opening the door and jumping out to hail a cab back to Park Avenue.

"Christine," Tracy began in an even and controlled tone, "be quiet unless you have something productive to say. I can't handle panic right now. Read the letters to me." Tracy was thinking, and scared.

I opened my letter first, holding it at the edges to avoid too much contact with it, and read, "'The family has finally reunited. I'm so pleased. Come home, and you will find the answers.'"

I threw the letter into the backseat and opened Christine's.

"'Girls, let's take a family photograph. A tableau vivant. I have so much more to show you.'"

"Okay, next mine." Tracy drove like a maniac.

"Where are we going?" I asked.

"To see Adele."

I felt a lump in my throat. "You don't think—?" I could barely finish the thought, as it dawned on me that she was the only person who knew where we were staying, other than the police and the FBI.

"That she delivered these letters for Jack?" Tracy finished for me. "I don't know. But either way I have a feeling that, like Helen, she knows more than she ought to, and it's time to make her tell us before we go any further."

I nodded and slowly opened Tracy's letter, forcing myself to keep from throwing it out the window.

"'You have studied so hard over the years, Tracy. So many books. I have written one just for you. In our special room.'"

I handed the final letter to Christine, amazed that she didn't seem to mind touching them, as I watched her neatly pile them together.

"How did he get these letters out of the jail without them going through Jim?" she said. "I thought the prison was all over this and they monitored everything going in and out of that place. All the other letters came through Jim. We have to call him."

I agreed, got out my phone, and dialed.

Jim answered, sounding like I'd woken him up.

"Did you get him? Did you arrest Noah?" I asked first.

"No. The place was empty—not a soul there. They obviously had a doomsday scenario mapped out, so they had an escape plan ready. They left behind some computers, though. Our tech guys are working on breaking the codes now. They must have some real pros in their organization, because their security is extremely sophisticated."

"Did you find any other girls?"

"No. But we could tell someone had been living there in some pretty rough circumstances. Listen, Sarah, this situation is very dangerous. We found—we found some shocking things in that compound. I can't emphasize this enough: the three of you need to remain at the hotel until this situation stabilizes."

"What? What did you find?"

Jim paused. But this time he probably wanted to scare us enough to make us stay put.

"The upstairs was set up like a church retreat: institutional furniture, bulletin boards, sign-up sheets. But underneath . . . Sarah, that entire compound sits on top of a labyrinth of underground rooms. That's where the real operations were going on. It was a hellhole. Chains on the walls, torture devices everywhere, blood splatter on the floor, buckets for human waste shoved in corners. And there were video cameras all over the place. They were filming it all."

"Filming it? Oh my God," I said, repulsed.

"Yes," Jim went on. "We ran image-matching software against some of the footage left behind, and it looks like some of it was recently uploaded to an Internet porn site dedicated to 'true slaves.' You can't get into it without sharing files of the same kind of content, so the users are all hardcore. That must be how Noah gets his clients."

I shut my eyes, as if that could keep the words he was saying out of my head.

"Jim. Listen." My voice was shaking. "Jack sent us letters. They were delivered to our hotel today—slipped under our doors."

"What? That's not possible."

"Oh, but it is. They are here. Christine is holding them in her hands right now."

"What do they say?"

"His usual stuff. They make no sense, but that's not the point. The point is that somehow he knew where we were. Doesn't that mean the person Noah had following us is also reporting to Jack Derber? Jim, there is definitely a link between these two. Listen, can you have someone on your team find out who uses or has ever used post office box one hundred eighty-two in River Bend? Noah Philben was sending letters to that address, years ago."

"One eighty-two?" I could hear his pen scratching over the line. "I got it, but listen, let me handle it. It's my job. You three have been through enough." He paused, perhaps realizing his under-statement.

At that moment the car swerved hard as Tracy maneuvered to avoid a vehicle passing in the other lane. She leaned on the horn, cursing.

"Sarah, where are you?" Jim sounded upset. "Aren't you in the hotel?"

I mouthed the word *fuck* and covered the phone. I didn't want to tell him what we were doing. We needed to find these answers ourselves. We'd come so far, we didn't want to be relegated to pas-sive victims at this point, sitting back, waiting for some junior agent to be assigned this piece of the puzzle. But if we refused to stay at the hotel, Jim might order us into full protective custody.

I changed the subject.

"Jim, what do you know about Jack's childhood?"

"Sarah—"

"Jim, just . . . for my information . . ."

"Sarah, let's talk later—but the truth is, we don't know much."

"Please, Jim. Tell me something."

Jim sighed the way he did when he was about to give in.

"He bounced around the foster care system for a while, until the Derbers adopted him when he was about fourteen. Before that, well, unfortunately the record-keeping system for Child Protective Services was not so great back then. His file was lost. His social worker was killed in a car accident about fifteen years ago. No one else has any idea about his past."

"Well, we might be piecing some of it together. Let's talk tomorrow."

"Sarah, go back to the hotel. *Now.* We'll double security. Leave those letters with Officer Grunnell. We'll find out what's going on. Someone called in a tip about Noah, so I'll most likely be gone all night, but I'll be by to check on you in the morning."

I pushed the off button on my phone and repeated to the others what Jim had discovered at Noah's compound. We all stared straight ahead, trying to piece it together, to understand what it all meant.

Finally, I dared to look at the others. Christine's hands were still now, but her eyes were darting right and left, her face flushed. She had appeared completely together, our savior, the meticulously assembled Upper East Side mother, just a few hours before. Now she was starting to remind me of the Christine I had known all those years ago.

Had this Christine been lurking behind her eyes all this time? Was this the real her, and everything else a plastered-over version held together by all her repressive might?

I looked over at Tracy to see if I could shift her attention to Christine without being obvious, but she was concentrating only on her driving, one eye on the pink line of the GPS system, hurtling us toward the campus. Tracy's grip on the steering wheel was turning her knuckles white.

None of us wanted to admit it, but we knew. Jack was telling us something with those letters. Sure, he was letting us know he thought he was still in charge, that he could still reach us anywhere, wherever we were. But he was also telling us he'd left us a clue there. There at that house. Some clue in his sick game that might yield something valuable. But at what price? I knew we all understood it, though none of us could bring ourselves to say it out loud.

We'd try anything else first.

We reached the campus, Tracy hitting every speed bump at five miles an hour too fast. The tires screeched as she pulled into a space in the empty lot next to the psych building. The streetlights over the parking area were just coming on, giving the sky a strange glow. I glanced at the campus security emergency call box on the other side of Tracy, as she emerged from the car. If only that call box could help us now, I thought.

As we walked toward the building, I could see a light on in Adele's office.

We made our way down the hallway, past the same security guard, who as usual didn't even give us as much as a sidelong glance. We stood still for a moment in front of Adele's office door, wondering whether to knock or barge in. I stepped forward and rapped lightly on the door. No answer. Tracy rolled her eyes at me and gestured for me to step aside. I obliged.

She turned the knob and flung the door open wide.

Professor David Stiller was kneeling on the floor, blindfolded, in front of Adele, in a pose of total submission. When she saw us, she jerked upright, her left hand behind her out of sight.

As she recognized us, a slow smile crept over her face.

"I'll be with you in just a moment." She said it as if we'd merely caught her busy on the phone.

She signaled for us to close the door. We stepped back out into the hallway stunned. When we recovered, we started whispering in the half-lit hallway.

"More fieldwork," Tracy said dryly. "She must have a grant."

I stifled a small laugh, and we moved farther away from the door.

"I thought David Stiller hated Adele, but maybe that was just their idea of foreplay," I whispered.

At that moment Adele stepped out into the hallway, the model of professional composure. David Stiller followed her, and carefully avoiding eye contact with us, he slipped down the hall back into his own office. Adele didn't even glance back at him.

She was calm and cool, her face, as ever, a mask. She politely offered us a seat. I took the chair in front of her desk. Christine and Tracy scrunched in next to each other on the small love seat in the corner.

Adele folded her hands in front of her on the desk and leaned forward.

"I thought we were meeting later. Is everything okay?"

"Adele," I began, "I wanted you to meet Christine."

Adele looked over at her in awe.

"Yes, *that* Christine," I said. "So here we are. A complete set."

I studied her face carefully to try to determine if it was all an act. If she'd delivered those letters, she knew perfectly well who Christine was and where she'd been for the past two days.

"Well," she said, shaking her head with astonishment, "I have to say I'm really happy to see you all here together. Safe and sound. After all you've been through." She paused. "So what really happened out there today? They aren't—they aren't releasing much information to the press."

"We don't know much more than you."

She stared at me. She must have known that wasn't entirely true. She changed tack.

"I see. Well, in any event, maybe the three of you will consider participating in our victimological study, especially now that you're all together again."

I knew I'd better steer us away from that topic before she could go any further. I had a feeling the word *victimological* would not sit well with Tracy.

"It looks like you and David Stiller have a—a very different relationship from what we thought."

"Oh, that," she said tonelessly. "Just reconstructing a scene for a conference presentation."

I didn't believe that for a second but decided to move on.

"Adele, do you know whether Jack Derber had a connection to Noah Philben?"

Her face was still for a moment. "Well, only what they said on the news: that his wife is a member of Noah's church."

"I mean something from . . . before. All those years ago. You've known Jack a long time. Did he know Noah Philben before prison?"

Adele looked straight ahead and blinked twice slowly, as if only her eyes would tell us anything, in code. Her lashes, in a thick coat of mascara, fluttered. She looked away, straightening some papers on her desk. I thought her smooth gears might slip for just a moment; then she seemed to gain control of herself, and she looked back at us, indecipherable as ever.

"How would I know? Jack and I were not *friends*. We were working on research projects together. I wouldn't know with whom he associated outside the university, except the people I've since met at The Vault."

With this she sat back and folded her hands carefully in her lap. I waited for her to look away, maybe to shift uncomfortably. But she didn't. She sat perfectly still.

I could tell that, if she had delivered those letters, we would never get her to admit it. Adele wasn't going to fall apart like Helen Watson. Maybe because she had more to hide.

I tried to imagine what was going on in her mind. This woman was all discipline, but there had to be something that would break her. I couldn't believe she was all power and control and ambition. I had to do something. Something big.

There was only one way left to push her. One place where I knew even she couldn't hold on to that composure. I had to get her out of her element. Make her face the past she seemed to brush aside.

But I knew it would push us as well. To go back there. Yet we all somehow knew it was the one inevitable place we had to go. The place we knew was calling us home, ready to tell us what we needed to know. Nothing could be more terrifying to me. Nothing. But I reminded myself that I had to be stronger now. I was following Tracy's advice. We all had to plunge in. With or without Adele, we had to go back there. We had to test ourselves. Test Jack Derber.

"Okay, we're leaving." I stood up. Tracy and Christine looked at me questioningly but stood up in tandem, prepared to see where I was taking this.

"We're going to his house," I said decisively. Much more decisively than I felt. Tracy and Christine looked stunned.

Even Adele blanched. "Why would you do that? You can't get in there. Isn't it all locked down by the police?" Her surprise seemed genuine, and I began to doubt whether she was involved.

"We'll have to break in then. He has written us letters, Adele. They were delivered to us today at our hotel." I scanned her face, searching for a sign of guilt. If she knew anything, she was hiding it well. "And everything in those letters suggests there is information hidden in that house. Papers. Photographs. Perhaps some of his *research materials*."

At that Adele stood up abruptly and grabbed her purse. She was on board.

As we marched down the hall, Christine sidled up to me and whispered furiously, "What the hell are you thinking? No way am I going back there without Jim."

"Jim would never let us go there at all. We have no choice," I replied, sorrier than anyone that it was the case. But this was our moment. I felt it. "Jack is telling us something is in there, and I believe him, even if it's part of his sick game. For this one last time, I think we have to listen to what he has to say."

CHAPTER 33

We returned to the rental car in silence, Tracy taking her now-familiar place behind the wheel. This time, though, it didn't bother me, because in some new and strange way I felt I was the one leading us on.

Staring out the window on the passenger side as we left the city proper, I wondered what had made me insist on going to the house. I hadn't had time to prepare myself mentally, and I reminded myself I had sworn never to return to this state, much less to that awful place. I looked at Tracy. She nodded as she shifted the car into drive.

"You're right, Sarah. We need to do this."

I found the address on Google, and we punched it into the GPS. Amazing how easy it was to find now, when so many had searched for it for so long. There it was, on Google Maps, street view and satellite. I turned to the backseat. Christine's hands were shaking again, as she ran them up and down her thighs.

I felt my breath coming a little faster and recognized with annoyance the dizziness that was starting to whirl the thoughts around in my head. If there was one thing I was not going to do, however, it was let Adele see me crack. This time I didn't bother with any sophisticated stress-reducing techniques. *Goddammit,* I thought to myself, *you are not going to have a panic attack right now. You can't.*

I held my breath and counted to twenty, squeezing my eyes shut. This was for Jennifer. I had brought her photo along again, and I pulled it out, taking a long look at her face. Then I slipped it back into my pocket as a talisman against the evil of this place.

I felt my head begin to clear and my breathing return to normal. And then once again, I began to feel that strange sense of elation. Maybe we would find something. Evidence. Explanations. Answers. Something we could use to keep Jack in prison, something that would take us to Jennifer's body, or maybe, just maybe, something that would explain why this had happened to us. I couldn't tell what was more important to me at this point.

When I finally made my escape, I had thought I would never be unhappy again. That there was no room for unhappiness as long as I was free. Why, then, couldn't I actually be happy?

Or is it the case that no one ever truly gets over anything? Is there really that much pain and suffering continuing right now at this minute, in millions of hearts, in bodies carrying on the burden of existence, trying to smile through tears for fleeting, passing moments here and there—when they can forget what happened to them, maybe even for whole hours at a time? Maybe that's what it is to live.

But I couldn't think about that now. I had to focus. However doubtful it seemed that we would find anything the FBI had overlooked, I reminded myself that they had been searching for something entirely different. They hadn't been exploring Jack Derber's whole existence back then. They had been looking for girls tucked away in crevices. The hard evidence of bodies.

And back then prostitution rings would have been low on the list of FBI priorities anyway. The Internet hadn't yet linked together the perverted of the world for more coordinated horrors. Back then it had been serial killer season. That was where the glamour was. That's what they wanted Jack to be—a mad, lone attacker.

None of us spoke for the entire forty-minute drive. We just listened to the GPS, its computer-generated voice filling the spaces where we couldn't connect anymore. *Recalculating* came the constant refrain, and I could see in all of our faces that that was what we were doing as well. Trying to adjust ourselves to this sudden new reality. We were approaching the place where we had thought we would die. The place where we had wanted to kill each other. We didn't know what this would feel like, but it would not feel good.

We found the driveway, which I recognized from the newspaper photos. Tracy stopped on the road, her turn signal flashing. A light rain started to hit the windshield, and without a word she flicked on the wipers. We sat there, still in the silence. The GPS reminded us that our destination was on the right.

"Are we ready?" Tracy finally said.

"No, not ready," came Christine's voice from the back. "But let's do it. Let's just do it."

I looked back at her. Christine's hands had stopped fidgeting, and there was a new resolve in her face. I nodded to Tracy, and she turned the car into the driveway, which twisted along up the side of a low mountain through a heavily wooded forest. I looked at the trees and remembered the time I had spent in those woods, after my escape, wandering, nearly dead from dehydration, naked. An animal in the forest, disoriented and alone. More alone than I'd ever been in my life. The weather had been the same then, and I remember opening my mouth toward the sky, tasting the rain.

As we drew closer, I noted that here and there, strewn on the ground or hanging from trees, were tattered bits of yellow police tape, hardly recognizable unless you knew to look. We finally pulled around the last corner, and the house came into view. A large A-frame lodge, dark green, blending with the forest, and a deep red barn over to the right. That barn, I thought. *That barn*. I shuddered as we pulled to a stop in front of it.

Tracy looked over at me, but I couldn't read her expression. Was she checking on me, or was she lost in her own painful memories? I couldn't tell.

I looked back at Adele, who had a look of wonderment on her face. I didn't know if she'd ever been here—if this place had been a secret haunt of hers as well—but at least she seemed properly in awe of what had occurred in this spot.

I looked over at Christine. She was calm and solemn. Her hands were still.

We got out of the car almost simultaneously, the doors clicking in unison as we closed them gently. We all stopped in our tracks, looking at that house with silent dread. It was overwhelming. This building felt alive to me, ominous and strange. It seemed to be watching us, a part of Jack he'd left behind.

Finally, I took a deep breath and started toward it, careful not to look at the barn. I almost laughed out loud at the irony of trying to break *into* this house that we'd spent years trying to get out of. But here we were. And we were all terrified.

I got close enough to look into the window by the door. It looked well organized and scrubbed clean inside. I wondered for a moment what lucky person had had the job of restoring the house after the ransacking by law enforcement.

Tracy, leading the way, walked over to the door and was reaching for the doorknob, when I interrupted her.

"Should we avoid fingerprints?"

"Well, we aren't exactly prepared with gloves, now are we?" Still, she stretched the end of her T-shirt to grasp the door handle. It was unlocked, and she flung the door open.

"So there we are. Our first experience as criminal trespassers—a great success."

"That's weird," came Adele's voice from behind me. "Creepy, in fact."

The door stood open before us. We looked at each other again. Who would take that first step?

I knew the answer. I had dragged us all here, so it was only fair that I should be the one to cross that threshold first.

I took a deep breath, trembling only slightly, then entered the house. I turned back to the others.

"See, it doesn't hurt at all."

No one cracked a smile.

I took another step in, and Tracy followed me.

"Well, here we are, in never-never land," she whispered, looking around at the prim kitchen. It seemed so ordinary. No one could have detected the evil residue his touch must surely have left behind.

Adele followed us in cautiously, eyes wide.

Christine stood at the door, immobilized by fear. I noticed her left hand start to quiver. Then, bracing her left arm with her right hand, she stepped over the threshold slowly and deliberately, inhaling deeply.

"Okay, then," was all she said.

I propped the door open with a small side table from the entryway, not ready to be fully enclosed in there, and then led the way down the hallway, fighting all the while to keep myself from hyperventilating. My pulse was racing, and that old familiar dizziness was creeping in. I knew, though, that for everyone's sake, I needed to keep it under control.

I went down the hall and stood for a moment alone in front of the double doors to the library. If anything relevant was hidden in this house, I knew it would be in that room, but I wasn't sure if I was ready to face it.

I put my hand in my pocket, reaching for Jennifer's picture. I clutched it. I could feel it crinkle up in my fist. I might be damaging it, but I needed to draw a kind of physical strength from it now, to let the ink from that image soak into my fingertips and bring Jennifer closer to me. I slid the door open slowly, hoping I could take in the room in bits and pieces, easing into it.

The first thing I saw was the rack, still there in the corner.

Tracy's voice was right in my ear behind me. "Ugh, why didn't they take that freaking thing out of here?"

"The room seems so much smaller," Christine said softly.

"That makes a lot of sense," began Adele. "This room won't have the same power for—"

"Shut up, Adele," Tracy and Christine said in unison.

Adele shut up. We all stepped into the room and stared up at the bookshelves, which ran up to the top of the double-height ceiling. The books were still there. Thousands of them.

I walked over to the heavy oak desk, with its roll top and its dark green blotter. It was expensive, clearly. Jack's adoptive family had not wanted for money, and neither had Jack.

In the dead center of the blotter lay an unmarked envelope. I lifted it up. It was sealed. The others came over to see what I'd found, Tracy and Christine carefully avoiding touching the rack as they made their way to my side.

"Should I open it?" I looked at them.

"Why not?" said Adele. "We've already broken and entered."

"We didn't have to break anything," reminded Christine, "and since he never wanted us to leave in the first place, I feel like we have full guest privileges."

I broke the seal of the envelope and slid the paper out, then unfolded it slowly. There, in Jack's writing, in clear bold letters, were the words *Welcome home.*

I dropped the paper as though it were on fire.

At that same moment we heard a door slam, hard, from the hall. The door we had come in. The door I'd propped open.

We all jumped to our feet and quietly pressed ourselves to the library wall. Tracy was in front, closest to the door. We listened, but I heard only our own breathing.

Tracy peered around the corner. No one could have gone farther into the house without passing the library door. She motioned for us to follow her, as she edged out of the room.

There was no one there. If someone *had* been in here, he'd gone back outside after slamming the door shut. But why?

Tracy made her way over and grabbed the doorknob, this time forgetting about prints. And then we understood. It was locked from the outside.

"What the fuck??" she shouted, as she banged on the door, to no effect.

"No way. There is no way we can be locked in this house. NO. WAY," said Christine, shaking.

"Let's stay calm," I said. "There are a million windows, and I have my cell." I pulled it out of my pocket and held it up. Only there were no bars in the upper-right-hand corner of the screen. In my crazed state, I'd failed to check it. "Except there's no signal."

"Too far up the mountain," said Adele. "That makes sense around here. Shit."

I raced from room to room, peering out the windows. There was no one in sight. But the house was surrounded by dense woods.

There were plenty of places for someone to hide if they were keeping an eye on us. Or planning something worse.

Adele walked into the kitchen and tried opening the windows. They were sealed shut. The locks would not turn. She pulled open cabinets and drawers and finally found in a closet a broom with a heavy wooden handle. In a sudden frenzy, she started beating on the windows in the kitchen. Glass broke and flew around the room. We shielded our eyes and backed out of the way as Adele struck again and again. She was surprisingly strong.

Tracy, staring at Adele in her fury, bent down, protecting her face with her hands, and leaned over to me to whisper, "Maybe I was wrong about Adele."

I shrugged as we stepped into the hall to avoid the flying shards. "Or maybe she knows even better than we do how dangerous this place is."

Adele finally stood motionless, panting, her face red, her hair a tangled mess. She still held up her broom, ready to attack, as we cautiously reentered the kitchen to survey the damage. The counters, sink, and floors were covered with broken glass. I moved closer and examined the mullion of one window that had splintered apart from Adele's thrashing. There was something there between the two thin strips of wood. I touched it. Cold metal. I realized then that each window was covered by a grid of iron bars. The painted wood built around them was only a facade.

The place was rigged.

At that, without a word, we split up, each of us going to different doors, pulling and banging at them all in turn, futilely. They were sealed shut, the doorknobs jammed. I heard screams of frustration from each corner of the house as every possible exit resisted our efforts.

Christine gave up first. She sat in a corner of the library, curled up, and began to cry, moaning words of apology to her daughters.

I couldn't stop myself, though. I pounded and pounded every available surface. Finally, dispirited, I stood at the kitchen counter, looking out of the broken window over the sink toward the barn.

"Only thinking can save us," I whispered to myself, drawing on the last bit of my fading inner strength.

As I turned to leave the kitchen, I saw Adele walking toward the door leading downstairs to our former prison. I couldn't face the idea of anyone going there.

"Don't bother," I said. "That goes to the cellar, and I can tell you with utter certainty there is no way out of there."

She flinched and backed away from the heavy metal door in horror. She didn't have to be told twice. A few minutes later I heard her hurling what must have been her whole body at the back door, grunting as she hit the solid wood.

Each of us gave up in our own time, then made our way, one by one, into the library. I sank down into the couch in the middle of the room, facing the large fireplace. Tracy slumped down beside me and put her head in her hands.

"He did it. He got us back," she said quietly.

I shook my head in disbelief.

"How could he have known we'd come here alone?"

"He took a chance, I suppose. What did he have to lose? Plus, if he was counting on us being stupid and arrogant, he was right."

"It won't take long for Jim to realize we're missing, though," I said.

"Jack knows that too," Tracy replied, "since he's obviously got someone following us pretty closely. That just means whatever he's got planned for us will happen sooner rather than later."

I scanned the room, wondering where the attack would come from. I felt helpless, panicked.

"We need some kind of . . . weapons," Tracy said, looking as frazzled as I felt. I nodded and we scattered, each of us searching for something with which to fight back. Christine returned brandishing the broom handle Adele had used on the windows. Tracy and I, clearly the most practical, each took a kitchen knife from the block, and Adele found a heavy frying pan.

When we gathered again in the library, I bolted its heavy wooden doors shut behind us. Without discussion, we spread out, as though taking up guard stations around the room. Tracy stood in one corner, I took up a post in the other. Adele squatted over by a window, her eyes just peering out over the sill, into the woods.

Christine pulled herself up and crawled into the window seat, as far from the rack as she could get. Her knees were tucked up under her, and she clung to the curtains, weeping. She had carefully propped the broom handle beside her, but I didn't have much confidence that she'd be of any use in a crisis this time. The old Christine was back.

"What was that noise?" Adele said suddenly, jerking to attention.

"What?" Tracy said, cocking her head to hear.

"That noise. I heard something, I think from the cellar."

"I'm not going down there," I said decisively.

Tracy shook her head. "I didn't hear anything," she mumbled. It's possible we were in denial.

"So that's it?" Adele said. "We just sit here and wait for someone to find us? And hope it's the good guys first?"

"I guess that's about right," Tracy said bitterly.

"Well, I for one," Adele began again, "plan to do what we came here for. I'm going to have a look around."

Tracy glared at her. "What's the point? You clearly don't understand what we're dealing with."

I sat in my corner, studying each person. We were starting to turn on each other already. I saw the obvious fear on the surface, but I could also see that other being inside each of us, poised to strike, poised to live at any price. I forced the thought away, telling myself I was only projecting onto them my own gripping fear of being returned once again to my animal self.

It was the place. It was being back in that house. I felt like a caged beast and once again felt I would do anything to escape. Anything. Just like before. I recognized it in a flash, the feeling that all my integrity, all my rational being, would be instantly displaced if it came down to it. Was everyone else like that? Or was I just a base person at heart, incapable of empathy for others, as Tracy thought? Could she have been right all along? And who would I sacrifice this time, to get out of here?

CHAPTER 34

When at last I pulled myself out of my dark thoughts, I realized Adele was poking around in Jack's desk.

"I still think," she was saying, her eyes focused on the contents of the top drawer as she rifled through it, "we can find something here to . . . help us. Maybe a key, or something."

She was beginning to look scared, and she was having trouble holding on to her otherwise extraordinary self-possession. Her movements were more frantic now, as she pushed aside pens and Post-it Notes to reach into the very back of the drawer.

"What are you really looking for, Adele?" Tracy's voice rose. Was she starting to feel panicked too? "Research papers? Do you think there's something in there that will make your career? You know, Adele, in case you hadn't noticed, you can't exactly have a career when you're dead in some house up in the mountains. Wait a minute—maybe I'm wrong. I suppose you could type up something now and have it published posthumously." She thought a second. "In fact, that's probably your fastest road to fame and fortune. A book written while held captive in a psycho's house."

She turned to me. "Sarah, why don't you get going on one, too? All about how you saved us once by accident but by hook or crook managed to get us right back where we started."

Adele stopped rummaging through the drawer and looked up.

"Wait a minute, Tracy. The way I understand it is, if it weren't for Sarah, you'd still be Jack's prisoner. And he'd be sitting at this desk right now instead of me." With those words, she got up and quickly stepped away from it.

I looked at her and thought I could sense a glimmer of feeling behind her eyes. Was she trying to help me here?

"Actually, Adele," Tracy replied, "in case you hadn't noticed, I am still here, and that's thanks to her, too. Back here anyway. So maybe the intervening ten years don't add up to all that much. It looks like I have a very good chance of dying in this house after all."

I could feel the color draining from my face. I thought Tracy had been on the verge of forgiving me. That this search together was healing our old wounds. I had obviously been wrong. And now the stress of our situation seemed to be forcing her true feelings back to the surface.

I knew Tracy thought I hadn't sent help for them when I escaped. She had told the press at the time that if it hadn't been for the police grilling, she was sure I would have left them there forever. Because I'd been upstairs for a while, as far as she knew, I'd been gone from the cellar for six days before they were saved. Six days during which Jack could have easily killed them to cover his tracks.

She was wrong. I *had* sent for help.

It would have been simple enough to explain what happened. But I had always been unable to talk about how I'd gotten out and had never even attempted to defend myself against her accusations. I had never discussed it before with anyone, not my mother, not Jim, not Dr. Simmons. They didn't know what happened, and any-time they had tried to get me to discuss it, I slipped into an almost catatonic state.

I could feel the panic descending upon me, but I knew it would only hurt me in Tracy's estimation if I let it show. *Still the poor PTSD victim*. Tracy had handled the past bravely, she had pro-cessed it and even used it for a purpose, shutting out the pain of the experience for herself and using it instead to promote an agenda—exactly as the modern world demanded. She had no time or pity for those who could not find a purpose in it all, as she had done.

If I wanted to explain, it was now or never. Maybe I wouldn't even have time. Maybe Noah and Jack's men were outside right now. But if there was one thing I wanted Tracy to understand, it was this.

I walked over to Jack's desk. I'd seen him sitting behind it so many times before, when I was there on the rack, exhausted from pain, and he would scribble away in his notebooks. In its perverse way, that desk was a symbol of peace for me. I knew when he started writing, I would at last have a few moments of respite, and there would be no more torture that day.

I pulled out the oversize oak swivel chair and sat down. I felt like a child sitting in the grown-up seat. It engulfed me, but in a strange way, I thought being there might give me the power to speak.

I looked over at Tracy, who would still not look at me; at Adele, who was watching me carefully, giving no hint of what lay behind her gaze; at Christine, who had stopped sobbing and was nestled in the window seat, her eyes staring vacantly ahead of her. She'd found a tissue somewhere and was wiping her eyes.

Finally, I picked up a pen on the desk, a Waterman, and started to push and pull the cap on and off in a steady rhythm. I waited, hoping that eventually Tracy would crack. She would look at me. She had to.

And then she did. She turned slowly to face me, peering out at me from under her dyed-black bangs. Only then did I start, in a halting voice, to explain what had happened that day. My throat was dry, but I pushed myself on.

Those last months in the cellar, I had worked hard to get Jack to believe I was coming around to his way of thinking. I was manipulating him, just as I knew he was manipulating me. I knew one day he would test me, though I didn't know how. He had been treating me differently now for weeks, no regular torture, just the large looming threat of it always in the air. He pretended to cherish me. Almost . . . almost to love me.

I knew if he believed I was under his spell, he might give me a longer leash. Might ask me to do chores for him outside, might even take me out of the house.

Finally, that day, he opened the door. The same door that kept us imprisoned in the house now.

He opened it. I was standing there before an open door. Granted, I was naked and sore and hadn't eaten in days, so I was weak, but there, there, there, in front of me . . . was an open door.

I looked ahead. Jack was right behind me, his breath on my neck. I saw the barn, the yard in front, his car. I walked slowly, steadily out the door, hoping I could get more than an arm's length away from him where he couldn't easily yank me back. I was in a daze.

He had told me I could see her, and he kept his promise. There on the ground, just at the edge of the barn door, wrapped haphazardly in a dirty blue tarp, was a long lifeless form. At the bottom I could just see a bloated chunk of flesh, blue and black. A human foot.

I had been begging, begging for months to see her body. I needed to say good-bye, and I thought that was the one thing he would do for me. And there she was. When I saw her there, when I saw that flesh peeking out from under the tarp, the body he had dug up for me to see, I suddenly didn't want to see her anymore. I realized, at once, what the reality of her dead body would mean to me. The finality. I had seen enough.

At the same time, I couldn't think clearly about whether I needed to put in more time convincing him of my loyalty. If I hadn't been so hungry, if I hadn't been in pain, if I hadn't feared the body I saw in front of the barn, maybe my own body would not have reacted as automatically to the sudden taste of freedom and the exhilarating feeling of fresh air on my skin. Something lit on fire at that moment, the innermost part of me that only wanted escape. My legs found their strength, and my heart found some current to lift it up. With a sudden start, I broke into a run. He must have thought I would be too terrified to do anything so bold so quickly, because there was a split-second pause before he followed me.

I knew if he caught me, all my hard work for the previous four months would be lost. He would never trust me again. I would never have another chance. This was it.

I ran as hard as I could, gasping for air almost immediately. My muscles had been deprived of even normal physical exertion for three years, so I was weak. My legs could barely carry me, much less pull me free of him. But my fear drove me on, and I bolted away from him. He was prepared for such an attempt, though. He jerked into swift action, running behind me. Fast.

At that point, the world switched into slow motion. I moved as though through molasses, my breath loud in my own ear. I could hear his steps behind me, crunching each twig, his feet pounding hollows into the earth. He was strong, I could feel it.

My lungs wanted me to give up. I couldn't breathe anymore. My arms and hands were numb. I couldn't feel my legs either, but I knew they must still be moving because he didn't have me yet. I turned the bend in his driveway, going down the hill. I couldn't see the end, but I could sense it far ahead of me. In a way I felt trapped, thought the gig would soon be up, but I knew I had the will to live on my side. He had only evil.

I made it another hundred yards, which, when I really reflect on it, was a kind of miracle. I had practically taken flight. But I didn't have the strength to keep up the pace, and he was driven by rage at that point, his body fortified by it.

Only a few seconds later I felt his strong grip on my right arm. I will never forget that moment. I knew what pains and torments I had survived for the past three years. And I knew my punishment now would be far worse.

I could hear it in the sound that came out of me, like something more from an animal than from a human girl. It was over, and I would suffer from then until eternity. At that moment I didn't have the wherewithal to reflect on the opportunity I had blown. I didn't have time to be filled with the regret of a lifetime, but later, in the many hours just after, I would feel a soul-searing pain, knowing I had been so close and had thrown it all away on an impulsive act from which there was no turning back.

He grabbed me and threw me over his shoulder. I immediately went limp, defeated. In my mind, my life was over. Just over. All I wanted was to have the mental strength to check out of the world entirely. I wanted to disconnect from the pain he was about to inflict.

Slowly over the years I had developed that capacity. I had learned to take my mind far away, to stop anticipating either pain or release from pain and to feel everything and nothing as one long continuum. No moment any different from any other, the feelings all evened out over time. *Disconnect*, I told myself.

He hauled me into the barn, and for a moment, the sheer disorientation of the new space made me panic. Then I willed myself to shut down. No feeling. No engagement. I entered that interior space in which my mind was set loose to wander. My body was an inanimate object, distantly floating in its own space.

I tried not to care. I tried to resign myself to death, or worse, a living torture beyond what I had experienced those years in the cellar. Enraged, he grabbed me by one arm and by my hair and flipped me over into a long wooden box deep in the interior of the barn. A box smaller than the one in the cellar, this one horizontal, coffinlike. He flung my weak body into it, then stepped away.

Instinctively, I grabbed onto the edges and tried to pull myself out of it. As I sat up, I was met by a hard fist, pummeling me back down into the box. I covered my face to protect it from the blows. Seconds later a long, putrid object was thrust upon me. Jennifer's lifeless body, heavy and cold, descended on me like a blanket. Then he slammed the top of the wooden box shut, and I could hear him nailing it closed, screaming something I couldn't understand.

For a moment, I felt relief. I was separated from him by a few feet at least, with the nailed door between us. His hands couldn't reach me. It took me a few minutes to register that there I was, sealed shut into a coffin with Jennifer's body, preceding me in death but clearly not by that much. With a final nail, and a shuffle outside, everything was suddenly still and quiet. Jack must have gone back into the house.

Eventually I could tell night was falling. I pushed my body into a corner of the box, making myself as small as possible, shrinking away from her body. I began to see and hear things. I thought I saw her move. I thought I saw her fingers reach up to caress me. I thought I heard her voice, asking me not to leave her. I heard it all too clearly. I don't know when I started crying, but soon enough my own hands were on my face, wiping away my tears and snot and spit. I wondered, despairingly, what would kill me first, dehydration or lack of air. But in that reflection, I noticed there was no lack of air. I could breathe just fine. There must be some small opening somewhere in that box.

I pulled back from my corner, careful not to tangle the strands of dry dead hair from Jennifer's corpse in with my own. I noticed that the box had been built directly into the side of the barn. And then I looked more closely and saw that something had been happening in that building. That maybe for years before me, somehow anticipating my presence, I felt, hundreds of tiny creatures had been unwittingly working to save my life.

The edge of the wall, the edge that met the outermost corner of the barn, was damp and chewed. Termites, carpenter ants, powder-post beetles—something had weakened the board. I pried at it. It was loose. I could almost break it away, but this time, I thought, this time I would not be so impetuous. I would not live in regret but would wait until morning, to see if he left, since it would have been his normal day for teaching. I was lying there in the darkness, smelling the decay of the body, the dampness of the earth, and all but praying to those bugs, those miraculous bugs, thanking them for living, for desiring the taste of wood. I could have kissed them in my delirium. But I waited.

The next day I heard the door of the house open, and eventually steps coming into the barn. He was checking on me. At first I held as still as possible, hoping he would think I had already died of sheer fright. He banged hard on the top of the box to stir me. I decided I didn't want him to investigate further, so I moved slightly to show I was there. He gave the box another thump with his knuckles and walked away. I heard his car start and pull off down the driveway. His schedule never varied—I knew he wouldn't be back for four days, but also that I couldn't live that long without water. My throat was parched already. The delicate moistness of the earth under me was tantalizing.

For hours I dug my fingers into the crevices of the wood and tried with all my remaining strength to pry it off. After what must have been a few hours, I managed to break off the end of one board, and I could see an open field behind the barn and, farther on, the woods behind it. It was the most beautiful thing I'd ever seen, that vista, and it was calling me to freedom.

I hit the board harder and harder with my fists, with my head, and in my frustration opened a cut just above my eye. In desperation, I tasted the blood, hoping it would quench my thirst.

The board was wedged in tightly, and I thought all my efforts might be of no use. I thought maybe I should give up, curl up on the ground with Jennifer, and meet her in whatever cellar afterlife we could conjure. But then I thought how, if I did that, my parents would never know what happened, I could never explain what Jennifer went through, and I could never bring justice to Jack Derber. That last point drove me on.

Eventually, I forced enough of the board free almost to squeeze my shoulders through the open space, but not quite enough. I knew I needed to turn around somehow in the box, so my feet could reach the top of the board, and I could use the strength of my legs to push it out. The box was just wide enough for the two of us, so I practically had to embrace Jennifer's corpse, which I had pushed to the far side of the box.

The stench was overwhelming, but I could have stomached that. I hated more the stiffness of her body and the coldness of her skin. I was crying, but no tears would fall. There was no water left in any pore of my body.

Finally facing the other way, I pulled my legs up underneath me, mustered all the force that remained in my pathetic form, and shoved my feet down again and again, pounding at the board, my knees shaking the corpse to the side, as we moved together in some kind of strange death dance.

It lasted for what seemed like forever, and then the board came loose entirely. Just like that. My breath came faster. I clenched my fists and closed my eyes, bracing myself to wriggle through the opening. It was a wide board, but I only just fit underneath it. I thanked Jack out loud for keeping me emaciated, and I slid under and out into the open air.

I turned around and carefully replaced the board in its old spot as closely as possible. I wanted to give myself as much running time as I could. For all I knew, he had these woods under video surveillance, and this whole setup could be just the latest game for him to amuse himself with. I knew I wasn't free yet.

I ran toward the woods. Going down the driveway would have been more direct, but I couldn't risk running into Jack's car if he decided to make an unexpected return.

I paused for a moment in front of the house. I thought about saving the others then, but it was too risky. The house was a trap, and I was sure he had coded locks on the doors that I would not be able to open. I would send someone as soon as I could make it back to civilization. I hoped those four days would be enough time before he made it back and discovered I was missing.

So I ran. Stumbled is more like it. I was naked, and the bottoms of my feet had lost whatever protective coating of skin they'd ever had. I felt every rock and stick. Soon my feet were bleeding. I was running hard down the hill, not caring. I felt . . . I felt uplifted.

Near the bottom of the hill, there was a stream, and I drank from it like I'd never drunk from anything in my life. It was then that I knew I'd survive. Then that I felt the first joy I had felt in three years. After that it seemed I had the strength of a thousand women, and I ran down the hill like a colt in an open pasture. I was still afraid, but I could see a large field at the bottom of the hill, and beyond that a dilapidated old farmhouse. Surely there would be someone there to help me.

When I reached it, I discovered it was empty and locked, but in the barn beside it I found a battered coat and some heavy work boots. Both were absurdly big for me, but I put them on and started out down the road, disoriented by the open space, yet determined to put distance between Jack's house and me.

A car stopped at last, a young couple with two small children in the back. I asked for directions to the police station. They looked slightly terrified of me, a dirty stick woman in a clownish getup slurring her words, but they seemed genuinely concerned. The woman hesitated, glancing at her husband questioningly, and finally told me to get in the car so they could take me for help. I started crying and said I couldn't, that I was too afraid. I couldn't get in a car with strangers. They asked what happened to me, and all I could say, over and over again through my sobs, was that I'd been in the cellar for a long, long time.

At that they looked horrified and told me to stay where I was and they would send the police. I figured I'd scared them off, and I'd have to find my way on my own. But I couldn't move anymore. I nodded at them, clutching the stiff fabric of the oversize coat, and sat down on the side of the road as they drove off.

I must have passed out, because when I came to, two police officers were lifting me into the back of the squad car.

On the way, in the back with one of them, a gentle woman who listened with pity in her eyes, I whispered our story in a garbled mishmash of words and phrases. I knew I was hardly making sense, but she was patient and managed to piece it together. I told her then about Tracy and Christine, and they called it in to headquarters right away. Hours later, at the hospital, I saw them being carried in. The police insisted, however, there were no bodies on the premises.

The doctors had me hooked up to an IV, pumping fluids into me. I could barely move, and I must have passed out again, but not before realizing our captivity, at least, was finally over. Over.

CHAPTER 35

Tracy continued to stare at her knees, as she had been through my whole story. Christine had stopped crying and was actually sitting up straight now, listening attentively. Adele, meanwhile, had been taking notes and was still writing feverishly when I stopped.

The silence was thick around me. I waited. Would this help Tracy understand why I hadn't gone back for them first? Would she believe that I sent help as soon as I could? I waited a full minute more in the silence, the only sound Adele's pen scratching on the paper.

And then Tracy looked me in the eyes and said, very softly, "Adele, put the fucking pen down."

Adele stopped writing and looked up. I let out my breath.

It wasn't much, but I'd take it.

"Sorry," Adele said, putting the pen down.

"What difference does it make?" I said quietly. "Now that we'll just die in here. One way or another."

"No," Tracy said, her eyes igniting with sudden fire, "we're going to get out of here. We just need to know more. Adele needs to come clean."

She stood up and turned to face Adele.

"Adele, you've been here before, haven't you? Whatever it is you're hiding from us, you have to tell us now. You may not even realize you have the key to get us out of here. Or maybe you do realize it. We need to know who else is involved. Who left those letters? Who trapped us? Who got this house ready for us? Who put out the welcome sign? Jack has to have had some help. He is in prison, after all."

At that we heard a noise, unmistakable this time, coming from underneath our feet. A thump. We all sat up, alert, leaning forward, listening. There it was again, a thump. In the cellar. There was no ignoring it now.

"What is that?" Christine spoke first.

We stood up simultaneously and walked to the door that led down to the bowels of the house, Adele following us a few feet behind, a look of sheer terror on her face.

We stood there in the hallway, in front of that cellar door. The coded locks were there, but the door was slightly ajar. As though someone wanted us to go down there. As though the very house itself was luring us down. Down into that cellar. Again we heard the noise.

Taking one deep breath, Tracy pulled the door open and took a step down the stairs. As her foot hit the first tread, Christine balked.

"I can't go down there. I really, really can't." She stepped back into the door of the library.

"You can go in *there* but not down there? That makes no sense," Tracy whispered in frustration.

"Leave her alone. I feel the same way, but we need to see what that sound was. Maybe she can keep watch upstairs," I said, motioning for Tracy to continue. Tracy shook her head but then went on.

We carefully made our way down the stairs. My nerves were rattled by the sound of those too-familiar creaks from my nightmares. I counted them automatically, without realizing I was doing it out loud. Tracy turned around and glared. I stopped.

But in that moment our eyes met, and the years we spent together flashed through my mind, blurred into a dark-gray haze of memory. Every pain, every sorrow, every regret was suddenly racing through my body, fused into a powerful sense memory of our past life. And here was Tracy, my rival, my enemy, my tormentor, and yet the only one who could truly share this moment with me. For a split second, we were worn-out soldiers fighting together in the same lost cause.

And we both recognized the electricity passing between us. A sinking in the stomach, a terror rising in our throats, a shadow of evil passing over our hearts, that only we could possibly understand. This energy, this current, this place. We looked away at the same time, unable to bear it.

Down in the cellar, I felt my chest tighten. The dank smell of it was exactly the same. The chains might have been gone, but the rings attached to the walls were still there, as menacing as ever. The box still sat in its corner, shut up tightly. There was no one there.

At the sight of the box, my stomach clenched again. Yes, it had all been real. Yes, I really did lose Jennifer. There it was. Wood and nails and agony. Unimaginable. Yet undeniable.

Then as Adele reached the last step, the sound came again. Only this time we could tell it came from inside the box. Automatically, my brain struggled to detect a pattern to it, just as I had listened for Jennifer all those years ago.

Hearing the sound, Adele turned around and darted back up

the stairs. But before she could make it even halfway up, Tracy grabbed her arm and held it fast.

"Oh, no, Adele. You're in this with us now," she said.

At that moment something stirred at the top of the stairs. Christine was standing there, clutching her broom handle for dear life. Her face was tense, her eyes looking past me to the box in the corner.

"I'm coming too," was all she said. She seemed to be holding her breath as she carefully made her way down the stairs. I pointed to the box, and we nodded, taking small, tentative steps toward it. Inching our way in the dark cellar toward the one thing we never wanted to see again.

The door to the box was fastened with a piece of thin rope, tied in an elaborate knot. Tracy was the only one brave enough to walk all the way over to it. The rest of us stopped a few feet away. We all stood behind her, raising our makeshift weapons. We froze for a moment, still, listening for the noise again in that box. No one wanted to touch it. It was like a living animal, dangerous and solitary, down here in the hell of our past.

As Tracy reached it, she seemed to summon every last ounce of courage in her, and she suddenly grabbed the knot and worked at it frenetically, her brow furrowed and teeth gritted. It was a byzantine tangle, loop upon loop, but finally it loosened, and in one swift motion she flung open the door.

There, in the box, was a man, tied up with more of the rope that had fastened the box shut. We gasped. I leaned in to take a closer look. Though his face was grimacing and red from fear, I could tell who it was.

"Ray? RAY?" I said, in shock.

He nodded but couldn't speak. There was a wadded rag in his mouth. His face had a look of extreme terror, but when his eyes adjusted to the light, he saw it was us, and his fright turned to relief. Tracy moved to untie him, but Adele held up her hand.

"Couldn't this be a trap? Isn't it possible that he's the one in league with Jack, and once we release him, he'll turn the tables on us?" Even Adele's voice had reached a frantic pitch.

"Let's let him explain," Tracy said, pulling the rag from his mouth instead.

"Water," he whispered hoarsely.

I nodded, and Christine went back up to the kitchen and returned with a glass. She held it to his lips as he drank thirstily and asked for another. After two more refills, he was able to speak.

"Thank you," he said. "Can you untie me?"

"We need to talk first," said Adele. "Who did this to you?"

It looked as though he might cry again, as if he were pained at the thought of telling us what had happened.

But almost in a whisper, he said it. "Sylvia. Sylvia did this to me."

"*What?*" We all said it at once.

"It's true.

"I was in town, on my way home from work, when I saw her leaving the post office. Maybe it was wrong to follow someone like that, especially a young lady, but I just . . . wanted to see if she was okay.

"I'm embarrassed to say that, as you can see, I ended up trailing her all the way here. I called Val and left a message letting her know I'd be late. I ought to have told her what I was doing, but I knew she would think I was being an old fool, and I guess—I guess I was."

He stopped and asked for another drink, then continued.

"When I realized where she was going, I was scared. I knew this was Jack Derber's house, but I wanted to see if I could help Sylvia . . . and I guess, if I'm honest, I wanted to know what was going on. The door was open so I walked in and found her in the library and confessed that I had been following her. I told her I was so happy to see her, that I had been so worried.

"I couldn't believe the look on her face. It was so blank. She shook her head at me and said I shouldn't have done that and that she was very sorry. Then she walked over close to me and pulled out a gun. She said she was sorry again, and then she forced me down here to the cellar and tied me up, and she—" Here he broke off and started sobbing. "I can't believe it. She left me here. She left me to die. In a cramped little box. Sylvia."

CHAPTER 36

Back in the library, we sat in silence. We didn't dare meet one another's eyes, as we let the truth sink in. Sylvia was not the victim we'd imagined. She was our captor. She had been here—alone—to set the stage for our demise.

Ray was in the worst shape, perhaps, still grappling with his new knowledge of who we really were and why we were here. But as we had recounted our story to him, it had seemed even clearer to all of us that we could do nothing but wait for Jack's plan to unfold.

Christine's soft moaning from the window seat finally broke the silence, then rapidly escalated into a steady mumbling, low and unintelligible. I knew those sounds. It was a flashback to her cellar days, her familiar ramblings, the mutterings I had learned to ignore. The house was invading us each in its own way, creeping into our very bodies, reverting us to the selves we had been back then.

I was afraid of what that meant for me.

Then without warning, Christine stopped crying and stood up. She made her way to the center of the room as we looked on warily.

She seemed troubled, gripping her hands tightly in front of her, over her stomach. But her voice was unexpectedly calm when she began.

"Sylvia isn't the only evil one here. I'm just as guilty as she is." She paused, pulling herself together. I waited, my breath held, wondering what could possibly come next.

"I was afraid to tell you when we were in the cellar. I was too ashamed. I didn't think you'd understand it then, but now . . . now I have to get this out. Before it's too late.

"This"—she waved her arms to indicate the space, but we knew she meant something much larger—"this is my fault. Everything that happened here is because of me."

She was silent for a moment, then steeled herself to go on. It was clearly excruciating for her to say this.

"When I was a student—his student—I wasn't just his research assistant. I was . . . I was having an affair with Jack. I thought I was in love with him. And that he was in love with me." We stared at her, stunned. I could not imagine voluntarily being close to Jack.

She was holding back her tears now, determined to get the words out.

"So he lured me here, and I was a fool. I was the beginning of it all," she continued bitterly, "his fucking test case, and I suppose when I didn't fight back hard enough, or outwit him, or break out, he felt secure enough to bring you down there."

Christine walked over to the spot Tracy and I knew so well. His place by the rack where he had always stood over us. She remained there perfectly still, her eyes staring at the floor as she tried not to break down.

She looked up at Tracy, then over to me, and went on, "But it's worse than that. I could never bring myself to tell anyone this before, not even the police. You see, there were two other girls before you got here. I"—she could barely say it—"I helped him abduct them."

"What—what do you mean?" asked Tracy, looking as if she'd been slapped. I couldn't move. I just sat there, staring at her.

"He brought me with him. I thought it was my only chance to escape, so I told him I'd behave. I didn't actually intend to help him. Then there we were in his car, offering a ride to a girl about my age. I can still see her. Her hair was pulled up in a ponytail. She had a navy blue backpack and kept checking her watch. It looked like her bus was late. She seemed so innocent. I'll never forget it: her eyes met mine, checking in with me. Checking to see if it was safe. I wanted to scream out that it wasn't. Not safe at all. But I held my tongue because I was afraid."

No one moved. No one breathed.

"And then we did it a second time. That second time I couldn't meet the girl's eyes at all until it was too late," Christine had to pause to gather her strength again.

"Neither of them lasted very long down there. They each went in the box right away, and after a few days each one went upstairs and never came back. I didn't dare ask what happened.

"And now, every night I see the faces of those girls in my dreams. Hell, every time I close my eyes. And I imagine I see them looking at me through my daughters' eyes. That's why I came out here right away when you called. When you told me there might be other girls, I thought . . . I thought we might find those two somehow." She turned to me, accusingly. "But now we won't. Because now we are going to *die here*."

Tracy stood beside her looking helpless, as Christine dropped to her knees and started to weep, slowly and softly at first, but then steadily harder and harder.

I was preparing myself for the worst when she sat up abruptly, then bent down close to the floor. She was peering at something.

"Wait a minute. What is . . . what is this?" she said, wiping her face and then pushing her fingers hard against a spot in the floor. That same spot. Jack's spot. "What the *fuck*?"

Christine ran her fingers along the board and found some sort of lever. She pushed it, but nothing happened. We all crowded around her.

Of course, I thought. Another of his sick games. Something placed there specifically for us to find. So we could know the answers, just before he had us killed.

"Here, let me try it," Tracy said. She pushed it harder, but the catch was stuck.

"Hold on, hold on . . . there we go." She eased it open.

The floorboard came up, hinged on one side deep within the crevice of another board. There was a hole in the floor, about one foot by two. Tracy reached in and pulled out a small wooden crate, then lifted the lid. There was a smaller cardboard box inside on top of a pile of spiral notebooks. As she opened it, we peered in over her shoulder.

"Photographs," Adele said, looking excited at first, until she saw what they were. They were not what any of us were hoping to find. Not even Adele.

Tracy flipped through them slowly, and the rest of us stood watching over her shoulder. As the photos flashed past, I saw image after image of young women's bodies, of all shapes and sizes, in both natural and unnatural poses, naked and clothed. In color, in black and white, in sepia tones. But it was their faces that disturbed us the most, blurred as many of them were. Some were smiling, some looked afraid, some were clearly suffering. And some were the faces of corpses, in various stages of decay.

Adele covered her mouth with her hands, her eyes wide. I thought she might throw up.

Tracy methodically stacked the photos, put them back in the box, and replaced the lid.

"I don't think we need to look at those right now," she said with almost unnatural calm.

She turned to Christine. "This should give you some comfort. Some of those appear to go back twenty years or more. You certainly weren't the start of it all." But Christine looked like the rest of us felt, completely horrified.

What did this mean? Again, I reached for Jennifer's photo in my pocket. Was there a picture of her in that box as well?

"Let's see the notebooks," I said, keeping my voice under control, even though I felt like screaming.

Tracy lifted them out and handed one to each of us. I turned the pages of mine slowly, careful to let only the tips of my fingers touch them, as though a poison might be embedded in the words he had scratched out onto the blank pages.

"What is this?" I finally said. They were filled with notes in Jack Derber's even scrawl. I read out loud, "'Subject H-29 withstands pain at 6 count.'"

We turned to Adele as one. Only she could tell us what this meant. She was clearly in shock. She took the notebook from my hands, but unlike me, she caressed the pages like a long-lost love.

"These are his . . . notes," she whispered in awe. "The ones I've been looking for. For ten years."

"Would you care to elaborate?" Tracy said, an edge creeping into her voice.

Adele suddenly seemed confused, her bravado evaporating as it dawned on her what this meant to us. What this would mean to any other human being. She tried to explain.

"It's not what you think. Jack . . . Jack said he had gotten access to highly classified government documents. CIA research on soldiers and civilians from the fifties on—on certain coercive techniques. You know, 'brainwashing,' 'mind control.'"

"But why is it all in his handwriting?" Tracy didn't sound convinced.

"His contact wouldn't allow him to photocopy anything, so he wrote out everything by hand. He wanted to publish a study, the definitive truth about mind control. This is what I was working on with him, but he wouldn't let me see any of his actual notes."

"Adele, I hate to break it to you, but I don't think this work was based on secret CIA records," Tracy said. She patted the box of photographs beside her. "Looks like this was original research. And I certainly don't think he planned to publish it, considering it's evidence of his crimes."

Adele shook her head. She looked confused, panicked. "I don't know what you're—"

Christine interrupted. "Brainwashing? Adele, don't forget I was a psych major too. I know about those CIA experiments using Chinese and Korean persuasion techniques. They've been discredited. The CIA gave up. Brainwashing does not work."

"Jack disagreed," Adele replied. "He thought the CIA only discontinued their studies because they got caught. Their methods were unethical, so they got shut down. But Jack said the documents he obtained proved the CIA was successful. And that his discovery would change the field."

Tracy interrupted her, "I see. And you figured if you were his coauthor, you'd surely be invited to join the Harvard faculty."

Adele turned pale but said nothing.

I remembered the books Adele had been reading in the library, and it started to make sense. But then I had another, even more horrible thought.

"Adele, how does this research connect back to your little secret society? I know it existed. You and Jack were in it together, weren't you? Does that have anything to do with torturing these girls? Tell us the truth, Adele. Were these girls part of this project?"

Adele shook her head, her face as white as the pages of the open notebook in her hand.

"No, no, I had no idea about any of this." She pointed to the photographs. "That's separate. That's Jack's madness. There was another side to him, though. He was a serious scholar."

"Then what *was* the secret society for, Adele? We know you were in it. Scott Weber told us." It wasn't exactly true, but I thought I'd take a chance.

"You spoke to Scott?" Her tone changed in an instant, and her eyes flashed with anger. She looked like a trapped animal. She was used to being in control, keeping her secrets. Yet here she was, cornered.

"Tell us, Adele," Christine said, her eyes rimmed with red from crying but her voice steely.

"The 'secret society,' as you call it, has nothing to do with any of this," Adele began, looking away from Christine's disturbing aspect. "It was just a . . . school project."

"Explain."

The word must have echoed painfully in Adele's head. In her mind, as we all knew, *she* got to ask the questions. She looked at each one of us in turn, perhaps trying to weigh the situation she was in, figuring out who had the power here. We sat in silence for a full minute, waiting while she struggled with what she would say next. Finally, she must have decided she had run out of choices, and she began.

"David and I were seeing each other that first semester. He introduced me to the BDSM movement when we met. At first I was interested in it intellectually, you know, as a topic for study, but then I was . . . let's just say I was drawn into it. We started experimenting, and it escalated."

She paused and took a deep breath. She seemed to be gradually resigning herself to telling her story.

"Then Jack walked in on us in the back stacks of the social sciences library when we were engaging in some . . . imaginative role play. His curiosity was, needless to say, piqued. At first we were horrified that our professor had found us out. Then we were flattered when he was so intrigued. Jack was so impressive, and I had just started working for him as a research assistant, so we were thrilled really to have something to offer up to him.

"Soon enough we were all going to The Vault together. And then, I guess when Jack trusted us enough, he invited us to join his . . . private study group, I think is a better term. He'd set up an exclusive little cadre to analyze this subculture in a way a state-funded university might not necessarily sanction. More hands-on, so to speak."

"It had something to do with that Bataille group, didn't it?" I asked.

Adele looked surprised.

"Yes, *Acephale*, but how did you—"

"The brand. It's the symbol for it," Tracy responded.

"I see," Adele said, looking stunned. She gathered her composure and went on. "Well, yes, Jack was obsessed with the literature of transgression: Bataille, De Sade, Mirbeau. He thought it would help us understand the psychological origins of perversions, fetishes, sadistic impulses—all of it." The words rushed out of her, like those of a proselytizer. "But he believed transgressive behavior couldn't be studied through mere observation. It wasn't like depression or schizophrenia or sleep disorders. We had to experience it for ourselves.

"So that's what we did. We altered our entire lives to get to the core of this work. We created our own rituals and incorporated these texts to, you know, get into the spirit of things, to help us to break free from societal norms and uncover our true selves. And from there we could reach an understanding beyond—" She stopped abruptly, seeing our expressions. She'd lost us.

Adele cleared her throat.

"So yes," she said, "as part of all that, we talked about human sacrifice, mutilation, bondage, and all kinds of other debased acts. But it was a game. It wasn't real. It was just like what we did at the club." She stopped and looked over at the box of photographs. Tears sprang to her eyes.

"At least, I thought it was," she continued. "I don't know. Maybe Jack was grooming us for something more, but it didn't get that far before his arrest. I swear."

We were all staring at her. None of us even dared to move for fear she would stop telling her story.

As she paused, I glanced quickly around the room, checking the doors, the windows, listening. It was silent, all was still. Jack was making us wait. I held my knife in my lap, squeezing the handle tightly, clenching and unclenching it in my fist.

Adele inhaled deeply and went on.

"Jack had also brought in his old friend—Joe Myers, he'd called him at the time—to join us. He was something else altogether. The most hardcore of us all, cruel and violent. He made me wonder sometimes if I knew what I was getting into. But I was too deeply involved by then. And Jack was still the one in absolute control of it all. At the time I stupidly trusted him to keep everything safe."

She paused and looked up at us, then said meaningfully, "It turns out I didn't know Joe Myers's real name until he made it onto the Most Wanted List yesterday." She saw the shock in our eyes as we registered her meaning. "Yes. Noah Philben." She let this sink in for a moment before continuing.

"On the day Jack was taken away, the news broke and then spread around the campus like wildfire. But at the very beginning, the FBI was focusing on the house. Before they got to his office on campus, I sneaked in. I knew I only had one shot. I took everything I could carry so I could continue this project, but I also knew he had kept crucial materials hidden at the house, and there was no way for me to get in there.

"Noah Philben—still Joe Myers to me then—also wanted to get Jack's things, though I didn't know why. And I was afraid he'd already taken something. I wanted to confront him, but he disappeared. I couldn't find him again after Jack's arrest because I didn't know his real name. I swear I only found out yesterday when they showed his picture on the news."

She turned to me. "When I saw his face and heard that Sylvia belonged to his church, I suspected that your search had somehow led back to him. And I was right."

"And you wanted to know exactly what we found, isn't that right, Adele? That's why you called us, why you wanted to come to the hotel," interrupted Tracy.

"But, Adele, Scott Weber said the secret society was still meeting after Jack's arrest," I said, challenging her.

"Sort of." She thought a minute and then said, "We met, but at that point it was just me and David and two others we knew from The Vault. We were regrouping, trying to make sure we didn't have any ties to Jack that could be traced back to us, that everything we'd done would be kept from the police.

"And yes, I was still seeing David. I was . . . I was only seeing Scott to keep him out of Jack's research. I didn't want him to find the notes before I did. He is a damn good reporter, so I had to keep him away. I know that doesn't exactly sound ethical, but you have to understand—this work has become my life."

"No kidding," muttered Tracy.

I turned to Adele. "Didn't you—weren't you at all . . . moved or disgusted or horrified or *something* about what you had just learned about your professor and—let's just say it, *friend*?"

She looked ashamed. "Well, I was. I was. Oh yes, definitely. I just also told myself I needed to be strong, because this was really an . . . opportunity for me."

"You are one revolting piece of work, Adele," said Tracy, looking away in disgust.

At this Adele turned on her heel and walked back to her spot by the window. She faced away from us, so I couldn't tell whether she was regretting her revelation or not. We left her alone.

As the rest of us sat there recovering from Adele's story, Ray began picking through the box of photographs. Suddenly, he jumped up and turned to me, looking panicked, "What were those 'subjects' called again? From the notebooks?"

I lifted one up. "Let's see, here's a Subject L-39, and here's an M-50 . . ."

"That's enough. Look." He handed me a photograph, flipped over to the back. I could just make out the words "Subject M-19" scratched in the lower-left-hand corner. I took the pile from Ray. Sure enough, the photos were carefully labeled with tiny letters, each using the same formulation, "Subject P-9, L-25, Z-03."

And then I found H-29 the subject I'd read about in the notebook. She was a blonde, wearing a tattered nightgown, her eyes closed, a swollen purple bruise on her left cheek, a chain around her neck. Her teeth were bared, her lips dripping red around them.

Tracy had been right the first time. These girls *were* Jack's study.

CHAPTER 37

Tracy stood up abruptly and wrenched the photos from my hands. She crossed the room in two strides and waved the images an inch from Adele's face.

"Can't you see what this means?" she screamed. "Do I have to spell it out for you? There weren't any CIA documents, Adele. This wasn't noble academic work. Jack was running his *own* mind control experiments. Using torture. On these girls." She paused. "And on *us*."

In disgust, Tracy threw the photos onto the floor in front of Adele. No one spoke—we only listened to the sound of their sliding across the wood. Then Tracy stepped back and looked hard at Adele, her voice calmer now. "It looks like Jack wanted to turn you into a very different kind of protégé than you thought."

Adele stared at the photos scattered at her feet. She bent down, picked one up, and examined the writing on the back. Here it was, her life's work, based on a maniac's experiments on abducted girls. And worse, this maniac might have been slowly making her party to his machinations. Grooming her to be one of them, to engage in some horrific study, a magnum opus of torture and degradation.

"I think I . . . I think I need to be alone for a few minutes," Adele said. She turned slowly and walked like a zombie out of the room, staring straight ahead.

"Should we let her go?" Tracy said after it became clear Adele wasn't coming right back.

"Yes, she's in shock. And she knows she was duped. She thought she was the great manipulator, but it turns out she was the manipulated one. She is another victim of Jack's. A different kind, but still." I paused, taking a breath. "So I think, for now, we should let her have some alone time."

Tracy looked back down at the notebooks. "Well, I could probably use some alone time myself. Or ten more years of therapy. Or a giant slug of vodka."

She bent over the photos spread on the floor, picking one up here and there, tracing the images with her finger. "So," she began, her voice barely audible, "were we just part of these . . . these experiments too?"

I sat down next to her, picking up a photo, this one of a brunette with the frizzy curls of a cheap home permanent, her eyes staring warily into the camera lens. Subject S-5. From the nineteen eighties I guessed.

Christine had returned to the window seat. Ray was pacing back and forth, wringing his hands. We were all shaken to the core.

"Are these the other fifty-four girls from Jim's list? Could any of them still be alive? If so, are they on the run with Noah Philben right this very second?" I asked.

Tracy shook her head slowly. "I wonder if Noah is a 'serious scholar,' too."

"Somehow I don't think so," I replied, absently stacking the photos back into piles. "Seems to me that Jack liked torture and Noah liked making money. They figured out a way to do both. And now that Jack can't be hands-on, I'm sure he loves hearing the stories of this sick world he set in motion. And probably still controls.

"Or maybe Sylvia is in control," I said, thinking about our situation. "After all, she set this trap for us. Maybe she's his proxy now."

"Like you were, Sarah?" Tracy said quietly.

I jerked my head around to face her, "What do you mean?"

"I mean, look at how you betrayed us. You were practically in Sylvia's shoes. There but for the grace of God—"

"I was nothing like Sylvia. How dare you say that?"

Tracy stood up and walked over to me. She was close enough to know I would be uncomfortable. I hated my body at that moment for shrinking back from her. "Sarah, have you been brainwashed to forget? Do you not remember what it was like those last months in the cellar? When you . . . when you . . . *went to the other side*."

I shook my head. "I didn't. I didn't."

"Really? You didn't? Well, then how do you explain the fact that you'd moved upstairs at that point? How do you explain that when one of us would be tied down on the rack, you stayed right there, in the room, helping him, handing him his tools and instruments, *smiling*? I guess his techniques worked on you, after all." Tracy was shouting at me now.

My thoughts began racing, fragments of memories, disjointed scenes, reappearing in my mind. I shook my head, as if that might wipe away the images her words had put there. I shook harder and closed my eyes. I bit my lip hard to try to stop the tears I felt forming in my eyes. I didn't want to lose control right now. I wanted to be strong.

I pulled myself together and sat up. The first face I saw was Ray's. I could see his shock and horror at what Tracy was saying, as he looked from her to me, and me to her.

"I don't remember that. That didn't happen," I finally said, exhausted from the effort of struggling with my memories.

Christine had risen from her perch and was approaching me slowly. "It did happen, Sarah. It *did*."

"And that's not even the worst of it, Sarah," Tracy started up again. "I could almost forgive you for that. We were underfed, our heads were screwed up. But there was a certain code I thought we had down there. A certain commitment to one another. And you violated that in a way that was so much more profoundly damaging than anything Jack could ever do to us."

I shook my head, still repeating, "I didn't. I didn't."

"You *did*, Sarah."

The room was quiet for a moment, and then Tracy said, very softly and deliberately, enunciating each syllable clearly, "You told him about my brother. You told him about Ben's suicide."

At that something unbelievable happened. *Tracy* started to cry. Actual tears. I stared at her in shock. I had never seen this before. All those years in the cellar, she had been so strong, she never let us see her like this, and now, here, not because of Jack, but because of something I did . . .

"*Why*?" she pressed. "He didn't need to know that. I understood what you had to gain by helping him with the instruments. I know you were trying to get in his good graces so he might trust you enough to let you go outside. I understand that.

"But to tell him about Ben. When you knew he would use it against me. I could take anything else. Being bound, gagged, electrocuted, beaten—whatever. But I didn't want to hear him use Ben's name. Once he knew about Ben, he was able to manipulate my mind, make me believe Ben's death was my fault, my fault entirely."

She stopped talking suddenly, wiping her face with her sleeve. Then she stared at me, her eyes narrowing.

"Well, I have another secret for you, Sarah. I know you think you're the only one who suffered here. But let me tell you, those first years out were difficult for me too. Much harder than they needed to be. Thanks to you, I couldn't stop thinking about the things Jack said to me in there."

She was quiet for a moment, then closed her eyes as she began again. "It was so hard, in fact, that I tried to join Ben at the bottom of that lake. Twice. And clearly I'd be better off right now if I'd just stayed down there."

None of us spoke. I stared at the floor, unable to meet her eyes. I couldn't believe it. Tracy seemed so tough, so powerful. The strongest one of us all. Had this experience nearly destroyed her as well?

Or maybe *I* had nearly destroyed her?

They were right. I hadn't needed to tell her secret to Jack. Why did I? My memories from that time were so convoluted, so painful yet indistinct. Maybe there was a moment, a few fleeting seconds, where my mind had gotten turned inside out, and I thought that being with Jack, helping Jack, was somehow where my whole life had been leading. I had believed in his twisted vision of the world. Some small part of me had been resigned to be with him for the rest of my life, furthering his sadistic goals, satisfying his perverse needs. I had needed to believe so that I could carry out my plan. Believe just a little to convince him. But had I gone too far? Had I crossed the line? Had I been a success story in his sick study after all?

I could only stammer out the words, "I'm sorry . . . I'm so sorry . . . I—"

But at that moment, we heard a new sound from the front of the house.

CHAPTER 38

We all turned to the entrance of the library, where Adele had left the double doors ajar. We heard footsteps approaching. The outline of a woman appeared in the shadows, like a ghost, gliding along the floor into the room. Then I saw it: she was holding a gun. And moving in closer.

"Sylvia!!!" Ray shouted.

I could not believe what I was seeing. At first the room seemed to spin around me, and then to disappear altogether. A world came crashing down in my head. A thousand worlds. My mind couldn't put together the pieces of the puzzle, so disorienting was the reality in front of me. No matter how hard I tried, I couldn't do the math.

"That's not Sylvia," I finally said, feeling all of my blood surging to my head. "That's . . . Jennifer!"

"Oh. My. God," I heard Christine say from the back of the

room, as Tracy stood there stunned, only able to mutter a quiet "What the fuck?"

"But that *is* Sylvia," said Ray again, in an almost pleading voice. "It *is*."

The woman with the gun walked closer to us.

Finally, she spoke. "Everyone get close together. Sit on the floor. Hands up in the air."

I felt confused, disoriented, split apart. And yet what I felt most was joy, a sensation of completeness that I hadn't experienced since before our abduction all those years ago. It *was* Jennifer. Jennifer. It was really her. We were reunited again, after what was surely only an aberration, a fluke, a thirteen-year detour in what should have been our lives together. It seemed to me I should be able to run over to her, throw my arms around her, and whisper into her ear the way we always had. She was safe. We were safe. We were both alive.

I was whispering her name, despite myself. I thought somehow that once she realized it was me, she would put the gun down and we could all go home, and the past thirteen years could be erased. We could write up a new Never List, and we would follow it to the letter and be safe, together, forever. Surely she was not the one who had imprisoned us again. Surely we had all the facts mixed up, and there was another explanation.

The gun did not waver, though. We did as we were told.

Then out of the corner of my eye, I saw it. The front door of the house was wide open behind Jennifer. Even in my shock, my mind, so set to self-preservation, immediately started calculating the odds. How could I get past her and out that door? Then I recognized that once again all I could think of was saving myself, leaving the others to their fate. I'd save them if I could, but only as an afterthought, once I had secured my own future.

The realization of what I was doing, even in that moment, forced me to face something about myself. Tracy and Christine were right. What had Jack Derber done to me? In that instant, a part of me was ready to give up. Now anything could happen, and in a way I didn't care what did.

But no, I thought, pushing away that despair, I wanted to live. I wanted to be strong. And I needed to understand.

"Jennifer, I thought—I thought you were dead . . . the body . . . with me in the box . . ." I stammered.

"Yes, I know you thought that. There were other bodies, Sarah. That one wasn't mine."

"'Other bodies'? Where were you then?" I could barely process the implications of what she'd said. I had thought *I* was the turncoat. Now I realized Jennifer had made it much further down that road. "Did you know . . . did you know I'd been left in that box?"

Jennifer's eyes flickered for a moment, and then she turned away from me. Tracy stirred, and Jennifer trained the gun on her.

"Don't move, Tracy, or I will kill you first."

"'*First*'?" shrieked Christine, who was right behind me.

"Shhh . . . shh . . ." I tried to calm her, careful not to turn all the way around and not to take my eyes off Jennifer.

I saw Ray's look of utter confusion, but there was no time to explain to him what must have happened. That there was a real Sylvia Dunham, but this was not her, and he'd never met her. That Tracy and I had met the real Sylvia Dunham's parents and seen her photograph. That she must have been abducted too, long ago. That Jack had handed over her identity to Jennifer, so she could be out in the world, acting under his orders. That they must have needed marriage documents for her to enter the jail. Anything could have happened to the real Sylvia, and everything probably had.

Then I saw her. Adele was walking back into the room behind Jennifer. I wanted to signal to her but wasn't sure how. She was our only hope. I could see she'd been crying, that she was lost in thought, not even looking up as she walked along the hall.

I hoped against hope the others would not show any sign that they saw her.

Christine caught her breath, and out of the corner of my eye, I could see Tracy nudging her knee into Christine's leg. We all saw at once how our fate now lay in Adele's hands. The seconds were painful. Adele's steps, one, two, three. Jennifer in front of her, staring at us with an odd sort of victory playing in her eyes.

Look up, Adele. Look up. I knew we were all thinking it. No one was breathing.

Then Adele looked up. *Don't scream,* I thought. *Don't fucking scream.*

After that, everything was in slow motion for me. Adele didn't scream. Instead she slowly leaned down and picked up the frying pan she'd left on the floor. She hesitated only a fraction of an instant.

I could see in her eyes, though, that even after all her years as a dominatrix, Adele was not prepared to inflict actual pain, and maybe even death, on someone else. And I didn't want that either. I was even afraid for Jennifer at that moment. Even then, I did not want Jennifer to die. Not after I had found her again after all those years. Not even after I was pretty certain she was about to kill me. Not even then.

Adele suddenly pulled the pan back over her head and in one swift motion brought it down on Jennifer's hand. The gun fired as it flew across the room. Adele tripped and fell from the weight of the pan, the awkward angle of her swing bringing her crashing to the floor.

I quickly scanned the room. Ray had been hit in the foot. He was howling, his blood spreading out onto the polished wood floor. Christine looked stunned, paralyzed by fear.

Tracy and I both jumped up, lunging toward Jennifer. I got there first. Jennifer was already turning, running for the open door, ready to slam it behind her. To leave us trapped again, this time for good.

This was the moment. I could tell Tracy was not going to reach her in time. I was going to have to do it. To grab not just any body, but the body I had so longed for and yet feared in my memory, from the box. The idea of it made me sick, made my flesh crawl. But I fought it. I fought through.

I ran as fast as I could and tackled her hard, throwing my arms around her in a sick embrace of reunion. I held her firmly, wrapping my arms far enough around her to clasp my hands together. She twisted around to face me, to push me off. I could feel her breath on my face. No one had been this close to me in years. Her arms flailing, she fought like hell, but this time I was strong. This time I would save us all.

Tracy was right behind me and helped me pin Jennifer's arms. Adele had gotten back up, raced out of the room, and come back with the rope from the cellar. Together we tied Jennifer up tightly. Afraid to stay in the house for a second longer, we dragged her out into the yard and stood around her, staring in disbelief.

CHAPTER 39

No one said anything. While we didn't understand the full details of the story yet, we understood enough to get a sense of what had happened. We would learn later about Jennifer's terrible ordeal, the years of torture and manipulation she had spent with Jack at the house and then, later, in Noah Philben's cult. The way they had passed her around to satisfy their sadistic needs, then used her as a go-between for Jack in prison. The things she had had to do to survive. The pain she had encountered and, worse, been forced to inflict.

Tracy walked down the hill desperately trying to find cell reception and eventually reached Jim. He arrived with blazes, lights flashing, sirens blaring. It was an echo of that time, ten years ago, when he'd come here to save Tracy and Christine.

I knew they would take Jennifer away to a hospital, and eventually, I figured, she would end up in a mental institution. When she was fully restrained by the police, I walked over to her.

It was really her. Older, her face bore the signs of a hard life filled with nothing but tragedy—it was prematurely lined, her skin colorless—but it was still her. After all these years thinking that the cold body in the barn had been my precious Jennifer, it was almost eerie to see her flesh move, alive and real. Like seeing that corpse from my dreams come to life. I wondered fleetingly who could have been in the box with me back then but pushed the thought out of my mind. The important thing now was that I had Jennifer here with me.

She was strapped down on a gurney, but the restraints hardly seemed necessary, for she didn't move at all. She didn't look around. Her eyes were fixed on some remote point in the distance.

Was she thinking of Jack Derber?

I didn't want to ask, and yet I wanted to know how—how could she have gotten to this point? I turned to her.

"Jennifer." I could barely speak. "Jennifer, what happened to you?"

She didn't look at me for a long time, and then finally she shifted her eyes to me without moving her head. Did her look soften? I wanted to believe I saw a trace of the Jennifer I'd known, somewhere in there, her eyes pleading with me, like in the old days.

Her voice was clear when she finally spoke. "I'm not afraid anymore," she said. "Now nothing scares me."

That was all. Then she looked away. The horror of it pierced through me like a knife. She wasn't the same person anymore.

I tried to console myself with the thought that, whoever she was now, she would be safe going forward. She'd be safe where they would put her. Where nothing could ever hurt her again.

I wondered if there was any chance they could restore her to that girl in my attic bedroom. I made a pact with myself then and there that I would be there for her from now on. I'd try to save her for real this time, if there was even the remotest possibility that she could be saved.

She had been taken away by the time Jim walked over to me, in a corner of Jack's yard, as far as possible from the barn. The paramedics were wrapping Ray's foot, and Christine was being interviewed by one officer, Tracy by another. Adele sat alone in stunned silence, watching as the police unspooled yellow tape around the perimeter.

Jim sat down beside me, plucking at a piece of grass he turned between his fingers. He kept his distance.

"That was pretty tough in there. Are you okay?"

"Okay? No, not really."

"I understand." He looked at me intently. "Sarah . . . Box one eighty-two? One of our guys took a photo of Jack Derber. Showed it to the postal agent who worked in River Bend all those years ago."

"And?"

"She called him Tommy Philben. That's the name he'd used on the form." He paused, letting me take that in.

"So they've always been in it together, haven't they? One way or another. Noah and Jack."

"Seems like it." We sank back into silence.

"Sarah, I spoke to Dr. Simmons. She wants to help."

"No, thanks." I turned toward him. "There isn't going to be any 'getting over it' this time. I realized something in there."

"What?"

"That no matter what I've been telling myself, at some level I was only looking out for myself all those years ago. I was selfish, weak. And that's how I'd gotten so close to becoming like Jennifer. Now that I see that, I have to change something."

"Change what?"

"The other fifty-four."

"What?"

"I need the list."

"Sarah, I can't give that to you."

"Jim."

I didn't look at him. I just waited.

We sat in silence for a few minutes. Then without another word, he got up and went over to his car.

A moment later he walked back over to me holding a manila envelope. He sighed, shrugged his shoulders, and handed it to me.

"You didn't get this from me," he said.

I took out the sheet of paper and looked at the names. The typeface blurred in front of my eyes for a moment. I took a deep breath.

"Got a pen?" I asked. He reached into his pocket and handed me one.

I clicked it open and wrote at the top of the list, in the familiar big block letters of those long-ago journals, SYLVIA DUNHAM.

I handed him the pen and the empty envelope, folded the paper into a small square, and put it in my pocket.

I wondered where Sylvia Dunham could be, that girl in the photograph. Junior year. The girl who was lost somewhere without a name. But I would find her. Find her somehow and help her parents understand that she hadn't chosen evil over them. I wanted to erase that pain at least, if I could do nothing else.

And I felt that sense of purpose burning inside me. Burning away the hollowness, the emptiness. Taking away my own sorrow, swallowing it up in this need. This need to fix things. To save them all.

I looked at Jim. He was smiling. We both stood up. I wondered if the change in me was visible.

I reached out my hand to him. He looked surprised but took it in his own, and we shook. His hand was warm, and his skin smooth. His grasp felt safe and comfortable. I looked into his eyes. I'd never noticed they were green before. Then we were both smiling.

ACKNOWLEDGMENTS

I would like to thank my brilliant agent, Alexandra Machinist, who expertly shepherded this book from the initial draft; Dorothy Vincent, for her excellent international representation; Tina Bennett, for opening the first door; Pam Dorman and Beena Kamlani, for their skillful and insightful editing, and the entire team at Pamela Dorman Books/Viking, for their hard work and commitment to this book; my husband, Stephen Metcalf, who helped me enormously, both emotionally and editorially, in bringing it to fruition; Stella and Kate, who are not allowed to read one word of it until college; my fabulous sister, Lindsy Farina; my best friend and inspiration, Lisa Gifford; the other dear friends who supported this book in a myriad of ways: George Cheeks, Emily Kirven, Michael Kirven, Corey Powell, Paige Orloff, David Grann, Jeff Roda, Jennifer Warner, Virginia Lazalde-McPherson, Mike Minden, and Marshall Eisen; and, for helping me make sense of it all, Melissa Wacks.